W9-BTQ-710

"WE'VE DESECRATED A CARDASSIAN TOMB!"

Kira Nerys leaned over the staring corpses of her long-dead enemies.

With skin shriveled and exposed veins collapsed, the corpses lay as if they'd tossed in their sleep.

Captain Ben Sisko picked his way through a carpet of dust. "Cardassia is looking for a reason to get control over *Deep Space Nine* . . . How will they feel about our breaking into a burial chamber?"

Dr. Julian Bashir frowned at his medical tricorder. "Sir, I'm getting some very strange readings . . ."

Look for STAR TREK Fiction from Pocket Books

Star Trek: The Original Series

Star Trek: The Next Generation

Star Trek: Deep Space Nine

Star Trek: Voyager

For orders other than by individual consumers, Pocket Books grants a discount on the purchase of **10 or more** copies of single titles for special markets or premium use. For further details, please write to the Vice-President of Special Markets, Pocket Books, 1230 Avenue of the Americas, New York, NY 10020.

For information on how individual consumers can place orders, please write to Mail Order Department, Paramount Publishing, 200 Old Tappan Road, Old Tappan, NJ 07675.

STAR TREK
DEEP SPACE NINE®

STATION RAGE

Diane Carey

POCKET BOOKS

New York   London   Toronto   Sydney   Tokyo   Singapore

The sale of this book without its cover is unauthorized. If you purchased this book without a cover, you should be aware that it was reported to the publisher as "unsold and destroyed." Neither the author nor the publisher has received payment for the sale of this "stripped book."

This book is a work of fiction. Names, characters, places and incidents are products of the author's imagination or are used fictitiously. Any resemblance to actual events or locales or persons, living or dead, is entirely coincidental.

An *Original* Publication of POCKET BOOKS

POCKET BOOKS, a division of Simon & Schuster Inc.
1230 Avenue of the Americas, New York, NY 10020

Copyright © 1995 by Paramount Pictures. All Rights Reserved.

STAR TREK is a Registered Trademark of
Paramount Pictures.

A VIACOM COMPANY

This book is published by Pocket Books, a division of
Simon & Schuster Inc., under exclusive license from
Paramount Pictures.

All rights reserved, including the right to reproduce
this book or portions thereof in any form whatsoever.
For information address Pocket Books, 1230 Avenue
of the Americas, New York, NY 10020

ISBN: 0-671-88561-8

First Pocket Books printing November 1995

10 9 8 7 6 5 4 3 2 1

POCKET and colophon are registered trademarks of
Simon & Schuster Inc.

Printed in the U.S.A.

Dedicated to Gregory Brodeur, my husband and collaborator, the man with the magic plot wand, who makes sense out of nonsense

STATION RAGE

CHAPTER
1

"CHIEF—LOOK OUT!"

Too late. Out of the shadows, a matte black club swung down and cracked against a human skull patterned with curly buff hair.

Miles O'Brien shook his ringing head and cursed himself for not reacting quicker to the warning from behind. "Oh, damn . . . damn that . . ."

He blinked up at the heavy lintel. It hadn't really moved, but sure seemed as if it had. This whole tunnel was on the hunt for the two of them. His bleeding hands, torn uniform, and now his swelling forehead told the tale.

Pressing a scored palm to his skull, he lay to one side and rested against the curved wall of the access cave. "I shouldn't have let you talk me into this, Odo. This is what I get. Look at me. I'm chipped as cordwood."

Security Chief Odo moved forward from the harsh slashes of shadow and blades of light cast by the illuminators they'd been dropping like bread crumbs behind him. "You all right?"

Wincing, O'Brien tried to nod, but it hurt. He fingered his head. "Swelling up like a soap bubble. Times like this could drive me back to the sod."

With a grunt Odo shifted his lanky body, leaned a knee on a broken piece of metal, and touched the lintel that had reached down from heaven and struck O'Brien. "Mmm . . . it's painted dull black, with some slashes of gloss black that go against the shape. Keeps it from being seen until someone gets struck on the head."

"Call the Cardassian Central Command and tell the bastards it still works."

This tunnel was more like a coal mine than an access corridor through one of the docking pylons that vaulted into space like a spider's legs. Its collapsed areas and false turnoffs had confounded their tricorder and turned what should've been an hour's glance into a daylong exploration. The widest place they'd come through had been back about an eighth of a kilometer, and it had only been four feet wide and six tall. Odo couldn't even stand up all the way.

Of course, Odo could be shorter if he wanted to.

The skinniest place had been all of twenty inches wide. Odo hadn't found it a problem, but O'Brien had done some fancy squirming to get his shoulders through, and taken a scrape or two or three on the odd edge.

Some of these edges were razor sharp—like the lintel, deliberately made that way. This was a danger maze, built to bump, bruise, or slice anyone who didn't know the way through. A misstep meant a fall, and a fall could mean losing a hand or leg.

"Inexcusable," Odo simmered, gazing now into his tricorder, squinting at the tiny screen. His blank face had more expression than he seemed ever to realize. "When Starfleet took over, I told them they'd better explore these pylons thoroughly. They didn't listen."

"There wasn't time," O'Brien defended. "It's a big station. Besides, you could've come down here anytime on your own, mate, instead of waiting until it was Captain Sisko's idea, so don't be so lofty. This pylon was collapsed during the fighting. There was no reason to come down here. I mean, how many back alleys do you bother looking down?"

"I look down them all."

One hand on a cobweb thick as cotton, O'Brien peered through the shadows. Odo seemed at home here as he gazed into his tricorder and the soft lights from the screen, normally invisible, brushed the lineless mask of his face. Somehow he was mystical in the darkness and dust, an echo of legends that called to O'Brien from long back and were hard to ignore even through the clutter of an engineer's logic.

"So nobody's ever been down this far since before the war?" O'Brien asked.

Odo looked up, his rough voice laden with a sudden meaning, his eyes like two thumb marks in clay. "Nobody."

"Right," O'Brien sighed, and pushed himself forward again. "Come this far, might's well keep on."

"Agreed. Would you like me to take the lead?"

"No, I'm fine. Here, watch your footing on that . . . here's another one of those black things topside . . . welcome to Hell'n Highwater . . . can I show you to your room, cell, or coffin?"

"I beg your pardon?"

3

"Nothin'. Let's roll."

This place had a life of its own. Not just the tunnel, but the whole of *Deep Space Nine*. Even evacuated, it would still pulse. He'd felt that since his first runabout approach, since he first saw the great unlubricated wheel cranking in space, cast in methyl violet and frosted with the cold light of the Bajoran sun, grizzled with patina not of age, but of overuse. This giant spool of incorrigibles was bazaar, dime store, rialto, community center, infirmary, refuge, precinct house, or hideout to the hundreds who came and went from it, and it could stir the neck hairs of any species that had them. Only a person's own odds could say whether the jaundiced silver sculpture in this dry veldt of space would turn out to be a safety net or a bottle dungeon, and the station ignored all hopes, turning coldly and whispering, *No promises, no promises.*

To Miles O'Brien, this crossgrained, cantankerous duty station was the back stair of space, and it still looked a little too Cardassian for comfort.

He coughed harshly, and it cracked him out of his haunts.

From behind, Odo asked, "Chief?"

"Fine . . . air's a bit stale."

Hanging with both hands from a steel rod overhead as he swung over piled trash on the deck, Odo huffed at him. "Only if you breathe it."

O'Brien paused. "Looks like we're up against a dead end here."

"Are you sure?"

"No passage right or left . . . I'm flush up against a bulkhead. Cold, too. Let's have a light."

From a suffering rucksack that had bumped along

on one hip all day, Odo tugged another of the small illuminators and clicked it on.

Gassy white light gulped at the darkness and finally swallowed most of it, enough to show a dust-shrouded wall made of several pieces of dented metal panels, bolted and welded to each other in a crude manner.

"Oh, the captain's not gonna like this," O'Brien muttered. "Not a bit."

Odo squeezed in to put a hand on the shabby wall. "Why not?"

"Look at the seams. Anybody with a can opener could break in through this mess in five minutes. You know the captain . . . sees every little disturbance as killing somebody's family."

With a twist of his flat lips, Odo tilted his head. "That's not a nice thing to say."

"I don't mean it poorly. We've had a streak of peace on the station lately. I just don't like to be the one to bring him trouble. Wish I didn't have to tell him about this."

"I'll tell him," Odo said. "I'm in charge of security. It's my job to bring him trouble."

"You sure there's no schematic of what's down these ruddy throats?"

"None. This pylon and the one directly above are the two oldest parts of the station. Though *Deep Space Nine* is only about 21 years old, some of the parts were cannibalized from existing stations. No telling how old they are."

"Crazy-quilt space station," O'Brien grunted. "Hear something new every day, don't we?"

"Yes, we do." Odo craned his long neck to look at the edges of the patchwork wall. "There's a sensor source behind here."

"It's not open space?"

"No. There's a six-point-four-meter pocket between us and open space."

"Air in it? Maybe there's a hull breach."

Odo keyed the tricorder and waited until it did its search. "Very little air. But no breach. It's vacuum-sealed."

"Let's put some air in it."

"Now? Without protective equipment?"

"Why not? We've had a hellacious time getting this far and I want to know what the Cardassians were trying to keep anyone from seeing."

Rather than waste time on a pointless agreement, Odo handed O'Brien the tricorder and toed around the clutter, then reached down and came up with a four-foot metal rod. Looked heavy. Maybe a forged rhodinium blend. Even Odo had a little trouble hoisting it.

He fixed one end of the heavy rod flush into the palm of his hand, supported the middle with his other hand, and aimed for a seamless patch on the bulkhead. His narrow shoulders flexed, rotated, then set.

"Take cover," he rasped, and braced his legs.

BANG!

Wheeeeeessssskkhhhuuuuuu

O'Brien clutched at the collapsia of ragged structural stuff around him as the sudden rush of air from here to there pulled him nearly off his feet. He came down on one knee, the other foot skidding out of control. A tornado of metal shards and bits of insulation material struck him in a sudden tidal wave. As he crammed his eyes shut, his last glimpse was of the rhodinium rod being ripped out of Odo's hand and the constable's thin body bowing forward.

O'Brien reached out and caught Odo's wrist, yanked back hard, and managed to keep the other man from crashing forward into the rattling bulkhead.

Ssscheeeeeeee

The sound was deafening, mind-filling. O'Brien felt his cheeks twist out of shape and grimaced to keep control and hold himself in place, waiting to be sliced in half by some soaring booby trap. His hand cramped, his fingers clawing into Odo's uniform sleeve. Strange how much it felt like real fabric—but there was a slight oiliness where his fingertips pressed hard. Was he imagining it because of what he knew? Confused by the noise, the rushing air?

He held on hard, teeth grinding. If there was a hull breach in there in spite of what the tricorder read out, even one that hadn't quite broken through, this would certainly break it and they were both dead men. All he could do was hold on and wait out the wind.

Hundreds of pounds of flotsam thrashed past them, all rushing for the four-inch hole Odo had punched in that makeshift bulkhead. They huddled for cover and only half succeeded in avoiding a hammering. O'Brien tried to pull Odo down, but the constable levered against him and maneuvered around behind to take the brunt of the pounding. For an instant O'Brien thought to shout at him, to tell him not to be protective, but then he realized that Odo could probably take the pounding better than he himself. Still—

Shaaaaahhhhh . . .

The whistle began to fall off. Took damned long enough.

He forced one eye open, just a squint.

The bulkhead was still there, though now dent-pocked and skirted with a talus of junk. But no structural collapse.

As he got shakily to his feet, O'Brien found his legs and back throbbing with pain, and glanced down to see if he was cut anywhere.

No blood. "All in one piece," he faltered. "You?"

"So far." Odo ran his fingers along the dented wall, then glanced into the tricorder. "The pocket is equalized. Not the best quality of breathable air, but it'll do. Still cool in there, but warming up."

O'Brien brushed crumbs of shaved hull material off his arms. "What now?"

"There's no time like the present." Odo handed him the tricorder.

"You be careful, now."

"I think we're beyond that point, Chief. Stand clear, please."

O'Brien stumbled as his heel came down on a solid block, but he skidded back a step and found a place to stand. When he looked up again, Odo had already stopped looking like Odo. In the constable's place was a mottled liquid pillar, arms and legs now melting out of form, shoulders falling and flattening. Another moment and there were no more knees, no chin, no hair.

With an involuntary shiver, O'Brien managed to hunker back another inch or two. The pillar mutated into a tower of silver jelly, lengthened, curved forward, and poured through the four-inch hole in the bulkhead. Stretching, it went through that hole like a snake into the ground, its last inch whipping like a tail.

He pressed close to the hole, but it was too dark to see through. He thought he heard another sucking sound, or squishing sound—or was it in his imagination?

"Odo?" His skin crawled. Shapeshifting . . .

Was the tricorder working all right? Was there really good enough air in there to breathe? Was it too cold—and would the cold be bad for a shapeshifter?

"See anything?" he tried again. "Odo?"

Just as he was about to take a blunt instrument to the hole—why hadn't they brought phasers?—there was movement behind the wall.

"Hand . . . a . . . through."

"What?" O'Brien went up on his toes to clear the skirt of junk at his feet.

There was another shuffle. "Hand me an illuminator through the hole."

"Oh—sure. Here you go."

The illuminator was barely small enough to go through, with a little encouragement from the heel of O'Brien's hand. In another second, frosty haze erupted inside the hole.

"Do you see anything?" O'Brien nosed up to the opening again. "What's in there?"

Bearing his weight as he leaned forward, his fingers started to cramp. He pressed his palms against the bulkhead, but the metal was too cold for him to do that for very long.

Aggravation growled in his stomach and crawled into his bowels. Damn this place . . . just when he thought he knew his way around, just when he had control, just when he'd gotten it safe to live here, gotten it in order, this giant set jaw in space decided to flex itself and show him what for.

He put one foot up on the mess of junk. "Odo! Can you hear me all right?"

"Yes, Chief." The constable's voice was faint.

"What's in there?"

"Call Captain Sisko. Tell him to get Dr. Bashir and the major and come down here right away."

"Why?" O'Brien put his eye to the hole, but saw only bits of dust floating in a band of ghostly light.

"Because," Odo rumbled from deep in the shadows, "we're in a lot of trouble."

CHAPTER
2

"ALL HANDS, STAND CLEAR. Let's have it down, Chief."

The bass voice drummed through the half-collapsed pylon tunnel, heavy and loud in spite of the quiet.

Not the place. The voice. There was no volume in it, yet it carried.

In spite of sonic disruptors and phaser cutters, sometimes there was nothing better for a job than a good old crowbar. Chief O'Brien put his shoulder to the iron bar he'd crammed into one of the patchwork bulkhead's seams, and leaned on it. Over his head, Captain Ben Sisko had a grip on the top of the bar and put his weight into extra leverage.

The wall creaked, resisted, then merrily gave, and O'Brien felt his legs straighten suddenly as he poured through the open gash even before he realized how hard he was pushing.

He came down on one shoulder and two cheeks, one on his face and the other on his backside. Had no idea he could twist in such a manner.

As he blinked and tried to roll off the pile of junk he'd made of the bulkhead, Benjamin Sisko's dark face loomed through the floating dust. The captain was reaching down to help him to his feet.

O'Brien forced his body to curve upward and managed to get up mostly on his own. He left the crowbar on the deck, and blinked into the chamber that had been closed for, as near as they could read from their instruments about the age of the chemical-bond seams, the whole time the station had been in existence. Eighteen years.

As he stood beside Sisko, O'Brien held his breath a moment and waved at the dust cloud.

"Cold in here." Behind them, Major Kira was just stepping through the opening, coming into the dark, small bay like Peter Pan stepping into a Neverland grotto. She was a quick trigger who knew what it meant to be kept from control and meant never to feel that again—certainly that was why she was here. It was never enough for her to let Sisko or anyone else see something firsthand and be deprived herself if she could wheedle into the front rank. Didn't always work.

The fine dust made a cloud around Kira's blunt-cut red hair, and dulled her eyes as she glanced at Sisko, a head taller than she was.

O'Brien was glancing at the captain, too, he realized.

Gazing forthright into a gathering cloud, the captain wasn't glancing at anybody else. He was just staring, fully involved in the ten thousand sudden implications flooding his mind and his experience. Yes, before him was a circumstance he had never seen or experienced before. Today, as O'Brien had come to expect, Sisko flickered to life when a chance for crisis popped up.

Framing Odo's narrow form as he stood in the middle of the dusty deck, along the cold outer-hull walls of this cramped chamber were twelve stone slabs, and upon those slabs, in unlikely repose, lay Cardassians.

Emaciated, sunken, grayer and more snakelike even than in life, with skin shriveled to paper and exposed veins collapsed, corpses so long dead were even more disturbing than if they'd been killed today, O'Brien thought as he gawked from behind Sisko's considerable shoulder.

They weren't covered with anything. No shroud, no protective covering, nothing. Only dust blunting the bright colors of their unfamiliar clothing and coating their bony faces. It wasn't death as he would have expected. It was a shade or two uglier. Nor were they lying in any particular position. Some were on their sides, some on their backs, some with hands on their chests, some with arms flopped over the sides of the slabs on which they lay, as if they had tossed around during sleep.

Sedate as a Vulcan, cloistering an unexposed temper, Ben Sisko didn't move much. At first he seemed only to be counting the corpses again, making certain there weren't any hidden corners or cabinets in here or anything tacked to the ceiling.

"Some of these tunnels are sensor-shielded, sir," O'Brien said. "That's why we don't know what's in 'em." As he watched, the engineer found a bizarre similarity between Sisko and the dead of their enemies—the same massive body structure, wide shoulders, broad chest, the same wide brows, and even the same black dots for eyes that could drill like an old-fashioned barn tool. He was built like them, as if given to *Deep Space Nine* to stand up against them, as if to say to the Cardassians in a subliminal manner that, no, they couldn't have the station back.

They'd lost it, and it was Ben Sisko's now.

"Oh, this is just great!" Major Kira blurted when the silence got to her. She swung this way and that with her hands out. "You've desecrated a Cardassian tomb!"

O'Brien blinked himself out of his stupor, and realized she was blazing at him.

"Well, how could *we* know?" he said quickly.

"You couldn't leave well enough alone? You had to explore these forsaken tunnels? *Now* what!" When Sisko flipped his enduring gaze to her, she gathered herself. "Sorry, sir . . . now what?"

"Now," Sisko rumbled, "we follow procedure."

"There isn't any procedure for this!"

"Then we'll invent some procedure." He tapped the comm badge on his chest. "Sisko to Dr. Bashir. What's your location?"

"I'm . . . somewhere in the tunnel . . . this is very difficult going, sir . . ."

"Take your time, Doctor."

"We should've beamed him through, sir," O'Brien said in empathy. "That tunnel's a sorry wreck."

"We'll get it cleaned out before we bring anyone else through it, Chief." Sisko picked his way through the two-inch-thick carpet of dust that made a *puff* every time his boots struck. "Be a hell of a field trip for the boys once we make it safe."

Kira was leaning over one of the corpses, her shoulders tight as she looked into the staring

Cardassian face, the mask of her lifelong enemies. "Shriveled," she muttered. "Doesn't look like anything recent."

"You don't know that," Odo pointed out. He wasn't going near any of the bodies, O'Brien noticed. "Don't touch any of them. You don't know what they've got."

"This isn't a time for jokes, Odo," Kira said.

The shapeshifter raised his chin. "I'm not making any. There's no sterile field here."

Kira shrugged, but looked at the corpses near her and stepped back. "I don't like this. . . ."

"Major," Sisko began and turned to her, "could they have been killed by the Bajoran underground who didn't want the bodies seen?"

"No one in the underground would treat Cardassian bodies so well," Kira admitted with a telling roll of her eyes. "A disposal chute would've been too good. Besides, we *wanted* the bodies seen."

A sound—a crackle and bump—in the tunnel made O'Brien turn back the way he had come. In the back of his mind he'd been waiting for this, knew it was coming, and reached through the craggy opening to help Julian Bashir stumble through.

"I knew it," O'Brien muttered as he drew the doctor in by one arm.

Bashir's boyish face was as gray as those corpses over there, his bronze hair indistinguishable from the dusty ceiling, his uniform sleeve torn and blood draining from his arm to his hand and from there to the deck.

"Doctor—" Sisko stepped toward them.

"I'll be all right, sir." Bashir's soft British voice was scarcely better than an unconvincing gasp, his large eyes wide with relief at finally finding the end of this particular tunnel. "Cut myself on something. I'm not even sure what."

"We should've provided a Security escort," Odo grumbled from near one of the Cardassian slabs.

"Oh, my . . ." Julian Bashir let his jaw drop as he leaned into O'Brien's grip and stared into the chamber. "My goodness, what is all this?"

Professional fascination capped his initial shudder as the doctor stepped past them one by one, to gaze across the chamber at all twelve corpses, then to focus on the nearest one. With his bloody hand he dug into his medikit and found a medical tricorder, and began to wave it over the body as it stared up at him. Its head was tilted slightly to one side, and seemed to be looking into his eyes, which bothered everybody but the doctor. And maybe Odo.

O'Brien, though, found himself leaning a bit off to one side to avoid those staring eyes. "Julian, don't you think we'd better tend that arm?"

"One moment." Already lost in metabolism.

Or what was left of it.

"Cause of death?" Captain Sisko asked straight off.

The doctor bobbed his eyebrows and frowned at his medical tricorder. "Something's interfering with my readings . . . I'll need better equipment."

"Never mind that. Just give me what you've got."

"Well . . . their heads aren't bashed in, there aren't any gashes, stab wounds, or other major trauma to the bodies . . . all organs are present—"

"Are they mummified?"

"You mean like the pharaohs?"

"I mean, has anything been done to the bodies after death, like the blood drained or anything put in there."

The doctor's brow tightened. "Not that I can discern . . . there's some reading of blood, but it's in a rather dry form. I can't tell about the amount."

"Doctor, I'm just trying to find out if this was done to them on purpose or if they were trapped in here and fell asleep in the cold, or what. Can you at least tell roughly how long they've been here?"

"This skin tissue is confounding my readings a bit, but the clothing"—Bashir recalibrated his tricorder—"seems to be on the order of seventy-five years old. At least, that's what I get from the state of molecular decay of the fibers."

"Any contamination that you can find, Doctor? Any danger to us here?"

"No, sir." Bashir hung on the word as if unsure. "I'm getting some very faint readings . . . might be bacteria, but they don't read as contagious. The skin is *so* strange . . . probably the age . . . and I've never had a chance to autopsy a dead Cardassian, so I have no experience, but judging from my readings here I think we're safe, sir."

"Safe," Sisko rumbled with that low voice. He strolled from the middle of the chamber to the farthest slab, looked into the face of the dead Cardassian as if to find something scratched in the paperlike skin, then came back again. "We won't catch a plague, but we're still trapped. They weren't murdered by Bajorans and therefore were probably left here by other Cardassians. How will the Cardassians feel about our breaking into a burial chamber? What do you think, Major?"

Kira flinched. She'd been about to touch, fingertips only, the arm of one of the corpses.

Suddenly she was set apart from them, away from

all humans and even away from Odo. All at once she was Bajoran. She was the soldier of the underground again, not an officer with a Starfleet field commission, but a spit-fisted fighter who had the longest and most antagonistic relationship with Cardassians of anyone on the station. At the moment, she was their only expert.

"Sir," she began, her eyes wide as Julian's now and filled with the responsibility shifted to her, "I'm used to dealing with *live* Cardassians . . . that is, unless I helped make them dead ones."

Sisko stepped toward her. "You must know something about their traditions. Is this a normal form of interment? I've heard they like to bury their dead in space. Is that something new? The doctor says these bodies are seventy-five years old. How can that be, on an eighteen-year-old station? Come on, Major— you've done battle with these people since you were a child. Don't you know any of their legends or beliefs? Superstitions? Religions? Voodoo? Anything, Major?"

"None that ever looked like this!" Kira smiled mirthlessly and gestured in dismay at the baffling scene around them. "I've never seen uniforms like these before either! If that's what they are . . . they could be some kind of tribal outfit. I've heard the Cardassians used to be divided into tribes. Or I suppose they could be burial clothing. . . ." She stepped from the corpse nearest her to the one near Odo and poked at the unfamiliar body-armor-type leggings. "Looks like something a Klingon would wear."

"But not these colors," O'Brien spoke up, and was startled by his own voice. Yes, he wasn't imagining it—there was an echo in here. How the devil could that be, with a ceiling this low? Damned Cardassian architecture. "I've never seen either Klingons or Cardassians in bright red and orange and purple like these people. Don't know that I'd wear it myself."

Julian Bashir straightened up, but leaned the heel of his hand on the slab under the Cardassian he was examining, and blinked and groaned. "Bit stuffy in here, isn't it?"

"Sit down." Sisko scooped up the doctor's good elbow and maneuvered him to a place where he could sit. "You're losing blood, remember?"

"Oh . . . yes."

"I'll take care of it." O'Brien grabbed at the reason to move, do something, distract himself from the grisly scene around them. He didn't have the constitution to be an archaeologist. "Where's the medikit?"

"Over there. Dropped it." Bashir pointed at the deck near the slab, then gazed at his bleeding arm. "I haven't the faintest clue what cut me."

"The tunnel is set up with booby traps," Sisko said. "We'll have a crew go through and clear it."

Plunging into the immediate task of cutting away the torn sleeve, sterilizing Bashir's arm, and putting a temporary bandage on it, O'Brien started to say something, but clamped his lips and made himself stay quiet. He wouldn't say anything the captain didn't already know. Diplomatic implications, military ones—a Cardassian tomb a quarter of a century old? Loaded with problems.

Sisko was an enigma of a man to Miles O'Brien, who always knew his purpose day by day. As an engineer, O'Brien had the comfort of dealing in tangibles. He liked things that way. Even when theories crept in, he started to sweat. Diplomacy—now, that was just asking for trouble. Sisko could have said goodbye to the bundle of problems of a deep-space station, never mind one where a stable wormhole had been discovered. Now DS9 was not only a way station but a gatehouse, a place coveted once again by the Cardassians, who had once abandoned it as junk.

"Seventy-five years," he uttered as he gazed at the dead soldiers. "Well back into the warring history of this sector. Long before the Federation found our way here. I imagine there aren't many artifacts or preserved bodies from that era. We've got ourselves quite a find here."

"What do we do?" Odo asked.

"I know what do to," Sisko said, and raised his hand to his badge. "We call our friendly local Cardassian."

CHAPTER 3

"Sɪsᴋᴏ ᴛᴏ Dᴀx. Patch me through to Garak, please."

They all paused and waited.

Something about this made O'Brien hold his breath. This would be one of those moments when their local, friendly—if there was a definition for conditional friendliness—Cardassian became more than a haberdasher, more than an exiled alien no longer welcome among his own. This was a time when Garak would become consummately Cardassian, though the Cardassians didn't want him. He was *their* Cardassian, *Deep Space Nine*'s, maybe even Starfleet's, from moment to moment.

O'Brien suddenly couldn't wait to see the tailor's smart-ass face and hear his explanation for this.

But nothing happened. No response.

"There's a haze of interference down here, sir," O'Brien said. "Try again."

The captain's brows twisted with dissatisfaction, and he tapped the badge again. "Sisko to Dax, come in—"

"Dax here, sir."

"Patch me through to Garak. I need his monumental wisdom about a little problem brewing down here. No—on second thought, never mind patching me through. Just get him, stuff him into a transporter, and beam him directly through to me."

O'Brien glanced at Kira, and it was as though they could both see Jadzia Dax smiling over her control board. She'd enjoy that.

"I'll have him there in a few minutes, Benjamin. Dax out."

"The Cardassians aren't going to like this, sir," Kira said suddenly, as if she'd finally let the attitude of her longtime enemies distill in a calm corner of her mind. "They might assume we did this."

The hum of a transporter made them stand aside, and in a moment there was another gray face in the crowd, this one animate and full-faced.

"Captain, how impertinent. Beaming me into the bowels of the station without so much as a pardon-me?"

"That's right, Mr. Garak," Sisko said bluntly. "Right into the bowels."

O'Brien gave in to the reflex to stand a little in front of the injured doctor—he didn't trust Garak. Everyone was suddenly tense again, for they all realized Garak had been beamed into the center of the chamber facing Sisko and with his back to the bizarre decor.

"I don't like leaving my store," Garak said. "I'm not an employee of the station, you know, I'm not one of your crew, I'm not at your beck and call. Constable, I'm sure *you* can explain the—"

The Cardassian expatriate swung around to lobby

Odo, but in his periphery caught the corner of one of the slabs, and that was enough. He swung all the way around, arms out at his sides, mouth gaping, eyes like balls.

A terrible thing, to see a person so sledgehammered with shock.

O'Brien felt his eyes tighten with sympathy, but also with curiosity. They were dead. So what?

Garak didn't even seem to be breathing. He was up on his toes now, pivoting to take in the whole picture of the twelve corpses arranged without ceremony on their slabs, their heads turned this way and that, arms frozen in whatever position they'd fallen into decades ago.

"I need your opinion, Mr. Garak." The captain spoke out through the spectacle before them as if asking for a merchandise list. "Who do you think I should inform about this first?"

"You can't tell anyone!" Garak choked, then shouted, "Not *anyone!*"

Sisko closed in on him. "Why not, Mr. Garak? What've I got here? It's just a tomb, correct?"

"Just a tomb?" Garak pressed the heels of his hands to his head and stumbled away, staring from one corpse to the next. "There's no such thing as *just* a tomb!"

There was a glint of victory in Ben Sisko's eyes as he raised a brow and looked toward his own crew, toward where O'Brien stood over Bashir, with Kira farther to their right.

"These are old." Garak was hovering over one particular Cardassian corpse, a sunken individual, not as massive as most of the others. His voice was barely there. He was speaking to himself. "Eighty

23

years, maybe. From the previous age . . . the age of the High Gul . . . remarkable!"

"Why is it remarkable?" Sisko prodded.

"Because these are soldiers!"

"How do you know that?"

"Because tailors don't get this kind of treatment!" Garak shook himself and straightened up, then stepped back to gaze upon the bodies longer. "For me, they'd probably just flush my body out into space. I'd be grateful if they just waited till I died to do it."

Kira lanced Garak with a blistering glance, then stepped between him and Sisko. "I think you should tell Starfleet before you notify the Cardassian Command."

"Mmm." Sisko continued looking at O'Brien as if waiting to see if he could goad another opinion out of him.

The engineer looked down and the doctor looked up. O'Brien knew what was expected of him—he'd served on a starship, not just a space station, and he'd watched his captain and officers tumble and brace under the flexing of galactic borders, interstellar personalities, and unthinkably long-armed protocol. Why didn't he have an insight or two?

So O'Brien threw in what he knew. "Depends how much control you want to keep, I'd wager, sir."

Sisko was watching Garak, who was now creeping from one slab to the next. Garak held his hands to his chest like a squirrel, and now reached out to poke one of the corpses, then flinched back as if he expected it to jump up. The silent faces of the dead gave them nothing.

"Notifying Starfleet," Sisko said, "triggers a certain

series of shiftings of responsibility. So-and-so is then required to notify such-and-such, who has to contact this and that, and of course along the way I get less influence and less control. Ultimately interstellar law and the treaty between us and the Cardassians kicks in." With a frown at the sudden complications, Sisko shook his head. "Maybe I should just hand these bodies over to the Cardassians right away and be done with the whole matter."

"I wouldn't," Garak said, twisting to look at him without really turning. He was working hard to control his voice, but his eyes gave him away.

With his teeth gritted, Sisko pressed, *"Why* not?"

"You'd better pull up the agreement between the Cardassians and Starfleet, Captain. It states, 'As long as there are Cardassian citizens-in-good-standing residing on this station, the Cardassian Central Command retains the right to inspect the premises.'"

"So what? Other than you, and you're not a citizen-in-good-standing—"

"Because the clause doesn't specify between *live* Cardassians and *dead* ones, Captain. For technical purposes, a dead Cardassian has all the rights of a live one. If you think they'll miss this opportunity, you haven't been paying attention!"

"I have been," Sisko droned. "There's a Critical Information Clause in the treaty that says each side must consider the beliefs and creeds of the other when confronted with situations like this one, even if we don't know what those creeds are."

"That leaves the Cardassians open to making up a creed to fit the situation," Odo said. "It's not a very well written treaty."

"We were in a hurry," Kira drawled. "We wanted them out of here. It can't be that hard to keep them out."

Sisko glanced at her. "You know as well as I do that Cardassia intends to get this station back and get control over the wormhole. That's in their medium-range plans and I'd be a fool to ignore it. The treaty's only a thin veil while they bide their time. I'm sure you don't want that any more than I do, Major."

"Well . . . no, sir, of course I don't. But I know the Cardassians." She didn't even offer Garak a look, but spoke as if he weren't there. "They're superstitious and possessive, but they're also manipulative. They'll want to do their own ceremonies around these corpses and anoint them and parade them as past heroes and use them to shore up current morale. If they discover we kept dead Cardassian soldiers here in this condition, unburied, unburned, just stuck on slabs, drying out like so much meat—"

"The Cardassians will *insist* this station be reoccupied until a proper investigation can be carried out," Garak said.

Irritated now, Sisko glowered at him. "Define 'proper.'"

"You define it! As long as they want, that's the definition. Such a performance can be unending. They could claim you or I or anyone did this, and investigate forever!"

"Pity's sake," O'Brien groaned, then realized he wasn't helping much. "Do you know how much mischief they could commit on a sanctioned stationwide inspection?"

Odo came out of his shadow, stiff with composed

anger. "After they evacuated, it took nearly a year to clean out all the listening devices, trip switches, booby traps—the whole station was like that tunnel out there. We'll never be able to have another secured meeting if we let them get their toes back inside our doors for sanctioned inspections!"

"And the resident Bajorans won't be happy about having a Cardassian presence on the station," Kira admitted. "We took this station at the cost of plenty of lives and we don't intend to let it slip back. Any number of my people would be pleased to slip a blade between some Cardassian ribs. We'd have to divert Security forces to protect the Cardassian inspection team."

"Then we'd be spread thin," Odo added, "and we'd have to ask for additional troops."

"Then everybody'll be here," Sisko picked up. "Cardassia, Starfleet—everybody. If I tell Starfleet, then they'll be under obligation to inform the Cardassians, who can then lever inspections on the station. That's *if* I knew about all this, and *if* my crew were efficient enough to tell me these bodies were here. Luckily I'm not very bright. Neither are any of you."

"Thank you, Captain," Garak heaved.

"Chief—"

O'Brien blinked, his mind tumbling with visions of armed, angry Cardassian inspection teams thumping through the toothbare corridors of this giant set jaw in space. DS9 would become an even hotter hell's kitchen than it already was. "Sir?"

"I want you to seal this area up again and put a 'contaminated' notice on the bulkhead. We'll lock it all up on both ends until I have a chance to do some unofficial looking around . . . find a path without thorns."

"That could take months, sir."

"They won't be any deader, Chief. All of you keep your mouths shut until I figure out what the next step should be. Until then, it's just going to be Halloween around here for a while."

CHAPTER
4

A SORRY, SAD little place to spend generations, with only cobwebs for banners. Not a flag, not a drum, no salutes nor any murmurs of appreciation for the grander age moved the stale air here.

What a place to hide a hero.

Damned Starfleet efficiency. When Chief O'Brien sealed something, it was bound to stay sealed. Breaking in made for a torturous hour of picking and chipping, with that bogus CONTAMINATED AREA sign glaring down. Couldn't use a phaser—it would be picked up. Couldn't do too much damage, or his tampering might be too easily discovered . . . too soon.

Garak's hands were cold and stiff, though he was working hard and breathing like bellows. His clothing was snagged and his thick skin scored by the long crawl through the tunnel. He knew what was hidden in there, and though those bodies had been in this room for eighty or more years, he was eaten up by the idea of leaving them in there alone for one more hour.

Every minute of his trek down the tunnel, and now every minute of picking away the sealed bulkhead, chewed at him without remittance.

Suddenly he flinched and spun around to look behind him. He thought he saw that large, dangerous living shadow of a man who could stop him from his task. But there was no one there.

Still, he continued to flinch and look. Sisko hadn't seemed bothered by what they saw down here, but then, Garak knew, he hadn't understood it. Yet, in Sisko's eyes had been a flicker, a hesitation, a clue that he suspected something.

He always suspected something. This was a man who was looking through the galaxy for a crashworthy seat and was enraged when anyone disturbed it—but not so much that he didn't want to keep his foot to the fire. He wanted a safe nest in which to raise his son, but he couldn't make himself leave the frontline. He had found an anchorage, but at the eye of the wormhole. He hunted excitement, yet roared when it came.

And he suspected it everywhere, Garak knew. Before long the eerie and inconsistent details of this tomb began to congeal in Sisko's mind, and he would be here again. Why were there dead Cardassians here, and why were the bodies so old, yet not dissolved to dust? Why had they been mummified, when in fact the Cardassians did no such thing to their dead and never had?

Shy of every collision, Sisko would before long be haunted by these questions and, just as he was the ghost of those he had been forced to leave behind in the tragedies of his life, he would begin to haunt the database of Cardassian culture, looking for what happened eighty years ago. It might start as a casual question to Jadzia Dax . . . *"By the way, while you're doing that, would you take a look at Cardassian history for me? When you get the chance."*

And the chance would come soon, and Sisko would be here again. That was all the time there was.

Garak's pipeclay-gray hands began to shudder and go pale as he forced back a panel of the bulkhead. Inches from his face, his knuckles turned bony with strain, every vein and ligament cracking to the surface.

It was a chamber of blighted hopes into which he stepped. Beaming in had been a completely other experience from this one, from putting his foot forward and carrying his weight into the presence of these elegant Cardassians of the past, of an age when Cardassia was the power of this sector, when the Federation trembled at their first meetings. Mmmm, such a time.

Garak fell back until his shoulder blades touched the ragged bulkhead, closed his eyes, and drew in a long breath of the dusty, brittle air. Eighty years . . . a long, long dream.

Crackle—he swung around. Noise in the tunnel—

He hunkered down, out of a shaft of light provided by one of the small illuminators left behind by the others. There was nowhere to hide but a pathetic shadow, no place to slip into or behind. He was stuck, found out. Into his mind flooded a half-dozen stories about why he was here, each a little wilder than the one before. None that Sisko would buy.

Insulation drifted from the tunnel ceiling onto the cluttered deck, making a crunching noise as the larger flakes fell.

His heart thundered against his ribs. His dinner

nearly made a second appearance, but he held control. And the edge of the bulkhead panel so tightly that his palm was bleeding when he let go.

He was still alone. In a way.

The thought struck him like a hand in the middle of his back, and he pivoted again to face the slabs and their dwellers as if they themselves had struck him. His legs were shaking now, too. If he were caught here, too soon, there would be fire, there would be slaughter.

The twelve bodies lay in casual mummification, each lying as if he had simply reclined to take a nap.

Garak blinked at his thought and leaned forward from where he was, squinting into the dimness. Yes, all these were male.

He expected that, but one could never be sure. Eighty years, after all. Things changed. Lies were told. Stories fermented. Customs cracked.

When he gathered his nerve, he went to the far left end of the curved row of slabs, to the body two from the end.

A Cardassian indistinguishable from any other, except to a Cardassian. Garak was thankful that Sisko didn't know many Cardassians, or there would have been a focus for the big man's instinctive suspicions. He would have seen the difference. He would have noticed the uniform.

Legs quivering, Garak lowered himself to both knees. From his pocket he took a standard palm-sized heating unit and attached it to the side of the slab, and turned it on.

Within moments, the unit began to hum, and the slab to change color.

He scooted back a few centimeters and looked at

the sunken, shriveled face of the Cardassian on the slab.

"I offer you all my honors, leader of my father, and I hear you whisper. This is the best time of all. Now I hand you all I have built here and turn myself over to you. I will bring you back to influence in this powerful age . . . and you will do the same for me."

CHAPTER
5

EVERYTHING WAS WRONG.

The ceiling was wrong first. Then the walls. Unfamiliar architecture. What planet was this?

The corner struts of this closet were unmistakably Cardassian, though. Not much of a clue, but a clue.

Yet, there was no building like this on Tal Demica.

Sight. His eyes were operating. And scent—dust. No moisture at all. Nothing musky . . . just raw, dry dust.

The revival palette was working beneath him. Only his face, hands, and toes were cool now, as if he were floating in a warm sea with a cool breeze dipping down.

No weapons lining the walls—stolen? But if stolen, where were their special mountings? This wall was unbreached, unmarred. No weapons had ever hung upon it.

So, even before he pulled his back muscles and forced his legs to rise and swing over the side of the revival palette, he knew it was he who had been moved and not the weapons.

Was he alone in this vault? Where were the Elite two thousand? Certainly not in this tiny room. Thus his relief as he gripped the edge of the palette, blinked his aching eyes within their throbbing bony goggles, and peered through the faint shafts of light cast by tiny fixtures upon the walls.

Along the walls on each side of him were several of his Elite Guard, most of whom were now rising. They seemed dazed, confused, sleepy, but those anchors were falling away. He had awakened first, and the other palettes had come into sequence, triggered by his. All these soldiers were younger, and awakening faster.

Six . . . ten . . . fourteen of them. Fourteen!

Where were his two thousand?

Possibly in other chambers in this facility. He gripped that thought and clung to it as he forced his fingers to flex, his neck to move.

Very stiff. Too stiff. How long had it been? Six months? Eight?

His assistants were supposed to be here to answer these questions. Where were they? Deserters, probably. So he would pick the answers out of the mountain himself. He had done it before.

He left his soldiers to shake themselves out of their daze and fixed his eyes upon the floor, working to clear his vision.

Dust. Plenty of it. They had been here a *long* time. Everything was layered with dust, including his own clothing and skin, but someone had been here very recently. There were fresh footprints in the dust layer.

And over there, footprints that led from nowhere. Had that person jumped from the entrance all the way to the far end of the row of palettes? What kind of beings had visited here?

The prints were of ordinary boots, not particularly large.

"Anyone who can stand, please do so."

Voice was terrible. Not a commander's voice. Scratchy, false, weak. Where were the survival supplies? There were supposed to be drinks ready for them. He saw none of this. His throat would have to make do. His soldiers would forgive it.

Still blinking, he looked around. Seven standing already. Very good. Three more with one foot upon the deck, seeking the strength to push all the way up. Two still fully reclined. One of those looking quite emaciated. Probably long dead. Obviously a malfunction.

What was this? On the side of his palette was an activator modem. Small, but recognizable. No dust on it at all.

"Wake up if you can," he encouraged. "Listen while you do. I am the High Gul, you are my Elite bodyguard . . . we are not where we expected to be. Our weapons are missing. The situation is unassessed; however, someone has been in this chamber within hours and presumably was responsible for keying the palettes and awakening us. That means someone knows we are awake. It may also mean we have a confederate in this place. The fact that our confederate is no longer here suggests collusion exists here, which suggests a volatile situation. Does anyone have a hand weapon? No? Well enough, we shall do what we can with what we find."

He forced himself to his feet. His own weight was foreign, and he became suddenly dizzy and weak, but managed to wait it out without falling. Managing to turn, he looked down.

"These are not our original revival palettes," he said as his soldiers began to move about and gather closer. "That means we have no idea how long we were in hibernation. Our palettes were scheduled to warm us after one year, but these have no timing mechanism that I can see anywhere . . . do any of you see a timing mechanism?"

Several of his guards ran their hands along the tops and sides of the other palettes; then someone said, "No, High Gul. Nothing."

He turned, and found himself facing his second-in-command.

The High Gul paused and smiled. "Elto, I'm glad to see you. So many of us are missing . . . I'm glad you're here."

"I'm here to serve, High Gul. I willed myself to stay with you," Elto said, his voice also weak and gravelly. The younger soldier was unashamedly devoted, and that was worth appreciating.

"I'm glad the conspirators who moved us here could feel your will," the High Gul responded, feeling the eyes of the others. What he said mattered down to the word right now. He would be the fulcrum on which their success would turn.

"We don't know what has happened to us," he said. "We have been moved and deliberately preserved. I see only eleven of us alive and I must assume there are only eleven of us here now, wherever 'here' is. Someone knows we are awake, but we don't know who knows that and who does not. We may have been captured by some Taldemi slime and kept here to be used as a bargaining chip. We may have been used against Cardassia instead of for it!"

His numb hands curled into balls and his elbows flexed at his sides. Control was a strain. His legs were trembling, his eye ridges pulsing.

They were all looking at him now, expecting encouragement, expecting him to know what he could not know yet, and expecting orders.

He steeled himself, turning away from the past but for the lessons it left.

"Our task," he began, keeping his voice in rein, "is to rise under the unsuspecting Taldem who hold this planet. They thought they won with their uprisings, but you and I are here and now awakened. We must find our two thousand warriors—that is our first priority, to gather our strike force. Then we will clear this planet for a landing. If we have been betrayed and there are only you and I left, those of us in this chamber, then we will do it ourselves. Afterward, we can contact the Cardassian Command, tell them to assemble their fleet, come back and retake this industrial base in such a manner that we will never lose it again. We will take this outpost first, and from now on hold this planet."

He paused, and looked at each face as the young members of his guard. Nowhere among them was a flicker of doubt, and he knew from experiences of his own youth that they were hammering back their fears. He cherished that in them.

They would do as he said. He must say well.

"I want you to recover yourselves, then divide out into this outpost. Wear your hoods and gloves so no one sees your face or hands. Look at the technology.

See where they store their weapons, for if we cannot find ours, we must gather from our enemies. Look at who runs the outpost. Find out what you can about them. If the first person you question will not talk, then move on. There is always someone who likes to talk. Then report back to me so we can assess the moment and plan to move it forward. If killing is necessary, it must be quiet killing. There is much we must figure out before we decide who we have to kill. If we have been used against our own kind, we will kill them all. Remember, we are the final defense in a great circle of action. That makes us the first offense here and now. We will do as we have been preserved to do. And we will slaughter anyone who comes into our path to stop us."

CHAPTER
6

"GREETINGS, GUL FRANSU. The salutations of the homeworld Central Distribution Authority are—"

"Idiot! Why hasn't my order number three-nine-four-eight-four been filled yet! The delivery is eight weeks late! I do know where your mother lives!"

"Order number three-nine-four-eight-four . . . one moment."

"I hate rotation! I hate it!"

"Acknowledged. One moment."

The voices were audible even when the door between the offices was closed.

Senior Red Sector Appropriations Officer Renzo nudged the door open and peered through to the miserable desk of his miserable commanding officer. All he could see beyond the pile of containers and requisition slides was the slick oyster-gray top of Fransu's head.

Every hair was tense. Amazing. But then, Fransu hated desk rotation.

Renzo maneuvered into the office, took a seat beside Fransu's desk, and began silently to regard his senior. Fransu was lavender with rage, exposed veins on the sides of his neck both corded hard and pulsing, his chin taut and teeth gritted.

Beyond that, he seemed as at home as any Cardassian behind any desk. Hence, nonoptional rotation of duties, without which the ships would all slowly fall apart.

Fransu's hot black eyes shot to Renzo and bored through as the seconds ticked away. Neither said anything.

"Gul Fransu, this is the Central Distribution Auth—"

"I know who you are. Get on with your explanation of where in the broad green galaxy are my shipments."

"The requisitions came through, but you neglected to attach Form Twelve to each requisition. I explained that to Glin Renzo—"

"I did include the Form Twelve. I did, I *did.*"

"But only one Form Twelve for the entire shipment. There must be a separate Form Twelve for each individual requisition. I told you that. According to Article Blue-Twenty-Three, I'm not allowed to move forward without that."

"Article Blue? A blue Article?"

"In the Blue section of the twenty-third manual. I can't take action without the proper form, sir."

"Oh, I know! If my own blood were on fire and I didn't have the proper form for a hose, you would turn me down!"

"Thank you for comprehending."

"Oh, I comprehend, you . . ." Fransu's considerable shoulders sagged beneath the weight of iron bureaucracy.

Only Fransu could see the face upon the viewer, but Renzo could imagine the pasty deskworker on the other end of the communication. Some people, even some Cardassians, reveled in detail work and inevitably they found their perfect place in the universe, usually making grief for field officers whose turn it was to run some desk somewhere.

Glancing again at Renzo and seeming to draw strength from his assistant's presence, the Gul leered with blunted rage at his private viewscreen. "What *else* do you need?"

"That should be all."

"Good."

"As long as you have your protocol clearances."

Fransu's lips peeled back against his teeth. "Yes. Yes, I've got those. I've got all of them. Boxes of them."

"Very well. I look forward to processing your orders. Salutations to Glin Renzo. This is the Central Distribution Authority signing off."

"Goodbye. Many goodbyes. Burning goodbyes. May you die of goodbyes."

The hazy light cast from the screen onto Gul Fransu's roundish face suddenly fell away, leaving only the harsh light from the ceiling lamp. His eyes once again flipped to Renzo, and he sank in his seat, shrinking like a beaten animal.

Renzo defied a smile and simply asked, "You don't know what a protocol clearance is, do you?"

"I'm not certain I could even spell it, Renzo."

"Would you like me to have him killed for you?"

"To what satisfaction? There are ten thousand

more of him, lined up to sit behind that desk and give pain to whoever sits behind this one. They are the 'Give Gul Fransu a Twisted Spine Consortium' and there is no getting to the bottom of them, not even with a Blue Form Article P-Nine Z-Four dash growl."

Renzo nodded. "Frustrating, I know. To have reached so high a rank as you have, yet suffer rotation."

"Rrrrotation," and here was the growl. "Ridiculous decisions by the barrel! All these minutia, pushed farther and farther up the command chain, because no one below wants the responsibility of having made a decision. Not even the smallest decision! Do you know that Gul Ebek contacts me every day during my rotation, just to needle me about it? He saves back all his needs until my rotation, then floods me with acquisition requests for his cursed squadron! I should push his promotion schedule and get him on this rotation, and on that day I will be needling, believe me, I will be needling hard."

Renzo fell to silence and waited for the Gul's mood to change. He wished he had better news.

Intuitive even through his fog of fury, Fransu was now staring at his aide, and there was no silence through which Renzo could shield his reasons for coming in here. He sat now on the crawling hint that he'd made a mistake.

"Tell me there's an emergency," Fransu snarled, and began to lean forward. "Tell me we're at war. Someone's blown up the homeworld. My mother-in-law has been unmasked as a Klingon agent. Tell me something to get me out of this, short of shooting myself through the head!"

A swipe of his arm plundered half of the desk's contents onto the floor with a bitter rattle.

"Nothing so insignificant as a war, I'm afraid," Renzo said. "We've gotten a private signal for you from Terok Nor."

"From where?"

"Terok Nor. Our occupied station near Bajor."

"So what? What do they want? We don't run that station anymore. Let them whine to Starfleet if they want something."

Gathering himself with what he hoped appeared to be an effort, Renzo didn't hide his foreboding. Perhaps if he stalled a few seconds, the age-old message would deliver itself.

It didn't. Fransu continued to glare at him as if Renzo were Form Twelve with boots on.

Renzo held himself stiff in his seat, lowered his chin, and raised his brows. "Sir . . . it's not from any of the people there. It's an *automated* signal."

The commander paused, peering at him, as memory nipped and tugged.

"A very *old* signal," Renzo added.

Fransu's eyes suddenly went narrow, then shot wide, and all other imprints of a bad day dropped from his face. "Not just that someone has broken in . . ."

"No, sir. That someone has activated the revive sequence."

"Revive!" Fransu seized.

They knew each other very well. Decades upon decades of mutual dependence, of spiraling up through the ranks together, of wars and wounds and rotations inward and outward. Renzo read Fransu's face as easily as reading a child's story, and knowing that, Fransu made no attempts to hide his roiling thoughts.

"Revive," he uttered. He stood up, and paced around Renzo's chair to the other side of the office. "Curse me that I didn't take care of this before . . . that I avoided making the decision all those ages ago, Renzo . . . what was I then, that I failed to erase the problem at the time?"

Quietly Renzo said, "You were a thief who couldn't sell a stolen piece of art, but couldn't bring yourself to destroy it either. So you hid it."

"I couldn't bring myself to kill him," Fransu agreed. "I should have. But I thought I could engineer the future."

He placed his hand flat on his desk and gazed at the clutter here and on the floor, and he sighed a great sigh.

"You were right," he said heavily. "I should have taken your advice then as I have learned to do since then. Now our grim harvest comes back to poison us."

Renzo stood up, but didn't move toward his commander. "I should have advised you more strongly. I was greedy, too. We were very young."

Without looking up, Fransu nodded. He stood in disturbed silence for many seconds, gathering the full realization that he had gone in a few moments from making piddling decisions to making quadrant-shattering ones.

"Very well," he scratched out. "Prepare my flagship. Pull the maintenance crew off. Notify my prime crew to report in two hours. Load the ship with full armaments. Talk to Glin Angat—he owes me his career. Tell him I want warp-nine drones launched into the Bajoran sector and every bit of communication blanked out. Tell him to lose any record of where those drones have gone. Make sure he understands that part. No one is to know where the drones have gone. If he gives you any problem, contact me immediately."

"He'll give us no problems, I'm sure."

"And call Gul Ebek. Tell him he's been promoted and his first duty will be to replace me on rotation."

Plucking the commander's uniform jacket from its hook on the wall, Renzo held it so Fransu could slip into it. "Command will be confused at your leaving rotation early."

Fransu neither nodded nor disagreed, for his mind was already far away from here.

"Once I make this problem die as it should have died long ago," the Gul said, "that will be the best trouble I've ever been in. If necessary, I'll leave an unexplained cloud of dust where that station is now floating. Then it and its foul contents will be in the dead past, where they all belong."

CHAPTER
7

"THE NEWS DOESN'T get any better, sir. I've checked into Cardassian customs, as much as we have information about, but it's almost impossible to get any information without arousing suspicion. I can't exactly tell them I want to set up a museum or I'm writing a school paper."

Kira Nerys squirmed in her seat. Cardassians weren't exactly her favorite topic of conversation, or research, or anything. She'd spent half her life fighting them and the other half trying to forget they ever existed, and felt doomed to be eternally confounded on both fronts.

Before her, Captain Sisko sat like a monument behind his desk, dark and quiet, absorbing whatever she said without breaking his smooth expression. "I understand, Major. Just tell me what you do know and we'll go from there."

"If we try to investigate too much," Kira went on, "we risk news getting out that we found a Cardassian mausoleum on the station. Never mind the Cardassians, I don't think the residents'll be very happy about that."

"I don't think we have a problem," Sisko said, "as long as Garak keeps his mouth shut, and he didn't seem as if he wanted to talk about it."

Kira leaned forward in her chair and leered as if at Garak himself. *"He's* just about as likely to—"

"Bashir to Captain Sisko."

Sisko held up a placating hand to her, then keyed his comm unit. "Sisko here. What is it, Doctor?"

"About our quiet residents, sir. On the cell samples I took, we may have another problem. I don't know precisely what was preserving those fellows, but I have reason to believe that now they've been exposed to air, their cell structure may begin to break down and they'll start to decay. I don't know how long you intend to take in making your decisions, but I doubt the Cardassians will be too pleased at getting their relatives back as bones and dust and strings of scaly skin."

"Can you do something about the decomposition?"

"We might consider putting sterile fields around the bodies to keep any microbes from—"

"That would be an absolute admission that we knew they were there. We'll leave them as they are for now and take our chances. Is that all, Doctor?"

"Yes, sir, that's all, but I thought you ought to know."

"Thank you." Sisko shook his head and looked at Kira. "So the clock ticks. All right, Major, what did you find out about Cardassian customs? I supposed you'd better speak faster now."

For a moment Kira couldn't tell if he was joking or not. "Well, I was right about the fact that they don't usually preserve bodies like that. I mean, they don't preserve them at all. And they don't leave the bodies of their fallen behind if they can possibly retrieve them."

"Which leaves us with the same haunting question . . . what are these bodies doing here at all, and why were they moved here, as they obviously must have been?"

"I say we flush them into the sun." At Kira's left, Odo finally spoke from where he stood near the wall in a shadow. Typical Security officer—always ready to be jumped. "Or phaser them. They're just corpses. Dead tissue. Bones and scales. I'm not afraid of dead Cardassians, but I certainly don't want live ones on this station."

"We can't do that, Constable," Sisko said even-handedly. "We may find we have a responsibility to the families of those individuals down there."

Odo shook his head and folded his arms tight around his narrow chest. "Dead is dead. What can the affection be for a lifeless corpse? I don't understand this attachment to bodies."

"That's because you don't have one," Kira sniped, running her forefinger along her mouth.

Just as she was about to turn to him with an apology for her joke at his expense, Odo came out of his shadow and stood over her.

"Feel free to discard me after I die, Major. I would find it an insult to have my dead remains put in some ornate bucket and 'visited' every few months."

Kira pivoted a calculated smile at him. "Okay, I won't visit you."

Odo fumed down at her, small eyes complex and

probing from within his smooth mask of a face, as if he couldn't decide whether to say thank-you or not. So he turned to Sisko.

"She's right," the shapeshifter said. "They don't leave bodies. That makes this either a mistake or a trap. And we'd better know which."

"So what you're both telling me," Sisko picked up, "is that I've either got a minor annoyance here or a major diplomatic problem, and I'm leaning toward assuming the latter. The Cardassians are high-strung. If they don't prefer to leave their soldiers' bodies behind, I doubt they'll prefer the idea of having their mausoleum desecrated. But if those were my relatives, I'd want to have them back and take care of burial myself. I know what it's like to lose someone and not have something to bury. *Deep Space Nine*'s not going to be part of that story for anybody else, if I have anything to do with it."

CHAPTER
8

"REPORT."

"High Gul, I have seen many corridors, but I saw no windows. There are science labs, at least three that I found—"

"Their purpose? What do they analyze or build?"

"I don't . . . know that, Excellency."

"Go on, then, Koto."

"But one of them is an infirmary!"

"Good. Go on."

"Turbolifts go everywhere, horizontal and vertical, as well as a honeycomb of accessways behind the walls."

"What is the architecture?"

"Pardon me?"

When the young soldier became confused by the question, Elto stepped forward to their leader, who was a head shorter than any of them yet could put them all spine-tight to a wall with a glance. "High Gul, it is Cardassian architecture."

"You're certain of this? I wouldn't want you to be mistaken, or our decisions will be bad ones."

"I recognize the corridor structure and the building material."

"Rhodinium?"

"Yes, High Gul, rhodinium sheeting with some molybdenite and other alloys used for structural support members. The power conduits and computer stations are clearly Cardassian. I can read them. But, Excellency . . . we see no Cardassians here. Many aliens of many kinds, but no Cardassians."

"Have you done a sensor scan for other Cardassians?"

"We are trying, but these controls have been altered and we don't trust them."

The High Gul tipped a glare at him. "No Cardassians in a Cardassian installation."

"None that we can find. And we see no one here who is Taldem either."

"None of our own people . . . none of the planet's natives . . . then who controls this place? Did you see anyone you recognize?"

"Yes, Excellency. Ferengi, Bajorans, and others who may be Bajorans, but have no ear cuffs."

The High Gul stood in one place and resisted his urge to pace. Any movement could give them away, and if he seemed nervous, then his men would become nervous. "Bajorans," he thought aloud. "Slaves from halfway across the sector. Why would they populate a Taldem installation? Unless, of course . . . we are no longer on Tal Demica."

"You mean someone has removed us from the planet?" Koto gasped, with such bald shock that he seemed like a child in spite of his bulk. "But why?"

"My political enemies have long claws," the High Gul said. He held his voice down, and managed to keep the venom out of it. They would all take their cues from him, from his attitude, and from his anger. He must stay calm until he understood the situation.

Then, however, his men would expect him to act, and he would do that. But there were so many questions here, and he would have some of them answered first. They were awake now, but they might as well still be in the sleep, as little as they understood about their surroundings. Elto, Koto, Malicu, and Ren were back with their perplexing discoveries, but Fen, Clus, Ranan, and a few others were still out on reconnaissance. Entertaining a fleeting hope that they would manage to keep themselves unseen on a populated installation with no other Cardassians behind whom to hide, the High Gul kept his posture in check. His demeanor was critical. Confidence, even if it was a lie, a temporary one.

"What else, Elto?" he asked, breaking into his own thoughts. "Reach for conclusions. Jump, if necessary."

Elto paused to think, as if determined to come up to the task demanded of him. "Excellency, the communications setup and computer junctions are Cardassian design, but there is something that disturbs me. These are modern devices, all up-to-the-minute technology, and some is even beyond my skill as an engineer, yet everything here is . . . old . . . showing signs of wear."

"Old?" The High Gul swung to face his bulky second-in-command. "New science that is old? How old?"

"I would guess by the wear," Elto said hesitantly, "fifteen, twenty years."

The High Gul turned from him to keep the worry on his own face from shining too sharply on Elto. With one hand he touched the gritty knuckles of the other and felt the silt of time.

"And dust . . ." he murmured, his gaze unfocused. "All this dust . . . twenty years . . ."

Koto's eyes bulged suddenly and he shuddered with realization and choked, "My wife! My daughters!"

The youngest of them, their thick-skulled, eminently devoted Inos, stepped forward with his fists balled. "High Gul! Who would dare keep us suspended for twenty years! To keep *you* suspended? You, who started it all!"

"We were put in suspension by our own command, to be the final gauntlet," Elto said. "To rise again from the talons of the enemy and destroy him! How did our enemies gain control of us?"

"We cannot assume it was only our enemies," the High Gul said grimly. "This may have been done to us by fellow Cardassians."

"What Cardassian would do this to another Cardassian?" Koto stammered, shaking violently now, seeing in his mind only visions of his wife and children.

"None," Elto snapped back.

"There are those," the High Gul corrected. He could provide a brave image for them, but he would not deceive them. All the evidence indicated that they had been stolen from their original place of suspension, taken right off the planet, moved to another planet, and hidden away in this vault.

But why?

"If this is true," he went on, "then our families are grown, our wives are old. We were left to molder here while our civilization, our families, our fellows went on without us. Worst of all is the probability that our suspended forms were used as bargaining chips or artifacts, trophies in some twisted struggle—used *against* Cardassia—I can scarcely think it! Our anger is easy and I am angry, but there will have to be action, too, and we must calculate very carefully our actions. We have advantages here . . . we must be clever to use them. Elto . . ."

"Excellency?"

"You say you can read the systems on this installation?"

"Yes, Excellency, though some of them have been integrated with new systems."

"Does that mean you can shut them down?"

The large young officer was taken by surprise, hesitated, then his expression changed. "I can surely try."

"I wish you to try. Shut them down slowly, one by one, so it appears to be a series of malfunctions."

"Which systems, Excellency?"

"It doesn't matter. All of them. This will serve to distract attention from us and also confuse those who occupy this outpost. No windows . . . we seem to be in an underground facility. Close down the lighting, the air circulation, power conduits, service umbilicals, turbolifts, or even just the turbolift doors. Anything to cause chaos. Enjoy yourself, Elto, shut down everything. If you make a mistake, we'll deal with it. The rest controls this place. Learn your way around. Malicu and Koto, I want the two of you to scout us a new headquarters. Someone knows we are here, so we shall not stay here."

"Yes, High Gul," Malicu answered, for Koto was still shuddering in his personal horror.

"Tactically," the High Gul went on, "hiding in these lower chambers and in the access walkways, we are in good shape. Try to keep your faces hidden, but if anyone sees you, kill them and hide the body. But kill as few as possible—we may have an ally or two here. Elto, shut down the internal sensors first. That will prevent them from finding us with biosignals. Yes, my strong young men, this is your chance to do what you were so carefully trained to do. Better than a simple battle, this is stealth conquest. We can gain control by chaos . . . and when the building is debilitated and the people suffering, we will all escape to the surface and leave the invaders to suffocate."

"Uff! What the—"

There were dignified ways to break a nose, crack a tooth, or scratch a smooth ivory cheek, innumerable manners through history for valiant cranial injury, but smashing full-front into the doors of a stalled turbolift wasn't one of them.

Kira Nerys felt her arms flail out to her sides and little lights blow in front of her eyes as she hit the flat surface of the panels. They rattled dully, but didn't budge. Too bad. She'd been in a good mood until now.

Every day, every hour of her presence on this station, the Ops turbolifts had slid graciously open no matter how hard she strode, ran, or dived toward them, except today. She clamped a hand over her face and stumbled backward.

Watching her from across the Ops deck, Jadzia Dax sat at her station and remained eternally calm, the humanoid embodiment of the low notes on a French horn. Soft overhead lights cast shines on her tied-back black hair, backcombed a little too high and a little too smoothly—well, that's probably what happened when a pretty young woman used to be a shriveled old man. But even a Trill who'd forgotten four lifetimes ago what it was like to be a woman couldn't muss up the fluid classic beauty of Jadzia.

Sure wish she'd try once in a while.

Suddenly feeling skinny and tomboyish, Kira hated the perfect hair and the perfect lights and the fluids and all that general perfectness as she stumbled back toward the control panel, fingering what was left of her nose and her aching front teeth. "Whu'muppen toofa turfolifs?"

"I don't know," Dax said as she worked her controls coolly, though her perfect brows were drawn. "But look at this. I'm getting red lights from all over the station. Two-thirds of the turbolift doors on the station just froze."

"Tell Dzoolian to get ready for a vunch of 'roken novves."

Dax looked over her shoulder. "Are you okay?"

The question only irritated Kira as she pressed her fingers in a peak over her nose and throbbing mouth. "No! I cut the infide of my yip. My mouff iv gonna fwell up now, I bet."

"Well, don't worry. We'll find the perpetrator and string him up. You can hold the rope."

"Iv anyvuddy ftuck infide a lif?" Kira forced herself to lower her voice and put her hands down, sufficing to explore the inside of her lip with her tongue between sentences. "Better check."

"Yes, I am checking. I'm not getting any emergency blips for anyone trapped in a lift. Not yet anyway."

"Have Security check them personally." Sniffing, Kira pressed one finger to the side of her nose. "Ow . . . that's never happened before. We've had our share of problems, but that's never been one of them. Why would the turbolifts freeze?"

"It's not the lifts," Dax said, tapping elegantly upon her controls. "It's just the doors. The lifts are still in operating order."

"Not without doors, they're not. The safeties won't allow them to move without doors. No doors, no lifts. Get the chief on the comm for me."

"All right. Ops to Chief O'Brien, come in, please."

Kira drew a breath to talk to engineering when the chief responded, which ordinarily would be virtually instant. But nothing happened. She let out her breath and had time to draw another. "Well?"

Dax frowned. "Chief O'Brien, please respond."

"O'Brien here . . . sorry. We've got our hands full down here."

"Doing what, Chief?" Kira leaned forward over the controls as if that would help.

Another ten seconds trundled by.

She glanced at Dax. "Chief, what's going on down there?"

"—isolinear op—cal chips—without any—and the internal sensor sys—shutting—"

"Chief!" Kira blurted. "You're breaking up. Are you using your comm badge or the main unit?"

"—hear you, Major. It won't—any—ence. There's a damper wash of—kind and I can't—cate it. Do you read?"

"Stand by, Chief, stand by." Frustrated with insufficiency, she realized she was raising her voice as if that would help. She looked at Dax. "Did you get any of that?"

"If there's a damper wash coming over the internal sensor system," Dax said, "it'll shatter all forms of communication whether coming through the main systems or through our comm badges. It'll crackle the signals on the fly."

Straightening, Kira glowered. "I guess you got it, didn't you?"

"That's my job, Major."

"Come on, don't gloat."

"Am I gloating?"

"Well, your hair and eyelashes are gloating. What could cause a thing like that?"

"Nothing I know of short of sabotage, but once in a while these old Cardassian systems find ways to feed into the new Starfleet mechanics, even though they're not really compatible. It's like an old warhorse trying to get back into the battle, not realizing its days are over. I'll see if I can't track it. Maybe a process of elimination—"

"And with the lifts out of order, we can't go down there to see what the chief is doing or tell him what we're doing. I *hate* little technical annoyances . . . I'd rather fight the whole Cardassian fleet. I'll flip you to see who reports this to Captain Sisko."

Dax passed along her sedate half smile that had an underlayer of pure devilry. "There are advantages to not being second-in-command."

"Oh, thanks, thanks very much. You just helped me decide not to tell him until we get this figured out. Mechanical glitches—what waste of time! We try to be a legitimate space outpost, and when we hit a stride, we fall back into hell's kitchen. If we can't keep control over this Cardassian tortoiseshell, we're just another semiautonomous jerkwater town with nothing to offer anybody at all. All right . . . now that I've gotten that out of my system, let's start with square one and figure out a way to get messages back and forth to engineering. Anybody got a string and a couple of tin cups?"

"You'll find string in the open cosmos," a heavy voice announced from behind, "and tin cups in my old camping pack. What's going on?"

Approaching the central control console, the heartbeat of Ops, Benjamin Sisko appeared out of a shadow as if he had materialized behind them. As Kira turned, it struck her how often she saw him that way, just popping in out of nowhere, like the ghost of cultivated grief that he once reminded her of, vacant, tranquil, grave, yet somehow second-sighted. If he didn't know what was going on, then he always suspected, and the suspicion put him one step ahead of everybody else.

Kira straightened and almost went up on her toes to meet his considerable height. "How'd you know anything was going on?"

"I saw your expression through my office viewport. You've got a lousy poker face, Major."

"A poker face doesn't do a resistance fighter much good, sir."

"No, I suppose not. What've you got?"

"Frozen turbolift doors," Kira said, waving a hand at the lift car that had attacked her, then at the console board, "and some kind of crackling in the internal communications."

"It's a damper wash, Benjamin," Dax filled in. "Breaking up any form of nonhardwired broadcast, including that from console to console."

"So we can't talk to the rest of the station and we also can't *get* to the rest of the station. Are all the lifts malfunctioning?"

"Ninety percent now, with others continuing to jam."

"Anyone trapped inside a lift?"

"Not that we know of," Kira said, "but with the communications going haywire, I'm not making any assumptions. I was going to have Security check every lift, but now I can't even do that. Anyone who's trapped is on his own for now."

"I don't like that very much," Sisko grumbled, circling around behind Dax's console. "Break out the old hand communicators and see if they've got enough gain to bust through the damping wash. Have Security assign two dozen yeomen to be communications runners and use the spiral stairways, cargo aisles, and crossover bridges to deliver messages around the station."

Kira watched him thinking his way around their problems, or straight through them, which sometimes worked better, and though itchy with these breakdowns and unready to run on vague feelings, she felt a sting of gratitude. She had accepted the Starfleet field commission for Bajor's sake and she would spit it back the day Starfleet abandoned the planet. But

Starfleet hadn't yet. She'd almost stopped wincing when the long-range comm twittered. The Federation had done what they promised, never mind the rare vacillation, each stepped on in turn by Ben Sisko.

She always watched him carefully, trying to read the explosion underneath, for that explosion would either destroy or defend her home planet.

"What ships have we got docked here at the moment?" Sisko was asking Dax.

"Three Ferengi traders, a supply ship from Starfleet, and two Bajoran mining transports."

"Try to contact all of them. Have them attempt to route communication through to other parts of the station. Find out who can talk and who can't."

"What should I have them say?"

"Well, first of all, have them tell people to stay out of the turbolifts."

To Kira's irritation, Dax broke out in a complicatory grin. Sisko wasn't smiling, but he did seem only slightly bothered by the situation.

Why didn't he get mad? Was he storing it up? He stood slightly away from the main console, watching as Dax fed her messages through with notable difficulty, only getting about twenty percent of them to the ships docked around the station. As dark as a shadow, with that cocoa skin and that gunmetal uniform, Sisko seemed hardly more than a human yawn, unplagued by the glitches that teased Kira until she wanted to kick something.

"Benjamin," Dax ultimately said, "I'm getting a telemetric communiqué from the captain of one of the Ferengi ships, who says they have a message from Chief O'Brien."

"Have him send it through."

"Sir . . . he wants to know what we'll offer them for it."

Sisko's incurious eyes came to life, suddenly bright with the audacity of the tease. "Tell him . . . I'll let him keep both his legs."

Dax smiled that reserved smile again.

For the first time today, Kira felt a grin break out on her own face—any chance to give a Ferengi a bad moment. That was worth having the communications crackle anytime. There was a certain beauty in imagining the simpering face and bloated head of a Ferengi captain throbbing with sarcasm, but twitching with that one immutable doubt, because they all knew Ben Sisko now, knew he was as much storm trooper as sentry and as likely to ignore regulations as live by them.

"Benjamin," Dax said suddenly, and her smile fell away, "I'm getting a relay from O'Brien through the Starfleet supply ship. We're getting malfunctions in our environmental support system—thermal control is shimmying . . . and atmospheric processing is being compromised."

Sisko's bland expression turned sour, and he pressed both hands on her control panel and leaned forward as if to double-check what he already saw. "Is anybody besides me absolutely certain that those Ferengi aren't doing this to cause us trouble, because I'd be perfectly happy to be dead wrong."

"No, it's not them," Kira said. "They wouldn't dare."

Ignoring both her and his own previous statement, Sisko said, "Go to auxiliary backups."

"Yes, sir," Dax said, slipping instantly into professionalism and working faster as she and Kira caught the caution in Sisko's bass voice.

"Are the backups coming on?" he pressed after two minutes of clicking and tapping.

"Seem to be, so far," Dax said. "Subsystems are pulling support from auxiliary, though I'm still getting some flux in the stability of the systems."

"What's causing it? Can't be the same damper field as what's affecting the communication."

"Or what's freezing the lift doors," Kira threw in immediately.

Sisko glanced at her as if agreeing. "Could there be some kind of general virus doing all this?"

"Yes," Dax said.

Unsatisfied, Sisko pulled to his full height. "That's not enough of an answer, old man."

The elegant woman turned to look up at him, and her voice was quiet. "But the accurate one. Yes, a single virus could theoretically affect all these unrelated systems. It's not usual, but it's possible. Do I know what variety of virus or where to begin looking for it? Not yet."

"What was the first thing to malfunction?"

"The turbolifts," Kira filled in.

"Then start with those."

Dax nodded, but said nothing as she bent to her work.

Sisko paced around behind them again. "Where's Odo?"

Following him, Kira said, "Off duty, sir."

"Does that mean he's resting in his quarters, or sitting around in the bar, irritating Quark?"

"I think he's at the bar. Quark never gets as many

patrons when Odo's there, at least not at the Dabo tables. Odo knows that and he likes to cause Quark as much harmless, legal grief as he can."

"I know he does. See if you can get a message through to him somehow about all this."

"Why?" Kira asked. "It's not a Security problem, is it, sir?"

"Potentially. At least, until we find out it's definitely just a mechanical glitch and not sabotage."

"Sabotage! Sir, why would you suspect that?"

"Any time more than two things go wrong at once, I always suspect somebody's doing it on purpose. I don't believe in coincidences, Major."

Kira shrugged. "It's a pretty ragtag station, sir . . . half the technology cannibalized from Starfleet, the other half left over from the Cardassians—things are bound to go wrong, aren't they?"

"That's fine, if it's the turbolifts and communications. But when it's environmental support, I don't take chances. Hanging out in space we can't exactly just open the windows for a breath of fresh air."

Kira didn't argue. Past experience had taught her about the underlying Sisko, the man underneath the cool mask of the arbitrator, always shy of collision, feeling as if he had to hang on to DS9 by the fingernails.

What must that be like? At least she was only miles from her homeworld, could comprehend what she was fighting for, and know that people like her and with the same background were right out there within reach. She'd never been to Earth, but she knew it was far enough away to cause nightmares of loneliness. For Kira, distance had always been a matter of hours, maybe days. She knew that for the captain and his teenaged boy, home had better be here, in this calcimine firedog at the wormhole's hearth, because it was many long, cold weeks away otherwise.

As she watched Ben Sisko stalk the Ops command center and poke at the controls, she suddenly wanted to go home for a day or two and knew that every morning he got up avoiding random thoughts like that. He'd run away from too many sadnesses after the war between the Federation and the bitter-cold Borg. As a Starfleet veteran of a particularly vicious war who was raising a son by himself, he wanted shelter and safe haven, but he wanted it on a wind-blown cliff.

Just how worried he was on any given day, during any given problem, was hard to read. Kira wore her biases on her belt and had no problem drawing them, but Sisko was more closed.

So she ended up watching him a lot, sifting for interpretations.

She didn't always get them.

"How's the auxiliary going?" Sisko designed his patrol back to Dax's station.

"I'm focusing on rerouting the connection to Chief O'Brien. I've almost got it . . . try now."

Sisko swung around toward the comm panel. "Chief, can you read me? Chief O'Brien?"

"This—infirmary, sir. I'm—up your—Chief."

"You've picked up Bashir," Sisko said to Dax, then spoke again into the comm. "Doctor, I'm trying to get through to engineering. Are you picking this up?"

"—es, I am, sir."

"Can you relay to engineering?" While Sisko talked, Dax fingered her controls with determination.

"I'll do my best, sir—have to say?"

"Tell them we've got malfunctions stationwide, nonrelated systems. This might include environmental control. Do you copy that?"

"Yes, sir . . . malfunctions, possibly environmental control. I'll see what—do. Bashir out."

"Well, that's progress," Sisko sighed. "Most of that got through. Good job, Dax."

"Sir, why don't you let me try to get through the service crawlways to engineering?" Kira suggested.

"I will, but before I send you crawling through those cobwebby shafts, let's wait a few seconds and see if the doctor can make contact."

She grinned at him. "Don't think I can take a few cobwebs, sir?"

"No, I think the cobwebs would have their lives at stake from you, Major, but let's do one thing at a time. If Dax manages to clear communications, we can tackle everything else in order."

At the panel, Dax shook her head as her long ivory hands played the board like a piano. "I doubt I'll clear it entirely, Benjamin. And then, not for very long. Conduits are still flashing on and off throughout the system. If I get you in contact with engineering, I may not be able to hold it, so be ready with what you have to say."

"Acknowledged. I'll be—"

"Captain? Do you read?"

"Chief! Affirmative, we copy you. Are you reading these malfunctions?"

"I can barely hear you, sir, and I don't—how long this'll last. Every time we mend something, something else goes down. We're—essing subsystems—oxygen

supply and the thermal levels. The internal sensor system is flickering too. I'm chasing down each glitch as it rises and trying to backtrack or bypass."

"Understood," Sisko said clearly. "We'll continue to—"

"Sir!"

Kira had almost let herself fall into the trap of being the second-in-command, of handing the trouble over once the captain showed up, and she'd been hovering at the other side of Dax's control panel, glancing from readout to readout, mindlessly watching the ones nobody was paying attention to. Everyone was minding the internal readouts as systems flickered and baubled within the complex, but nobody was watching the external ones.

When Sisko and Dax and the other officers manning Ops all looked at her at once, she realized what hammered-in training had made her do.

And she stuck by what she saw.

"Look!" She pointed at the screen that had caught her attention. "It's not just internal communications—there's a complete sector-wide blackout!"

CHAPTER
9

A DIMMER PLACE even than the vault in which they had slept, this hole provided the ideal seclusion sought by any saboteur, a grotto from which to extend affliction into the nearby community.

They had followed the web of Cardassian architecture, doggedly familiar once they let it work for them, left their gray mausoleum and now crouched within a low-ceilinged maintenance chamber whose walls were grouchy blue and marked with repair-coded panels of mustard yellow.

There was much less dust in here, but enough to inform them that the chamber had been undisturbed for years and probably would remain so, at least long enough to serve their purposes. The High Gul was pleased.

He congratulated his men twice when they found this place, this hole with open circuits whose connections could be fanned to life and made to scourge other systems in the complex. He told his men they were superior, because in their eyes he saw their need to hear it. They weren't feeling much more now than the blistering fear and fury and shock of what had happened to them, and none of those were helpful. The disfigurement of those feelings would impair them, torment and maim them, and he wanted the slates of their emotions to be blank for him. He did not yet know what the situation would demand of them, and he wanted to be able to play any card as he saw fit.

And what good would it do to let them fester in misery? Yes, they had been deceived, yes, their families had been told they were dead, yet their still bodies used in some hideous bargain, but he chose not to fan that flame yet, lest it burn itself out before he could make use of it.

These things required careful development, like excellent cuisine.

"Working quite well." The High Gul rearranged his stiff legs and watched the small auxiliary monitors before him, meant only for repair purposes. His eyes once served him better, but he could still see well enough for his ends.

"I don't know what I'm doing sometimes," Elto said as he picked at the exposed conduits.

"It doesn't matter. As long as there is chaos."

"Internal sensors are down, I know."

"We must keep those down."

"There are no Cardassians in the building," the younger officer said. "These people will probably not think to look for us with bioscans."

"Better they can't look at all. And remember, all of you, *someone* knows we are here and awakened. Someone wakened us, then left us there. Until we know who and why he remains silent, we make no assumptions." The High Gul leaned back and sighed. The cool dryness of the chamber was making him itch. "Besides, we still don't know what we're doing here, to whose purpose . . . even in ignorance I intend to find advantage."

Elto paused in the work that hunched his bulk into a tiny space, and looked around at him. "Your command is our will, High Gul."

Instantly he was echoed by the others huddled in the long, narrow space.

"Thank you," the High Gul said with a glow of appreciation, but in a tone that implied he fully and eternally expected their devotion and was entitled to expect it. "One step at a time. There is no hurry. Except . . ." He leaned forward again. "I *am* hungry. Has anyone seen food?"

"I saw a commissary," Ranan said. "But there was gambling."

"A public house. Gambling . . . that proves this is not, at least not entirely, a military base. Good . . . Ranan, Koto, you go there and see if you can bring food. If you find an easier place to get food, less populated, bring it from there."

"Yes, High Gul!"

"Yes, High Gul."

"And keep your heads covered, remember."

"Yes, High Gul."

"Elto . . ."

"Yes, High Gul?"

"Can you see any long-range sensor equipment tied in to these conduits?"

"Not here, High Gul. In these outlets I see only short-range sensors registering."

"Mmm . . . I wonder if there are any ships here. I

would feel better to steal one and get back in space, have room to maneuver, to make attack . . . it is a long desire of mine. I do not believe it ever went to sleep in me."

His men were watching him as he spoke, though he met none of their eyes. They were mystified by him, and properly so. Part of his job, of the responsibility of being High Gul, was to maintain the sense of magic and awe he saw now in their eyes. He felt the curiosity of their youth, the respect of students for an elder.

His many victories flew before his mind, and the success these had brought him in the Cardassian culture. He was High Gul—there was no other alive of that stature. He alone bore such a title, created for him. His approval or disapproval of a maneuver, political or military, could sway so many that the maneuver wouldn't even have to be performed to have an effect as if it had been. So strong was the muscle of cooperation beneath him that it was as if he had become de facto dictator.

This, he knew, was because he had never forgotten that his many victories had been as much good fortune as skill and bravery, and his influence only extended as far as his latest exploit. Such was the way with any leader in the Cardassian force.

The thought, plaguing him since first he had thought it, of his being used against his people was not only personally abhorrent, but was a negation of his entire life, his entire service. After twenty years, if indeed that was the count, or if those years were even more, was he unimportant among the current powers? Perhaps even an oddity to be patronized like a senile old relative?

If so, he must find and destroy the forces that hid

him in this place, and if they had forgotten the High Gul, he would make them remember. If they had used him, he would make them die.

Sharply he forgot his thoughts as they began to burn and pointed past Elto's noticeable arm. "What is that blue light flashing there?"

"A monitor of functioning inertial damping fields of some sort."

"Why would inertial fields be needed in a complex like this?"

"I don't know, High Gul. This equipment is highly sophisticated, elite extrapolations of what is familiar to me. It seems very advanced for twenty years, but . . . perhaps they are running experiments of some kind with inertial damping."

"Turn them off, then."

"Without tracing them first?"

"Chaos, Elto, chaos."

"Yes, High Gul . . . chaos."

The big second-in-command squinted to see better in the dimness, and punched the necessary button.

They didn't expect anything to happen. Expected in fact to have to risk their lives exploring out into this complex to discover what damage they had done and decide what to do next.

But the strangest occurrence descended upon them—they began to float.

Malicu shouted an unintelligible syllable as he tensed suddenly from his squatting position and propelled himself wildly from one end of the narrow chamber to the other, and smashed headlong into the High Gul's shoulder, which in turn sent both of them bouncing like balls into the others. If they had all managed to sit still, they would simply be hovering in place, but the activity caused equal reactions, and off they went, bumping and grasping in the dimness for a way to hold still.

Disorientation struck the High Gul along with a wave of nausea as his empty stomach reacted to the sudden weightlessness.

He flung out his arms, found a piece of structural metal, and held on, indifferent to the gulps and grunts of his Elite Guard as they also struggled for balance. He stared out into the narrow chamber at the bulky uniformed bodies that tumbled before him.

"Gravity!" he choked. "Artificial gravity! *That* was the purpose of inertial damping! We aren't on a planet at all! We're on a space vessel!"

His reaction caused him to flex his spine, which sent him convulsing forward to a place where he struck the side of his head. Reaching upward, he managed to catch the beam that had sent his brain ringing, and hold himself in place.

"Not a space vessel, High Gul," Malica said. "It must be a space station."

"How do you know?"

"I saw docking facilities."

"Yes . . . yes, a space station, then. Keep calm. Don't push around, hold yourselves in place . . . a space station, a space station . . . this changes everything!"

Elto, nearly turned upside down, with a flop of his black hair flopped from one side of his face to the other, one hand still clutching the housing of the bared circuits with which he was bedeviling this complex, blinked at him in the dimness. "How, High Gul?"

"Because a space outpost is here for a reason. No

one goes to the trouble and energy to place an outpost all the way out in space without some valuable consideration. A planet, a nebula, an ore-rich asteroid belt, a strategic location . . . something valuable enough to require guard. Much more important than simply a ship. If we can control the outpost, we can also control the reason. And don't forget—this is a Cardassian-built complex, without Cardassians living in it. Has it been captured? If so, what has happened to the Empire? When we answer these, we'll find our next duty."

"Do you wish me to turn the inertial damping back on, sir?" Elto asked, looking truly ludicrous now, pressed in a great hulking arch from the ceiling around almost to the floor.

"Not yet," the High Gul said, fighting to think in this unfamiliar state. "Now our chaos must be more careful and specific. We must debilitate these people and incapacitate them from acting against us, but we must leave the station functional in order to keep ourselves alive, and so we will have it to use when we take control. Very interesting, invigorating, this new challenge . . . you, all of you, pay careful attention and think very hard about whatever you see from now on. Unless your life is at stake, take the second action rather than the first. Do you understand? If you allow for that extra second, that extra breath, you may discover something that we can use. You may be risking everything, but you must now take the dangerous pause. Think, my young brigade, will you, of the dangerous pause."

He gazed at them, hanging as they all were, including himself, in this preposterous design as if illustrating what he was saying to them. Whether they comprehended or not quite yet, it didn't matter. When the moment came, they would recognize it.

"Go out now," he added, "and capture someone wearing a uniform. The time has come for me to have answers, and understand this prize of mine."

"Everyone, stay calm! Hold on to something! No, no, don't push off the deck or the walls! Madam, will you please hold onto that child before he turns into a projectile? Quark! Close your doors! Keep the people inside the bar!"

"Big talk from a walking water balloon! Why don't you just spread yourself into a big fish net and catch everybody until the gravity comes back on? You think I can keep fifty free-roaming patrons inside a dark bar at a time like this? I'm a wizard, aren't I? Talent worth a fortune! I wish!"

Odo coiled one leg around the handrail of a spiral stairway and watched in frustration as panicked station dwellers spiraled into the air like seed pods in a breeze. Their own forward momentum as they walked *Deep Space Nine*'s Promenade Deck now sent them soaring and bumping in midair, propelled by their own startlement that had prevented them from holding still and waiting out the mishap.

It struck him abruptly how many people were living on this station who in fact knew nothing about space travel or life in space or the eccentricities of either and who had never been trained to deal with such malfunctions as those of gravity control. They simply came here in a controlled-environment craft, and stepped out into the controlled-environment station without lending a thought to the effort and energy necessary to create and maintain this environment or what to do when it broke down.

"Quark, you have low ceilings in that bunco rat-trap!" he called across the open space of the corridor. "You can put people underneath them. When the gravity comes back on, these people out here in the corridor are going to—"

Plummet like rocks to the deck and smash every bone in their fragile nonfluid forms. No, better he didn't say that just to get a rise out of the station's number-one flimflam man.

From inside the open doorway of the bar, Quark offered a snaggletoothed grimace and communicated with his rodentlike eyes that somehow this must be Odo's fault, or at least that he would happily spread lies to that order.

"Keep as many people under the overhangs as possible," Odo finally told him, measuring his words and using his long cold stare to make an effect on the resident Ferengi woolpuller. "Tell them to get toward the floor and stay as close to it as possible, so they won't fall far when the gravity comes back on!"

"Sisko and O'Brien aren't stupid enough to turn the gravity back on too fast," Quark called. "Nobody's going to fall!"

"We don't know the extent of general damage," Odo called back, frustrated that he had to let so many people in on what was happening. "They may have no choice. We have to be ready for any circumstance."

He was saying as little as possible, but he saw in the eyes of the people around him that they were paying attention and reading in the complications.

A big fish net. Merited a thought or two . . . just

how far could he extend his substance? How thin could he stretch? He'd never tried that.

Still, he might catch between five and fifty floating victims, but there was a whole station full of people here. He was more use in this humanoid form, yelling at those who recognized his voice as the supreme custodian of common sense, order, and police action on DS9.

He rather liked it that way.

"See what you can do about getting people to hold themselves close to the floors. I'll try to get to Ops."

"You'd better try to get to engineering instead," Quark called, wrapped like an envelope around the very end of the bar, his bulbous head canted to one side to keep his sensitive wide-brimmed ears from striking anything. "Communications are down stationwide. If this gravity glitch is localized to the Promenade, Chief O'Brien's going to have to know about it before it can get fixed, and you're the only one who can turn to grease and squish under a door panel!"

Not sure whether he'd been complimented or not, Odo barked a few more orders to the wide-eyed patrons who were turning heels-up all around him and took the time to think about the logic of where he should go. Report to the captain, yes. But Sisko was no fool and probably already knew about this and the other malfunctions rattling through the station. Certainly everyone knew about the comm shutdown and the faulty lifts. He had personally extricated five people from the frozen lifts and he was already in a bad mood about it.

Odo hooked a toe around the stairway railing and glowered.

He hated when Quark made sense. Even more when he was forced to admit to Quark that Quark was making sense.

Might better be worth letting the whole station go to pot.

Suddenly a blunt sensation of solidity struck him—and all around it began to rain people.

Citizens dropped from midair and struck the deck in a gaggle, heads-first, knees-first, in piles, yelping and howling with pain as they slammed to the deck, powered by their own weights.

For Odo, variable mass was something he took for granted. He slipped to the deck also, but not with the punishing hammer blows of the poor souls around him. Around him he heard bones crack and flesh strike metal with bruising unforgiveness.

And someone began to sob.

So it was true—his guess was right. There was more going wrong than just the gravity. The systems to fix the gravity, and everything else, were also botched. Even the automatic safeties that would have prevented what just happened must be off-line or somehow compromised.

The whole station . . . compromised.

"Is everyone all right?"

With a gushing groan, Kira Nerys pulled herself up off the deck and custodially counted heads around the Ops center as everyone else stiffly got to their feet around her.

"Well, that was fun," she grumbled. "I always like a little fly around the ceiling before lunch. Artificial gravity now—what next?"

"I don't know," Sisko said, glancing at the readouts. "O'Brien must've managed to get control over it and get the inertial dampers working again. I wonder why he didn't turn it back on gradually, lower everyone to the ground slowly—there must be more breakdowns than just the obvious. Even the automatic safeties failed."

"And now," Dax added, "we also have to worry about how many people are hurt from the fall and can't get to the infirmary because the lifts are out of order." She pulled herself back into her seat and checked her equipment. "Long-range sensors still operating, Benjamin, and now I'm picking up two . . . possibly three warp-nine drones in the sector, distant but functioning. I think it's safe to assume there are more, which we're not picking up yet."

"It would take more than three to cause a sector-wide blackout," Sisko said, as if discussing a point over a game of cards, and rubbed the shoulder on which he'd landed when the gravity popped back on.

Kira had been watching him and Dax in silence for several minutes before the gravity went wild, keeping quiet as they sifted through the problems and tried to pick out which were homebound and which were external. As for any second-in-command, once the commander came on deck she was shunted to observer status, until she came up with something to contribute. That was fine—this series of events was bizarre to her.

She found herself asking two questions for every answer they got, while Ben Sisko was working through the situation one element at a time without getting mad at it.

Kira knew she would've been mad by now. In fact,

she was mad the moment her nose hit the lift door. Now they were all bruised too.

It was becoming a game, to see when Sisko would get mad. How much would he take before that stoic Vulcan-imitation exterior would crack? She's seen it crack before, but she'd never had a chance to actually watch the process.

"It's not precisely a blackout," Dax explained. "Blackout would mean hundreds of comm systems on planets, stations, and ships all shutting down simultaneously. It would be impossible to coordinate without the cooperation of every government and captain. What we're experiencing here is a whiteout—excess communications noise being flushed into the area, so much that it simply outshouts everything else, floods every frequency, and clogs the gains."

"In other words, no cooperative effort, no accident, but a deliberate act of sector-wide intrusion. Do you concur?"

"I concur, yes."

"Can you identify those drones?" Sisko asked. "What's the gain on their broadcast? Any propulsion mixture we can break down?"

"Very faint," Dax said. "Not enough for identification breakdown."

"No beams, semaphores, or signals of any kind?"

Dax looked up at him, and from the other side of Sisko Kira noticed a change. Dax's expression was layered with knowing. And Sisko's voice had gone indicatively mellow, his words specific.

"No beacons," Dax said, and continued to look at him.

Kira watched her, watched him—what did they

realize that she was missing? Suddenly she understood why she had fallen so quiet and let events play out before her. Something was changing, and her instincts had told her to shut up and notice it, pay attention and learn.

"Then it's not Starfleet," Sisko muttered to himself. "Are there any alert signals or blips that might suggest a drill or test of any kind?"

"No blips." Still turned up to him, Dax didn't even bother with her controls anymore. She obviously already knew these answers and was taking each in lockstep. "No alert signals."

"What are you doing?" Kira finally overflowed. "What am I missing?"

Sisko straightened and paced away, then turned back to say, "Several years in Starfleet Academy and Command School, Major."

For the first time in minutes, Dax looked away from him to Kira. "He's asking a series of proper questions before regulations allow him to come to a certain conclusion."

"What conclusion?" Kira felt like a child pestering her parents for answers about grown-up things.

Sisko was now pacing the deck as if playing out his role as the dad, sifting his experience for a simple way to deal with a complicated reality.

"Sector whiteout can be taken as a prelude to invasion, Major," he said. "And that's how I'm taking it."

Invasion. Not just a word, but the very sound, the embodiment of the action, the painting of horror. The settled galaxy had few corners any longer that had been isolated from the horror, and everybody knew what that meant and how high modern space science could execute such a concept with glaring, burning physical reality. Certainly Kira had never been protected from it in her life. Rather, her whole life had been one long response to such infliction.

It wasn't supposed to happen anymore. The Federation was here, Starfleet was here now. She had almost convinced herself the dangers of the past were over.

"Who is it?" she blurted. "Is this a move by Cardassia to get control of the sector back? Or could it somehow be the Dominion trying to extend control through the wormhole from the Gamma Quadrant?"

"At this point, there's no way to know," Sisko said evenly, but with smoke behind his eyes. "But I know what the Dominion is. I've been willing to take extreme measures to keep them out of this quadrant, even to destroying the wormhole. I'll carry through with that if I have to."

Feeling her body temperature drop, Kira pressed her fingertips to the buffer of Dax's console. "Without orders from Starfleet?"

"Major, I *am* Starfleet. That's why I'm in command here. For times like this."

His words were so simple, so unatoning, that Kira almost lost them in the hypnotism of his solemn eyes. He wasn't making any proclamations.

With a little spasm of her hand Kira pushed off Dax's console and took over the pacing. "This is a fine time for things to be going haywire all over the station," she ground out.

Even as she said those words, she realized the foolish blindness of them and felt her facial expression change. It gave her away completely as she looked up and saw Sisko looked at her knowingly.

"It's no coincidence," Sisko said in a confirming

way. "It's a good bet there are enemy operatives already on the station."

The headache just kept getting bigger.

And there hadn't been a single shot fired yet! Not a threat! Not a scratched line in the sand! Nobody had even spit on anybody else.

Somebody should at least spit.

"So," Kira shoved out, "what do we do? How do we fight an enemy we can't see, can't identify, and who may or may not already be here?"

"Tactics will be different," Sisko said as if ready with his answer, "depending on who's about to attack us. As far as actual punitive actions, we'll have to wait for them to make a move. Until that happens, we'll tighten security on the station and see if we can't flush out the birds who are sneaking around in the weeds."

Dax indulged in a quirkish grin. "So we start at Quark's, right?"

Sisko didn't respond. He was already involved in tactics. "Major, I want you to start evacuation of the station."

"Evacuation!" Kira interrupted. "Sir, the whole station?"

"All non-Starfleet personnel, and all the children first."

As she stared at him, he suddenly turned harsh and glared back. "I lost my wife in an enemy invasion, Major. There are lots of non-Starfleet people here and there could be lots of death coming."

"Commander," Kira began, slower this time, her brow tight, "don't you think . . ."

But she hadn't the conviction to say what she was thinking, to tell him he was being drastic, to explain to the man who knew what she would say how involved it was to evacuate a station the size of *Deep Space Nine,* or even that there wouldn't be any way to keep such an action confidential. He evidently didn't care whether it was kept confidential or not.

Sisko drilled her with a haunted and daring stare, brows down, the whites of his eyes showing like two reclining crescents beneath them, his mouth in a single straight line.

"I've been through an invasion before," he said. "I've seen it. I've paid for it. I know how much worse an attack is when the soldiers have their families with them. Heads aren't clear. Risks are entirely different. Innocent people die. Whoever will attack this station knows the station's defense—I have to assume that, because I wouldn't attack a place until I knew all I could know about it. There are saboteurs on board who are very likely equipped to overcome any resistance we initially offer. I don't have any intention of doing things in the order they expect, is that clear?"

Over the invigoration rising in her chest, Kira said, "Yes, sir!"

"Good. Get messages through to all docked vessels and tell them I'm issuing letters of marque that will allow them to act as de facto Starfleet ships and that their first mission is to take full loads of passengers down to Bajor."

"If this is an invasion," Dax said, "the planet'll be in danger, too."

"Taking a planet is a lot harder than taking a station. And they'll still have to get past me first."

He stared at nothing, fanning his inner flame, the flash of anger that would carry him through.

Kira recognized that anger, that flash—she had one, too. But she had rarely possessed control over it, to bring it to the fore as Sisko was doing right before her eyes.

His eyes grew hard and he drew a long breath. "A sector-wide communications shutdown and a series of debilitating malfunctions smells of a plan, exactly what I would to if I wanted to take an installation with minimum damage. If that's what's happening here, then we're going to be ready for it."

Kira glanced at Dax, and in that brief glance received the solidity she was looking for.

"Yes, sir," she said. "We'll be ready."

Sisko's dark cheek flinched, and somewhere under the conviction and the anticipation was a buried smile, of the kind that makes spines shiver.

"I'm betting Starfleet won't miss a sector-wide whiteout. All we have to do is hold our own until they get here. First we turn our attention to the internal sabotage, try to stay one step ahead of it and find out who's doing it. Major, as soon as the station has been evacuated of sixty percent of its non-Starfleet personnel, I want you to issue weapons to the staff. We're going hunting."

CHAPTER
10

"ODO, STAND STILL! Don't move!"

The shapeshifter bumped into Ben Sisko's thick arm as it was thrust out before him, and he stumbled back a step. The cool, dim passageway was like a coffin around the two of them, its long tubular shape stretching out before them into the undefined darkness. They might as well be in a cave.

"What?" Odo asked.

Sisko tipped his head forward just enough. "Look."

Odo peered deep into the shadows of the narrow corridor.

Two . . . three black-cloaked figures stood in the farthest shadow. Tall creatures, shoulders as wide as Sisko's, faces undefined in the darkness.

"It's them," Sisko said.

Odo puzzled, "How can you know that?"

"I just know."

There was no turning back—they'd come through four tubes no wider than wine drums in order to get to this passageway. They couldn't crawl away fast enough. It was time to stand and fight.

"Do you think the translators are back on-line yet?" he asked Sisko, keeping his voice down.

"I'll take the chance," Sisko said.

He stepped forward, his wide shoulders squared, knees locked, and his deep voice boomed under the low ceiling.

"You there! I am Captain Benjamin Sisko, commander of *Deep Space Nine*. Identify yourselves!"

Odo could see in the set of Sisko's jaw that he knew it might be useless, but that there was justice in announcing identity before demanding the same of others. That was the Federation way. No stabbing behind unidentified backs.

The beings in the shadows remained still, almost as if they themselves were shadows. For a moment it seemed as if there was no one really there and Odo thought the dimness might be playing tricks, but then the invaders moved.

They knew they had been seen. They were speaking to each other. Every few seconds a head would turn, a shoulder would dip, just enough to show that they were deciding what to do now that they had somehow cornered Sisko.

Odo realized with bitter self-recrimination that this was a deliberate trap. He'd imagined they were being followed, that someone had been watching them all morning, and now he knew his imagination had been more than the fantasy of a suspicious mind. He'd warned Sisko, but there was no stopping Sisko from going out on his own, pounding his way through the station, trying to get to engineering and help put back on-line the systems that were the station's heartbeat and blood.

And here, in the middle of some obscure corridor barely two men wide, they had been headed off—and there, only meters before them, was a cluster of cloaked infiltrators, right here, just like that!

Odo fumed that the station's security had been breached. The concept was poison to him, his only nightmare, because security was his responsibility and he had failed it. The station was his whole life, his pond and planet, and any adulterant his poison.

Beside him, Ben Sisko fully shuddered with fury like a leaf under the breath of a predator. His was an even deeper insult at the station's invasion. Odo watched and thought he understood, and was humbled by Sisko's restraint. He was letting the invaders make the first move, even giving them a chance to surrender.

"I should have suggested you bring your phaser," Odo uttered. "It's my fault."

"It's mine," Sisko grumbled out of the corner of his mouth. "I gave my phaser to Kira for Ops security. There are a dozen phasers in the lower core—I thought we'd get to the lockers before this happened. We're on our own. Just look armed."

"*Look* armed?" Odo whispered in horror. "How should I *look* armed?"

"Do what I do."

Sisko put his right hand into a fist and raised it to his hip, then hid it a little behind his back, as if going for a weapon. He bent his knees like a gunfighter Odo had seen in a holodeck plot.

"Insane!" Odo breathed.

Sisko held his left hand out in an accusatory gesture at the clutch of robed beings down there. "You! Surrender immediately!"

With a wonderful tin-box echo, the demand bumped on the low ceiling and set the thin plates to vibrating.

Suddenly provoked, two of the cloaked figures broke out of the shadow and charged.

Sisko shoved Odo back to get kicking room for himself. "Here they come!"

It was a kick that would knock a head off. A fabulous, unforgettable, heel-first kick, delivered to Malicu's shoulder, luckily, rather than his skull.

The High Gul stood in his face-shading cloak in a shadow of the narrow corridor. He had wanted to see for himself these people who had kicked out the Cardassian occupation of this place. Not even occupation—ownership. He had wanted to watch this fight between his Loyal Elite Guard and one of the occupying force.

When Malicu had come to him with an opportunity to kidnap the commander of the complex, the High Gul had hurried to agree. He wanted to talk to his opponent, understand his enemy. These moments of conversation were as fascinating to him as any battle. In many ways, they *were* battle.

So before him down the narrow corridor, the commander of the space outpost threw his kick at Malicu while Ranan held him from behind. Ordinarily, this positioning of one before and one behind would work well, but today the two strong young guards were helpless to possess this man. Malicu couldn't get anywhere near him.

It was something to see.

Strange how enjoyable, watching his own men be throttled so. Yet, the power of the beating was a thrill, and the High Gul knew his guards couldn't ultimately be beaten two-to-one. Only a matter of time.

Thus he enjoyed himself, kick by kick.

So this was a "human" . . . Elto had found the word in the computer banks and managed to translate it with the old Cardassian program.

As big as Malicu, shoulders wide as Elto's, thighs as thick and hard as Ren's, skin dark brown as toastberries in his home valley, eyes even darker—

Human. A race unheard-of in his time. How in twenty years had they become so powerful, enough to throw the Cardassian possession off a station in space? They must have come from outside, perhaps from another quadrant. Perhaps they were an army of settlers, unable to turn back. Yes, that would foster the fury he saw kicking and flexing before him like a rutting animal. As much as he wanted to destroy this man and possess what he possessed, the High Gul wished to talk to him for a few minutes before the destruction.

He pitied himself and mourned the time he did not have, to listen and learn.

But the man had said words the High Gul recognized now, even without a translator. *Deep Space Nine . . . identify . . . Sisko.*

Sisko.

The man in the muted uniform threw his weight back in a single great heave that threw Ranan back into a bulkhead strut and cracked that iron grip. Instantly the brown man was free, spinning like wind to land a blow upon Malicu's available face. Malicu jolted, but remained in place, feet braced, knees flexed, and leaned into yet another blow, which this time he managed to block with one meaty forearm. Even down the corridor, the High Gul heard the *thunk.*

Malicu raged forward and released terrible punishment upon the man, but his enemy soaked up the pummeling and would not falter. Blow after blow they rung off each other as, behind the man, Ranan struggled to find his senses. For a tantalizing moment the dark commander bent fully in half and committed the unthinkably bold move of grasping Malicu right around the middle as if to spin him up on his head. The weight was too great, though, and the heave put Malicu on the deck on one knee, and suddenly he and the commander were rolling in a bitter embrace toward the High Gul.

They never reached him. Ranan's instincts roused him from his daze and he threw himself forward so violently that he tripped on his targets, flew over them, and landed on the deck to become a solid brake.

There was vast invigoration in watching three such giants fight! The High Gul parted his lips as if tasting fine wine.

A fleeting thought interrupted the High Gul's enjoyment as he noted to congratulate his men for having singled out the leader of the complex, and for trapping him in this confined space alone. The High Gul had no idea how they did it, unable as they all were to understand the language here, and thus it was good work. Perhaps they had seen him giving orders.

Perhaps he wasn't the overall commander at all—perhaps he was only a brigade leader or a team captain or a corridor guard. Malicu had seemed so sure when they began following this one . . . mistakes were too easy in such a situation.

Down the dim corridor the embrace abruptly came apart and again there were three giants circling in a dangerous dance, with the human in the middle and the two Elites blocking his lines of escape. He was facing this way, facing Ranan now, and glancing expertly over his shoulder to measure Malicu's position and make sure he wouldn't be jumped on without knowing it, pacing himself to stay in the exact middle.

He was catching his breath, the High Gul noticed. Smart.

The dark man suddenly paused, stopped stock-still with both fists raised and his shoulders set, and stared down the corridor to its end.

And he saw.

The High Gul felt the flinch of his muscles as he realized without even thinking that he had been seen here in his shadowed nook. The commander spied him and now wouldn't look at anything else, though he erupted out of his pause and countered the punches that flew at him and hammered relentlessly on Malicu and Ranan.

Suddenly everything was different. Now the human refused to look away. He stared and stared, drilling down the corridor at the High Gul, and somehow, through the dimness and within the shadows of the hooded cloak, he found the High Gul's eyes and bored into them. Somehow they understood each other.

Yes, no doubt now. Sisko.

So they had entrapped the right man. Sisko himself, not just someone invoking the name of his leader. This was the commander of the complex, the ruler of everyone here, the person responsible for all lives, all success, all failure. This was communicated perfectly in that ferocious glare, unbreakable by the blows of the two Elites. No one else could have such an eye.

And the fight was different now, too—each chance he got to grab Malicu or Ranan and spin the action along the corridor, he took it. He volleyed punches and received them, poured forward into his task like a blade swinging, bright white teeth visible in a gritted square within his peeled-back lips and streaks of blood showing upon them. Now each blow, each kick, each shoulder up or down, each knee flung upward brought the brown man one more step toward the shadows. He was fighting his way to the High Gul.

Such ferocity! This man—what was he doing here? To administer an outpost, that was why the bottom of the barrel needed scraping. Such a creature as this, behind a desk? Why?

What if this were the most timid of these humans, if this were the kind considered most expendable by them? Imagine!

The commander still locked his glare upon the eyes of the High Gul, even as he punched his fists and drove his shoulders into the hard bodies of Malicu and Ranan, and centimeter by centimeter made headway down this narrow shaft toward the High Gul. There was instant communication between them— the commander knew this was the creature who had botched up his complex, scattered his peace, endangered his crew.

The High Gul raised his chin, only a touch, but enough to acknowledge the glory of the anger spinning in his opponent's eyes. And in that instant they understood each other perfectly. In a few moments they would be together.

The High Gul's attention shifted to the other human—

No, not human—the face was wrong. There was no expression, no lines or creases, no signs of wear, but only piercing blue eyes filled with excitement. A tan uniform—what did that signify? The Gul made a mental note to find out what the colors meant.

The other person was formidable, despite his thin body. Weight seemed to have no meaning to him as he dug his fingers into the shoulders of Ranan's cloak and wrenched the Elite off the brown man with a tremendous heave.

The abrupt change threw Malicu and the commander off balance and they struck the deck with a thunderous slam. Malicu took the chance to roll away from the commander, who lay for an instant and sucked a great sustaining breath before he too rolled to his feet. During that instant Malicu plunged to the side of the corridor, applied his brute hands to a wall stanchion, and wrenched it free from its place. Metal squawked, but the attachments gave. The long, thin pole came away from its braces.

Malicu spun around, let loose a ghastly shriek as he charged the newcomer, who was chest-to-chest with Ranan, up against the opposite bulkhead. Charging with his pole at his side, braced in both hands, Malicu drove the end of the pole into the spine of the stranger in the tan uniform.

The High Gul, who for his entire career had practiced not being surprised by anything that happened in a battle, sucked a quick breath in shock as the pole went straight through the newcomer as if he were hardly there, and plunged with Malicu's full force into Ranan's body.

The newcomer's back separated and his head kicked back a little, but he turned to look at Malicu without the slightest hint of having been pierced through. Where the pole went through him, his uniform and skin turned orange-red, separated, became liquid, and pulled out of the way, leaving Malicu staring into the stunned face of his fellow Elite. The newcomer dissolved to liquid across his middle, stepped out from between them all the way, spun against the bulkhead, and reassembled into his original form, his face twisted into a grimace as he expended effort.

Skewered to the wall, the pole driven cleanly between his lungs, Ranan stared with eyes almost as wide as the surrounding bone circles, his mouth that wide also, arms spread outward to his sides as if he were about to embrace Malicu in the terrible welcome that brought them together.

As well trained as the Elite Guard were, Malicu let out a yell of fright, as if waking up covered with insects, at what he had just seen—

Shapeshifter!

As the impaled attacker exhaled his last breath and slid to the deck, taking with him the pole that had pierced not only his body but the wall behind him, the other big assailant stumbled away and ran down the dark corridor with astounding speed for somebody so bulky. He grabbed wildly for the individual who had been watching them from the dark nook down there, and the two of them vanished into the folds of the station's bowels.

Odo growled an insensible noise and tilted to follow them.

"No!" Sisko said, and drove an elbow into Odo's chest. "You don't know what's down there, Constable." He shook his arms to get out the tension and huffed, "Cardassians! Dammit, I'd hoped it wouldn't be so simple!"

Tense and panting, still feeling his innards gathering back together, Odo stepped fully over the twitching body of the dead Cardassian attacker to Captain Sisko's side. "Sir, are you all right?"

"Dammit!"

"Sir?"

"Yes, dammit, dammit . . ." Then Sisko seemed to collect his senses, bury the steaming fury he'd needed a moment ago, and glanced at Odo. "How about you?"

"I'm all right." Odo heard the gravel in his own voice. Anger came out in it, disgust at having had the enemy, the saboteurs, within reach and having lost them. He *knew* he should've insisted that Sisko take a personal bodyguard with him everywhere as he crawled up and down the access ladders in the guts of the station as he went from area to area, trying to wrest control from confusion.

"I know what you're thinking, Constable," Sisko said, prodding the dead Cardassian with one toe. "But if I'd let you assign someone to me, then maybe these jokers would never have tried this, and we still wouldn't know who they were."

"Interesting logic," Odo rasped. "If you weren't my commanding officer, I'd have a smart response."

"You can go ahead with it." Sisko crouched beside the dead man and pulled apart the dark blue cloak. "I thought so! I thought I saw this! Look—it's one of those uniforms from those corpses you and O'Brien found."

"Why would anyone steal those uniforms?"

"Better question—how did these Cardassians find out about *those* Cardassians? And how far does the knowledge go now? Did these people contact the Cardassian Central Command, or do we have the whiteout on our side this time?" He looked up at Odo. "Do you recognize them? Did you see Cardassians on any ship's passenger manifest or crew roster?"

Odo battled down a sense of insult. "I would've investigated them if I had, sir."

He managed to keep from adding "don't you think" to either end of that sentence.

"All right, all right," Sisko grumbled, stood up, and dabbed at his bleeding face. "Have this one taken to Dr. Bashir. Tell him to do an immediate autopsy. Questions—is he really Cardassian, how old, and any identification."

"Yes, sir," Odo said. He wondered what else to say, if anything would do for this moment. Sisko was hot, bleeding, pumped full of anger, and flushed with aftermath, and Odo wondered if there could be true logic in such a physical condition. So far there had been, but would the anger crash in again? He could never tell. These humans were hard to measure.

"Sure you're all right?" Sisko asked him.

The question jarred Odo, and abruptly he realized he had been flexing his shoulders and back as he thought his thoughts. Ignoring the attention that made him uneasy, he gestured down the skinny corridor. "Do you want me to get a team and follow them?"

"Not yet. Let's wait and see if Dax can get the internal sensors back on-line, and we'll track them down with a bioscan." Sisko stared down the corridor as if he wished to disobey his own orders and plunge down there after those who had attacked him. "Something's very strange about this ... those uniforms ... why would anybody ..."

The captain paused, his brow drawn as he involved himself in thought.

"He was the leader," he continued. "That one watching us from way down there. He was in charge of them."

Odo peered at him, curious. "How could you tell?"

"I don't know. Something about him ... maybe his posture. He wasn't just hiding ... he was observing. And when I tried to get to him, he didn't even flinch. And he looked—strange. This one does, too. The bones show and the face is hollow. They look more like ghosts of Cardassians than living Cardassians."

For a few long seconds Sisko stared down that dim corridor again, past the shadowed angles and the ghastly poor lighting, as if he could still see that face in his mind and was still memorizing its lines, its complexities, preparing for the moment when he would meet it again.

Sharply, then, he said, "Get O'Brien. And get a crowbar. We're going back down that tunnel you found. I've got an ugly hunch."

"Your Excellency! We went after someone with a uniform, and we found, instead, this!"

The new headquarters, pitiful and dim though it was, with its sad mustard walls and its senseless angularity, was lit only with a few tiny work implements stolen from other places in the tunnels.

And in that light was a Cardassian face. Not unusual, given the moment, except that this was a face unfamiliar to the High Gul.

A Cardassian he did not know—a branch into this new era.

He paused before the individual who had been forced to sit between Koto and Clus, and who looked particularly small between two such individuals. The High Gul took a moment to appreciate his chosen Elite. They might or might not be the brightest lights, but certainly they were the biggest and they were the most loyal. With their devotion and purpose, he would gladly do the thinking for them.

The visitor—captive—stared at him. It might have been shock or appreciation; he couldn't tell. A signal, the High Gul realized. This was not only fear he saw, if it was fear at all. He recognized that look—one of possibility, risk, not awe but certainly expectation. Instantly he changed his plan of approach to accommodate what he read in the visitor's face.

"My son," he said, his voice low.

The visitor's eyes changed, but very little. His mouth opened, but he said nothing.

The High Gul offered a step closer, but only one step, with a controlled swagger of his shoulders and with his chin slightly raised and his eyes gazing downward in just the right manner to cultivate what he saw in the visitor's face.

"Do you know," he began slowly, "who I am, my son?"

The visitor cleared his throat and blinked into the dimness. "You are the first and only High Gul."

"Very good. You're correct. Be calm, for I have many questions for you and I need you to answer them. Are you cold here? Would you like a cloak?"

"No, Excellency. . . ."

The High Gul glowed with satisfaction. This response! This impassioned shock at seeing him, at recognizing him—it told him many things and gave him tools. He thought about it.

With another step he drew even closer. "Are you the only Cardassian resident of this outpost?"

"At the moment, yes."

"What is your name?"

"Garak."

"And you are the one who awakened us, also yes?"

"Yes . . . I did that."

"And I presume you went away, didn't let yourself be known to us because you were afraid. You didn't know how we would react to you? Is that true?"

Garak was waffling between the truth and lies, balancing which would do him more favor, or at least get him out of the Elite's grips. Quite a process to watch. An argument with self.

"No," the High Gul finally said. "Not the truth. Tell me the truth, then."

"I thought I might observe your actions and . . ."

"And find leverage from your position of silence?"

"Actually . . . yes."

"I appreciate that strategy, Garak."

This seemed to relax the newcomer further.

"Let's speak to each other, then," the High Gul continued. "Talk as fellows. You know who I am, you know I need to know things about this place and its people. You awakened me from my trance, and so you must want me to know these things, is that right?"

The visitor's eyes kinked tight as he pondered this, but there was no other answer.

"Yes . . . High Gul."

The High Gul held silent and let Garak slowly convince himself of what he had just heard. Clearly he had already run through all this in the hours since the awakening, but only now was able to absorb the reality.

"Tell me," the High Gul began, pacing his words, "who is my enemy in this era?"

"Unfortunately," Garak said, "everyone here is your enemy. Even Cardassia is your enemy. There's a new government structure called the Central Command . . . but also there is the Obsidian Order. Sometimes they work for the Central Command . . . sometimes they work for themselves."

"I understand." With his expression the High Gul communicated just how deeply he did understand such webs of power. He knelt, and sat on a piece of metal jutting from the wall, then gazed into Garak's tension-frosted face. "You are alone here among our kind, is that right?"

"Yes."

"Are you in exile?"

"Of a sort."

"Sanctuary, then."

"Yes, of a sort."

"Sanctuary here is provided by what agency?"

"They're called Starfleet, High Gul. That's the military and exploratory arm of the United Federation of Planets. It was started by humans—Terrans—people from a planet called Earth, but now it's made up of many species. They came here a few years ago and shored up the Bajoran government following the evacuation of Cardassian troops from the planet Bajor—and from this station."

"What other forces exist now, that you know of?"

"Oh . . . Romulans, Klingons, Orions, Ferengi, Tholians, Eridani, Rigelians, and there's the Dominion beyond the—"

"So many! An interesting time to live. Tell me about Cardassia. Tell me why this Cardassian outpost is held by others now. How is it that our powerful forces were thrown off. Are we no longer powerful?"

"In ordnance, yes," Garak said with a shrug. "Ships, weapons, numbers . . . but our leaders have lost their talent for . . ."

"For choreographing assault? I understand. Go on."

Another shrug. "They attack at the wrong times, they retreat at the wrong times, they're brutal for no gain, thereby making resentment in conquered people, which comes back on them. And they rarely see it coming. They're also more suspicious of each other than of their enemies." He blinked upward. "And wisely so."

The High Gul nodded. "So Cardassia has become its own enemy. And therefore weakened."

"Yes."

"I see. Tell me this . . . where are the rest of my Loyal Elite? Are they asleep elsewhere in the complex? Or perhaps on that planet nearby? If so, we must awaken them also, that I might have strength with which to approach the forces I must face here. We shall face them together, my friend, and you will no longer suffer exile."

Garak flushed at the new burden. He shifted where he sat, glanced up to one side at Koto, to the other side at Clus, and around him at the other Elites who stood like statues around them. "High Gul . . . it's in all the history records of the Cardassian Prime Order that . . . the Loyal Elite of the High Gul . . ."

"Say what you have to say," the High Gul prodded gently. "I am able to accept anything."

Drawing a steadying breath, Garak looked as if he expected to have his head removed for this. "Two thousand of the Loyal Elite—" He swallowed again. "—came back and were paraded before the populace to confirm the death of the High Gul and weld into place the power of his . . . of your opponents in government."

Garak squinted into the High Gul's gaze.

And what a gaze it was. The High Gul stood up sharply, felt his eyes burning, his skin shrivel, his arms and legs grow tight with horror. Two thousand *bodies,* his handpicked force, his most loyal, paraded in gruesome death as leverage against all he had tried to build. Used, used against him, against Cardassia, for political gain!

Now there were only these who were with him now, this loyal handful, his personal guard. Not only had these sicknesses happened to his civilization, but his own army had been used against itself to make these things happen. His own men, his own name—

As his blood boiled and tornadic rage quaked within him, he battled as he ever had against an enemy to keep control of himself. He *must* appear eternally composed, the ultimate countenance, self-assured and unirritable before Garak, because he needed Garak. He needed, now more than even a moment ago, someone who could walk freely in this outpost. The rage must be reined within.

In his effort to rein it, he turned his back on Garak and strode between the pillars of his remaining Elite, forcing himself not to look into their faces or communicate his grief and desperation.

Two thousand of them. What a sight it must have been, body after body, open-eyed, shrouded, and utterly still. A powerful demonstration that must have rended many hearts and attracted others.

At once a question burst into his mind. He turned.

"Garak . . . how many years has it been?"

The exile blinked at him from down the hollow tube in which they had hidden themselves. At first he seemed not to understand the question, but soon a realization crossed his face and he fought with the answer. He glanced at the Elites, then looked again at the leader he had awakened.

"It's been rather a long time, High Gul . . . it's been almost a hundred years."

CHAPTER
11

RAGE! IT BELLOWED. *Eighty, eighty, eighty years!*

It shouted, it howled.

Not twenty years, but eighty. Years piled upon years in dumb hibernation, frittered away for nothing. Wives, families grown old, grown apart, even dead.

Power and governments built, squandered, fallen, built, fallen again, struggling foolishly under the scattered directives of those who had somehow silenced him.

The High Gul could feel his own heart hammering in his chest, his nerve endings tingling through his entire body. At his sides, he felt the shivers of his horrified men as they, too, battled to control themselves, to let him take the first step and decide which path they would take in this new . . . century.

Even in his misery, in his rage, he was proud of their restraint and knew it would not be so if Garak weren't here. This was a vast shock to absorb without exploding.

In his mind he saw their shriveled bodies lying on slabs year after year, so much longer than expected, then their slow awakening only hours ago as shades of purple blush seeped into the gray skin, the bony goggles around the eyes pulsing with so-subtle life, arteries down the neck throbbing as they struggled to come back from hibernation.

Eighty years was a very long time for a process meant only to last a few months, a means of short-term survival, perhaps under water, perhaps on an icy tundra. The airless void of a chamber at the abandoned end of a docking pylon hadn't been one of nature's considerations.

His family—his wife. The image he had banished until now came breaking through. Older soldiers had mates they considered no more than that—many Cardassian women had donated themselves, to make his force stronger. It had been his idea, because he knew so personally what happened when devotion turned to distraction. All his professional life he had fought that, all for her. Hers was the only worship he had ever wanted.

"Eighty years . . ." His voice was rough, taxed, as he turned again to Garak but did not approach. "Has memory of me faded then," he asked, "or become quaint?"

Garak straightened abruptly. "The opposite, High Gul! You've become more revered with every campaign! In every strategic meeting, all sides invoke your name to their purpose—'If the High Gul were here he would do this,' 'The High Gul would never accept that,' 'This will do honor to the High Gul's memory,' 'The High Gul would be on my side'—and every one of your words has been recorded and is memorized by students, by advancing forces. You're sanctified—almost deified! And now you are the glory of the past returned!"

He stopped suddenly, as if afraid he was saying too much or insulting the High Gul in some way.

The High Gul let the sudden silence molder. Not just his accomplishments, but his *words?* What good was that? He had been a soldier, not a philosopher. He found himself standing here, neither doing nor saying anything, rummaging through his memory to see if there were any embarrassing remarks.

"High Gul," Garak began again, "you must escape from here! I would help you steal a ship, but right now all the ships are in use. They're evacuating the station of all non-Starfleet personnel, but I don't know why. Something else is going on. But you have to get away from here and make a plan. When the people of Cardassia realize you were betrayed, there will be a revolution!" Sharply Garak stood up. "I will go to the Cardassian government with proof that you still live and were betrayed, talk to someone, or a lot of someones. The inept, shortsighted fools will have to listen! If you had been here, none of this would have happened to us! But first you must get away from this station."

"No, Garak. As we both understand, I am the only High Gul. I don't sneak off. But tell me, what is it like to live on this station? What is the common denominator between the people living here?"

Thrown off his excitement, Garak settled down and made a facial shrug. "The only common denominator on *Deep Space Nine* is that no one really cares what anyone else here thinks of him. It is a place where lines are not clearly drawn. Everybody encroaches on everybody else's job a little. Everyone oversteps orders a little, crosses boundaries, glances to see who is around before deciding how far to overstep . . . the only duty each can be sure of is who does the reports when the smoke is cleared."

"A dark-skinned man, large, strong."

"Yes."

"Tell me about him. I must know what I will be against."

Garak resisted the pinching of division that suddenly ran through him. Sisko had always defended him, given him sanctuary, protection, even a chance to build a business, make his own way rather than sit on charity.

Before him sat an individual who, legend said, could smell lies. How did one speak, never mind lie, to an icon?

But also in the embodiment of the High Gul were Garak's own chances to return to power—not only return, but leap beyond his former influence in Cardassian government.

What could it hurt to talk about Sisko? One step at a time, even if someone yelped beneath him?

"Sisko is . . ."

"Yes?"

"Broad-minded, certainly. A good arbitrator when he wants to be, occasionally lenient with those of us who bend the rules, because he likes to be free to bend the rules himself now and then. He has a good perception of how far out in space we really are . . . he knows he can be sovereign if he plays circumstances correctly. I believe he . . . there is a praetorial guard in him who is frustrated at being on sentry duty here."

"More."

Garak sighed. More? What did the High Gul want? Complication? There was nothing complicated about all this. Escape from the station, go back to Cardassia Prime, foment revolution, and make Garak Vice-High Gul.

Yet the High Gul's steady manner affected him. After all, this was the individual to whom Cardassian success over the past two-thirds of a century could be traced. Even for a practiced spy who was out only for himself, awe was a powerful narcotic.

All right, more.

"More . . . Sisko is distant at times. Afraid he will spend his life in administration, listening to his bones vibrate. That's another reason he bends the rules . . . excitement."

"And how is he when he isn't fierce and battling to devour enemies?"

Garak buried an urge to lick his own lips, going dry as they were with empathy as he watched the High Gul's dry mouth shape the questions. "Tranquil, sad . . ."

"Why sad?"

"His wife was killed in a battle. She was trapped under collapsed debris. Sisko was forced to leave her behind during evacuation."

"Alive or dead, left behind?"

"Dead, although I think he had some doubts at one time. I think he wonders sometimes."

"Does he have other family here on this outpost? Children from this wife?"

The answer popped instantly into Garak's mind, a skinny teenaged human boy with a simplicity about him.

"No," he said. "No children."

The High Gul strode nearer to him, strong and impressive even though he was older and less bulky than his own guards. "Too bad. Garak, you've been instrumental today. Be assured, I am not the kind who forgets. You will reap the rewards of your loyalty and your risk. One more thing—and think most carefully about this—is there anyone on this station we *shouldn't* kill?"

Pausing now, the High Gul gave him time to answer, plenty of it. He had just promised Garak what he wanted—rank, privilege, restoration—and now he requested something in return. But Garak had been living on this station for a long time, had fostered relationships, however tenuous or teasing, with the people here. The High Gul knew that, and Garak felt the skitter of excuses to keep a few of those people alive as the High Gul and his men watched.

"Well," he admitted after quite a few moments, "no, I suppose not."

The High Gul reached out now and did the unthinkable—he touched Garak upon the shoulder, and Garak nearly shrank from the contact. There was a haunting reputation, legend again, that the High Gul could strangle with a glance.

"Remain silent, my friend," the ancient leader said, his voice echoing faintly in the chamber as if throbbing from the past. "We will contact you when you can help us again. We will foment war between everyone, and they will destroy themselves for us. Together we shall restore the true Cardassia."

And this leader from decades ago turned to what was left of the Loyal Elite.

"Let him go," he told them.

"Eighty years. And two thousand Elites . . . dead." The High Gul paced like a woman, shuddering with the rage. His hands were ice cold. How long had his wife endured the personal chill and public humiliation of his disappearance? All those long years she had thought him dead, those interminable years, knowing his memory was being used to pervert all he had struggled to build—an empire that should have lasted a millennium, but was crumbling already.

Then he thought of the most sore wound. What if she still lived? What a cruel trick, that she could still live, and he would be here again, the same as he was eighty years ago.

The rage grew and grew.

"Should we let Garak show us to the weapons, High Gul?" Elto asked. "Show us the way around this station?"

"Not yet. Garak isn't to be entirely trusted. When he described Cardassia, in some ways he was describing himself. He awakened us, but I'm sure for his own purposes."

"How do you know that?" Elto asked.

"It's what I would have done. I dare not accept his suggestion that he was exiled here because he is nobler of heart than the standing order."

"Wise, Excellency," Koto acknowledged, though it was plain he didn't entirely understand.

The High Gul continued pacing. "I don't completely accept his story that Cardassia has been despoiled. He may be lying, or his point of view may be skewed. He is in exile, after all. However, there's no denying that this station was once Cardassian and is now occupied by others. Garak may be a liar, but no one is a good enough liar to put the respect and awe in his eyes that I saw there when he looked at me. I know now that whatever happened eighty years ago and in the years since, I am still High Gul."

He stopped pacing and touched the wall, gazing with unfocused eyes as he thought hard about what to do next. In his periphery he caught his men glancing at each other and knew he must be decisive, demand quick and specific action of them in order to distract them from the rage boiling in them also, or it would rip them apart.

He raised his head and looked at them.

"We'll ask Garak for something small first, something easy, and draw him in step by step. His doubts will fade away."

"Food, High Gul?" Clus suggested. "So we can sustain ourselves. He won't find it a threat to give us something so simple."

The High Gul blinked at him. "Are you hungry, Clus?"

The big Elite shifted and shrugged. "Well . . . a little, Excellency."

"I understand." The High Gul laughed. "After all, you haven't eaten in eighty years."

Clus stepped back into a shadow to hide his flush of embarrassment, and Elto moved forward to say, "Excellency, we could ask for translators. The time will come when we may want to speak to the intruders."

The High Gul gazed at him. "I'm proud of you. We'll ask tonight, after Garak has had time to be impressed. Until then, we'll work to our own purpose.

I must have this outpost, and I hardly believe they will simply give it to me, therefore the first order of business is to chop off the head and leave the body sagging. I have no idea how to kill a shapeshifter, but he must be put out of our way. We'll find some way to incapacitate him. Once that is accomplished, the way will be clear to kill Sisko."

CHAPTER
12

ZZZZZTT . . . ZZZZZZTT

The walls shivered in their unthinking revulsion. Old ceiling tiles crackled overhead as the turbolift cab thundered behind its doors—doors open only two centimeters.

Just enough to see Security Ensign Ibrahim being electrocuted to death inside.

Not precisely—so far he was still screaming. The "to death" part hadn't happened yet.

Odo stood aside as two other Security men worked feverishly on the doors, but had only succeeded in making them rattle.

The deck thrummed, and he knew someone was running this way, someone with substantial mass and a strong, long stride.

"Captain," he said, without even glancing to his side.

Sisko arrived and bumped to a halt beside him. "What's happening in there?"

"Ensign Ibrahim is caught in some kind of electrical field. Possibly a faulty security loop."

"Can't you cut it off at the field source?"

"We're attempting that also."

"The doors?"

"Are absolutely jammed. We may have to phaser them open."

Sisko's face went hard. "That'll take an hour. That man's being tortured in there."

"Yes." Odo watched his men's shoulders as they threw themselves into forcing the doors open with the jaw-wrench that was braced between them. Another centimeter. At this rate they'd have that man out in four or five days.

Ibrahim's nerve-throttling screams were turning higher in pitch, affected by the man's exhaustion and panic as the fight was zapped out of him and he dissolved to agony, and every few seconds that hideous *zzzzzttt zzzzztt*. . . .

"Did you investigate the tunnel?" Odo asked, giving in to a need to fill the air around them with something other than those two terrible noises.

"Empty," Sisko said. "Either the bodies were stolen and their uniforms taken by the infiltrators, or—"

"Or the infiltrators *are* the bodies?"

Those fierce black eyes struck Odo hard. "Did you have a suspicion or were you just extrapolating?"

"Mostly extrapolation, but I've learned not to trust Cardassians . . . not even Cardassian biology. Now we have to wonder who put them there, and why, and what woke them up."

"We may have made them wake up when we broke into that chamber and let air in. I think we can guess some kind of hibernation process that we just have never heard about." Sisko looked at him. *"You've never heard of anything like that, have you?"*

Self-conscious about the years he lived with Cardassians and somehow failed to note such a proclivity, Odo sighed in frustration. "No, I never have."

"Well, there's one of us who has. When we get this man out of here, I want you to find Garak and gently drag him to me."

"You don't really think you'll get answers out of Garak, do you?"

"Depends on how tightly I close my fingers while I'm holding on to his neck."

"But Garak wanted them sealed in. Why do you suspect deception?"

"That's like asking why I suspect there's snow on top of the mountain." With a deep sustaining breath, Sisko leered at the lift doors as they creaked open another half centimeter. "I'm beginning to question *why* he was so passionate about having them sealed in. Or about our *believing* he wanted them sealed in. Garak's not a simple man, Constable, and it's not wise for us to accept simple answers from him. I'm afraid I did that."

"Well," Odo grumbled, "they *did* look dead, they were neither breathing nor moving, they read dead on the doctor's tricorder, and it's not asking too much to assume that dead is dead. Some things simply *are* what they seem."

"Quite a statement, coming from you. I want the station's Universal Translator checked. It doesn't do any good to yell 'Stop or I'll shoot' if they don't understand."

"It's not only the words, but the sentiment they may not understand," Odo said bitterly.

Sisko pushed past him toward the door, and received a crackle of electricity that snapped through the tiny opening between the door panels. He winced, then said, "I need a phaser. I've had about enough. Let's get that man out of there."

"I'll go in." Odo had tolerated enough too, and pushed his Security men to get them to move out of the way.

"Wait a minute—" Sisko caught his arm. "What'll that electrical field do to you? I don't want two casualties."

Caught between the mind-wrench of those screams and the responsibility to himself, and even to Sisko's command sense, which would stop him from going in there if he implied the truth—that he didn't know what those flashing fields would do to him—he shored his posture and said, "I'll be fine."

Perhaps it was the relentless *zzzt* or the pitiful whimpering that had come into Ensign Ibrahim's shrieks, but Sisko accepted the lie, though Odo knew he hadn't fooled the captain. There were times when a volunteer was acceptable, even for a suicide mission, and when officers knew to keep their mouths shut. Even such a silence, at the right times, was a command decision.

Grateful for the chance to save his man's life, or at least to make the gesture, Odo threw his mind into its most relaxed mode and allowed himself to dissolve from physical form into the liquid state that would let him melt through that two-centimeter crack.

The lights changed, the sounds became muffled, and he was in the turbolift, feeling electricity strike him and crackle through his substance until it dissipated somewhere in the deck. There was not precisely sight in this liquid condition, not so much as there was sense, awareness of space and place, and a foggy perception of movement, as if seeing shadows in his mind of the beings and things acting around him.

Once inside, he reintegrated instantly into his humanoid form like pouring into a mold, and was struck with a perception of why evolution had come up with hands and feet. Sometimes he simply needed fingers.

Ensign Ibrahim was crumpled, exhausted, battered, on the turbolift floor, flinching and moaning, as jets of electrical power continued to crackle from floor to ceiling. Odo stood over him immediately, hoping to block some of those strings of energy, and wedged his fingers into the jammed access panel. Ibrahim had kept his head long enough to try breaking into the panel, and had the sense not to use his phaser on it without knowing what circuits he was breaking. Valiant, considering the swords of electricity slicing back and forth at unavoidable diagonals in here.

Odo flinched as the electricity shot through him, but concentrated on the panel, pouring his strength into simply wrenching the cover off. Once he saw the conduits, he was able to push his hand in and rip out the guts of the electrical power unit. Simple enough.

In a moment he was standing over Ibrahim with a handful of shattered and torn electronics, and the zapping had stopped.

He bent over to put his hands on Ibrahim, and he was struck from behind between the shoulder blades—

Pok

Not a punch, but a puncture, as if hit by a marble from a slingshot. Something small penetrated his substance. He straightened quickly and turned to look around.

Pok pok pok pok pok

His arms, his back, his shoulder, his other arm—it was as if insects were dive-bombing him. He flinched away, only to be struck again and again. Something solid was hitting him, a dozen solid things—he tried to morph away from the tiny pellets striking him, but there was nothing solid left. Somehow the pellets were dissolving inside him, melting into his body.

Pok pok pok

"Ow!" Ibrahim gulped as he lay on the floor, and twisted to grab his left thigh. Suddenly there was blood on his thigh, oozing slowly from a small round wound. "Ow—"

"Odo, open the door!"

As abruptly as the stinging had begun, it ended. The turbolift fell to silence, but for Odo's own ragged breathing and the shocked gasps of Ibrahim on the floor.

"Odo! Open the door!"

Sisko's voice was a stabilizing force. Odo latched on to it and willed himself to concentrate. From in here he could manipulate the lift doors mechanically. In a moment they reluctantly scraped open.

"What happened?" Sisko demanded. He snapped his fingers, and the two other Security men dragged Ibrahim out of the lift. "Get him to the infirmary. Odo, what happened?"

Dizzy and suddenly nauseated, Odo parted his lips and worked to form the words. "Something hit me. . . ."

"Electrical bolts?"

"No . . . after that . . . some kind of pellets."

Taking him by both arms, Sisko glanced at the ceiling and wall panels of the lift, bodily pulled him out. "It was a booby trap! Let's get out of here."

"He is evacuating the station. Did you hear him mention that? Certainly not due only to our little presence. So far we've been hardly more than a slightly debilitating nuisance to such a man. He would not buckle so for merely us. So why is he evacuating the station? Elto? What do you think?"

The High Gul strode up and down the small line of his men, permeated with appreciation for his few men who had offered him not so much as a wince of doubt or resistance despite the costly revelations of the past short hours. Foggy memories had become crisp as to why he elected these particular children to follow him at so near a proximity, to rest upon their strong backs the empire of the future.

Elto's face flexed as he contemplated the question, but he didn't appear embarrassed that he didn't know the answer. Rather, he seemed concerned that he was somehow failing to comprehend something important about the situation. "High Gul," he said finally, "I cannot add it up. What am I missing?"

The High Gul smiled. "You're missing a broader thinking process, my son. Realize that we are on a space station . . . and imagine why you would evacuate it. If he is evacuating, then he is expecting . . ."

A light popped on in Elto's eyes, and the High Gul was gratified to see the same light flare in several other eyes at the same time, though none of the others begged for attention. Elto had the floor.

"Invasion!" Elto caught his breath. "Someone is coming here!"

"Yes," the High Gul said. "Someone is coming for *us*."

"For us?" Koto interrupted.

"Of course. You don't think this is a coincidence, do you? No, no, it isn't. Someone has been notified of our awakening."

In a flush of anger, Ren came forward a step. "By Garak?"

"I don't know . . . possibly. Though he could have notified anyone he wished, without awakening us first."

Ren's anger faded. "Oh . . ."

"I would rather guess there was some kind of automatic signal sent by our warming slabs, something integrated into the mechanics decades ago. Therefore, shall we assume this is to be a welcoming arrival?"

"No," Elto said.

The High Gul nodded. "No. It is probably our betrayer who comes to us now."

"Why assume it is our betrayer, High Gul?" Clus asked freely. "It may be someone glad to have us awake."

"Possibly," the High Gul allowed, "but if that's so, then why didn't he awaken us long ago, and revel in our presence?"

The anger started to simmer back into place as his logic worked on them. The anger, the indignation of having been betrayed, this would be good, but he wanted them to think hard right now, to understand why they would take the actions that were coming. He wanted them to believe in his process of thought and decision.

"Let us contemplate carefully," he said. "Arbitrary killing will get us nowhere. We will only enrage our enemy, and his rage will serve him, not us. Even if we kill at a ratio of ten to one, we will still lose. Our tactics must be more exacting, more specific. We have already managed to debilitate their chief of Security. The shapeshifter will barely be able to function and will probably be forced to leave the area. Now we will concentrate on pushing Captain Sisko out of the way."

"I volunteer to do it, High Gul!" Fen said.

Ren pushed past him. "And I volunteer to do it, High Gul!"

"Thank you, thank you," the High Gul told them, holding out one hand in a settling gesture. "When the moment is right, the honor shall be yours together, and the two of you can wrestle for the final blow." Then he chuckled as he regarded them both. "You know, I should really have one of you change your name, lest you confuse me."

"I'll change my name, High Gul!" Fen blurted.

The High Gul watched him for a moment, seeing in this dim light the haunting skull features on a face that was too young to look so gaunt. In fact, they all looked gaunt, bony, as if death had not quite let go of them. They were awakened, but somehow their young skin had no luster, their eyes were still sunken, the skin around their mouths like vellum, lips thin and unfilled, showing faintly the shape of their teeth. It was as though the hibernation had indeed gone on a little too long, as if they couldn't come all the way back.

Why hadn't he noticed until now?

He wondered how he looked.

"No, no, I was only joking with you, my son," he said, with a smile that suddenly felt skeletal. "Both your names are dear to me and will go down in the history of our people. Don't be so serious."

"Yes, High Gul. . . ."

"As you will, High Gul. . . ."

"Now, think, think, think. Using information Garak can give us about the station, we can cause the computer to speak in ways that will do us well. This way we can capture their operations center without destroying it. Better to capture an intact station than a destroyed one. Contact Garak and bring him to me."

"Garak! How fulfilling it is for me to see you again in the alleyways of this hinterland city. Strange, but I've become accustomed already to your presence. It consoles me somehow."

"I'm most honored, High Gul . . . here are the rations you requested. I couldn't bring you a replicator without arousing suspicion, but I stole these from a life craft."

Garak raised his eyes hesitantly, finding the role of the supplicant rather natural, considering in whose presence he stood.

Still, his innards protested. Burrowing about in the veins of *Deep Space Nine* was grating on the ego, and the High Gul's enthusiasm should have been validation, yet he was tentative. His hands were pale, clammy, his motions mechanical. He found less and less satisfaction in meeting the High Gul's eyes, and when he did it seemed the allure had gone out of them.

When had he come to question himself so? Out of a thousand schemes, devices, contrivances to get himself back into the fond eye of the powers of Cardassia, why did this one seem so fraught with artifice?

Probably because the High Gul was not yet in true power, and that always posed a risk. Surely that was to come. Destiny had put this wonder into Garak's hands and he had conjured it awake, and now it was his responsibility to see the phantasm through to substance. Perhaps all custodians of destiny shivered now and then.

The High Gul wasn't a large person in comparison with the Elite Guards, yet he fired the mind with his manner. Though he seemed animate, in fact he moved very little. His steps, his motions, his very breathing, the shifts of his eyes were carefully considered for style and impact. Though he seemed to speak often, in reality, if one paid attention as Garak had begun to do, the High Gul paused many times to scan the effect of whatever he had just said.

The result was many moments of expressive silence, which tended to humble the lower caste and to enhance the stability of the High Gul. It was effective, and Garak envied it.

How many years of practice had been required to devise, practice, and perfect such elegance of control? Control not of self, but of those around. Indeed a much higher attainment.

The great old man was looking at Garak that way now. It was humbling, haunting, and Garak shrank beneath the sound of his own awe. He lowered his eyes.

As if sensing, perhaps measuring, that thoughts were beginning to stray, the High Gul moved close to him and attended Garak as if he had nothing else in the universe to attend.

"You could find no translators for us?"

"Oh—translators . . . well, there aren't any portable ones. The station has a universal translation system built into all the communications. All you have to do is feed power to a unit that hasn't been compromised by your . . . by the damage."

The old leader's eyes gleamed. "Built in? Universal Translators in daily use? So integral? Such a place!"

Garak tucked his chin. "Yes. It's quite a place."

"And the schematics you delivered to us have been instrumental in our understanding of the station. We will find a way to free the translation system, that we may speak to these people. We stand in the midst of technical majesty! It is a wonder of modern times, this clawed outcast."

He waved both hands in an encompassing gesture, communicating his own kind of awe. Then he reached to the side of the narrow passage, and touched the wall.

Garak wondered if he were being manipulated, but this icon from the past seemed genuinely appreciative of the giant station, like a trainer looking at a wild animal. To Garak, *Deep Space Nine* had been, until now, little more than a hideout where he could lie low from those who wanted him dead and stand firm against those who would make him a puppet.

Today, somehow, it was something else.

"Garak," the High Gul said, his haggard face a canvas of wisdom. Somehow he moved a step even closer. "I sense your difficulty."

At his ancient leader's insight, Garak put up thicker

defenses. Suddenly he realized how much he had given away, even in silence that had been meant to hide his evasions.

"I am committed to you, Excellency," he attempted, curing his tone as perfectly as possible in this dusty hideout.

"But I see sacrifice behind your eyes," the High Gul went on, "and I understand it. As an exile living here, you must have feelings for these people, yet you have the inner mettle to take this chance for a change in the balance of powers. I wish to assure you, my goal is not to destroy these people, but to alter rule at Cardassia."

He placed a weathered, steady hand upon Garak's shoulder, and stepped back, an enticing movement where others would have stepped closer.

"For you," he granted, "I will give these people an opportunity to surrender."

At the right moment, he squeezed the shoulder just enough. The effect was like a change in gravity, and Garak forced an expression of innocent appreciation onto his face.

Whether or not the High Gul believed the face—that was something else.

As Garak and the Elite Guard gazed upon him, the High Gul gazed from one to the other, absorbing them one by one into his power.

"I will awaken the Cardassians, divide the Bajorans from the Federation, ignite the Klingons, tease the Romulans, infuriate the Orions, combust these Terrans who have come among us, and all the others who already bristle, and foment the war that should have happened a long time ago. They'll all be warring each other, and I will win. With the galaxy once again on fire, I will be at home."

"They knew you could get through small openings that would keep the rest of us out. They trapped Ibrahim in there and used those electrical bolts to make us want to get him out. The trap has your name all over it. They wanted to get to you into a place where the rest of us couldn't go, and we fell for it."

"We had no choice," Odo chafed as he lay on the diagnostic bed with Sisko glowering down at him. "A man was trapped and being tortured."

"I should've seen through it." Sisko paced to the end of the bed and back up the other side. "They've been one step ahead of me all the way and that's got to stop. How do you feel?"

Odo grimly resented Sisko's attentiveness. "Infiltrated," he said. He knew his answer was inaccurate, that Sisko was really asking him if he was fit for duty at this time when each of them was critical.

"They put something in me," he went on. "I can feel it. And I can't get it out."

"Describe that feeling."

Disturbed by this colorful vagueness being forced upon him, Odo damned the guilt of being helpless. He struggled to find words that could only be frugal in explaining what he felt.

"It's not heat, precisely, not cold, but . . . I'm aware of not being . . . completely pure."

How foolish, how cheap it sounded. How unscientific.

He pressed his lips flat, irritated at himself, and at Sisko for not becoming angry with him. Though cosmetic, Sisko's sedate fury allowed for too much latitude. It made Odo self-conscious, vulnerable.

He hated that.

"I can't help you, Captain," he said finally. "I don't know what they did, but although I'm somewhat tired I guarantee I am fit for duty."

"We'll let the doctor decide that."

"The doctor can do exactly nothing for me. He doesn't have a medical file on shapeshifters."

"Even if he did, it would probably leak." Sisko prowled the end of the diagnostic bed as if unaware of his own quip. "I saw him. The leader. He wasn't just hiding in that shadow—he was watching the fight, looking for weaknesses. When you had to morph to get away from that spear, he saw one and he acted upon it. He figured out how to weaken you. I'm not going to let anybody else get cornered. I'm going to start pushing."

Odo raised his head from the bed, and felt his neck ache and stretch. "How?"

Sisko's jaw jutted as he ground his teeth in determination. "Without internal sensors, we're going to have to quail hunt. We have to flush them out."

Letting his heavy head fall back, Odo asked again, with more force, "But *how?*"

"Section by section, we're going to turn off the station, that's how. They have to breathe, they need warmth—we'll turn off the air, the heat—they'll come out or they'll die. We'll start with the docking pylons, right where we first found that tomb, and the unused reactor chambers. Starfleet *will* get here, and when they do, they're not going to be facing an armed station that I lost to the enemy. The first thing I'm going to do is prepare a shuttle for launch, and I want you to—"

"Captain Sisko! Constable!"

Dr. Bashir rushed into the area carrying a sealed sterile beaker, eyes wild.

"For heaven's sake, Odo, don't revert to your liquid state!"

"Doctor," Sisko interrupted. "Calm down and explain that."

Bashir looked at Odo, then at Sisko, and held the beaker out. Inside was a very tiny pellet floating in inert pink juice. "I took this out of the soft tissue of Ensign Ibrahim's thigh. It's a pellet of nonreactive material, used, I presume, as a housing, a bullet. The nonreactive material remained solid in Ibrahim's tissue, but if it fell into liquid, like Odo's physical substance, it would dissolve immediately!"

"Yes, I felt them dissolve." Odo shoved himself up onto one elbow, and the doctor winced at the movement. "So what?"

Bashir swallowed hard, then said, "Embedded inside is a tiny amount of Element One-ten!"

Sisko pushed himself straight and paced away, one hand over his mouth, his eyes troubled.

"What is it?" Odo asked. "What would that do?"

"To Ensign Ibrahim, nothing," the doctor said, animated as a squirrel in a tree. "But in your physical makeup, the inert casing would dissolve right away and leave the element to integrate with your . . . body. At room temperature, it's in gaseous form, and it's penetrated you completely!"

"Doctor, please, you're not making sense," Odo growled. "I don't feel any different!"

His expression inflamed with frustration, Bashir looked desperately to Sisko.

Odo took the cue and also glared at the captain. "Could they have gotten it from one of the shut-down reactors?"

"If they did, then they killed the guards I put on station down there." New anger blistered across Sisko's face and he paced again, but only a step. "More heads for this witch-hunt."

Odo looked at the doctor, then back to Sisko. "What does this material do to me?"

Face stony and jaw set, Sisko forced himself to face him again. The ugly truth wasn't getting any more palatable. "Element One-ten is highly fissionable material, very unstable. When enough of it is rammed together in a small space, it reaches critical mass. Its own decay sets off a chain reaction. A small amount turns spontaneously and instantly into energy . . . and you get an explosion. A big one."

Suddenly conscious of his hands, his legs, of even his most minute movement as he looked at the doctor and at his captain. Odo felt the gravel in his voice. "But what does that *mean?*"

"It means," Sisko said, "you can't return to your liquid state to rest, or morph yourself into any other shape, certainly not anything the slightest measure smaller than you are now. You've got to hold this form indefinitely, no matter how exhausted you become. Or you'll erupt like an antimatter bomb."

"Doctor?"

"Garak? What are you doing lurking about in there? Come out into the light. Why aren't you off the station? Non-Starfleet personnel are supposed to be—"

"I know, on Bajor. Almost everyone is there, except for some Starfleet people still running about. The station is echoing like an empty dumpster."

"You're leaving the station, of course," Bashir said, and raised his eyebrows. "I hope?"

Cautiously, Garak stepped out of the shadows, but couldn't avoid glancing about to make sure the two of them were alone. The infirmary was dim, quiet. Strange how he had gotten used to the comforting protection of crowds.

"Of course I will," he said. "After all, I want nothing more than to cooperate. But what about you?"

"Me?" Bashir's boyish eyes widened within the frame of his narrow face. "I'm one of the department heads. I have a duty station. I can't abandon it."

"But why? There's no one lying ill or injured here, all your injured have been moved—are you staying here to guard a dead Cardassian?"

"No," Bashir said smoothly. "Because I'm a Starfleet officer."

Garak clenched his teeth briefly. "I suppose so. At times I have trouble thinking of you in quite so severe a persona. Tell me, have you found out who the individuals were who attacked Captain Sisko?"

"Nothing gets by you, does it? How do you know about that?"

"Oh, I keep my ear to a few select walls . . . the attackers were Cardassian, I hear."

"Well, the dead one certainly is. No remarkable qualities of any kind, give or take a shedding of dead skin cells here and there. Is that normal?"

"Skin cells? Oh, very normal, yes. It's seasonal for some regions," Garak conjured.

"Really," Bashir murmured, clearly troubled. "I've never heard of that. It's not in my medical files."

"Then I'm delighted to supply it."

"Mm, yes . . . and he was malnourished as well, poor sot. Very gaunt. Eyes were somewhat sunken. Veins were thin."

"What is that in front of you? On those two monitors?"

With a sorry sigh, Bashir shook his head at the screens before him. "I'm using computer simulations to try, rather unsuccessfully thus far, to help Odo."

"What happened to Odo?"

"He was cornered. His body was impregnated with a half-dozen or so pellets of neutral material that dissolved immediately and left a fissionable substance in him. Element One-ten, if you've heard of it. If he returns to his natural state—"

"He'll take the station with him and probably a bite out of the planet!" Garak swung away to catch his breath, stared into a blank wall, and whispered, "Ingenious!"

"Ingenious, and not a little diabolical," Bashir said. "He's getting weaker by the minute. I feel so helpless. I don't know what to do for him. I'm the station's chief medical officer and it's my job to know how to care for everyone who passes through. I've gone to great lengths to accumulate a library of biological conditions and treatments . . . but I've utterly failed to serve Odo. He's always seemed so invulnerable—physically, if not emotionally. . . ."

"Don't torture yourself, Doctor," Garak offered. "In a galaxy full of variations, sometimes the only people who can help someone are his own people. Unfortunately, we're too far away from other shapeshifters to get advice, not that they'd be particularly accommodating if we *did* ask. Things don't always work out."

Bashir looked over his nose in a scolding manner. "That's a soldier's thinking."

"Yes, it is. It's a different kind of survival than a doctor thinks about, but it's still survival. Odo knows that. You should learn it, too, and forgive yourself."

Garak's own words pounded in his skull, swirling beside the words of the High Gul. The Gul represented a change in government that might be friendly to Garak, yes, yet he was haunted. As the fog of excitement at this possible shakedown of powers was clearing from his eyes, he began to entertain other complexities. Doubt crept into his thoughts. Until now he had thought only of himself, the Gul, and Cardassia—a simple formula with a reasonably predictable result.

His eyes had been pried open by the words of the man whose presence had fogged them. The High Gul had been made chaste by history, polished to an image of brilliance, wisdom, and he was those, of course. Brilliantly inscrutable, wisely ruthless, capable of grand sacrifice, even slaughter on a large scale. The ages of memory had scrubbed him clean, leaving only a pristine paper image.

Garak could live with all that. Every leader had to choose men, legions, even whole populations to die. Strength and resolve were sometimes measured in those terms.

But the High Gul was a man out of time, and that

changed things. He wanted to foment panic, set the Klingons, Romulans, Cardassians, Terrans at each other's throats, but he thought he was dealing with the civilizations of eighty years ago, with weapons eighty years behind the times. This was a deadlier galaxy than the days of power eighty years ago.

Today, the Romulans, the Klingons, and all the others possessed strengths the High Gul had scarcely imagined in his own time, a time when the Cardassians were in control of all their known space, and just barely beginning to run into races who might stand up to them.

Now there were plenty. Today, any one of them could lay waste to whole planets, especially in the midst of panic.

The High Gul had no idea about the Dominion plunging through the wormhole to wrest his victory from his very hands and possess what he thought would be his. He saw too clearly in his mind a Cardassia that had long ago shattered. And Starfleet, the force that had managed to tame a dozen viperous forces, had yet to be provoked by Cardassians. Some said that was the only reason Cardassia behaved itself here and now, opting to chafe in silence.

Yet he was the first and only High Gul, clever, quick, and all that, hero of the past, and all knew him. He would have no trouble raising armies, igniting the youth, calling up the misty-eyed veterans.

And how would it all turn out? And when the end shook out, would it be Garak's fault, because he hungered to go home too soon? What good was it to be Vice-Gul in a smoldering graveyard?

"Doctor, by the way," he began again, "because the

communications are down, Captain Sisko sent me to tell you you're needed at the relief station on Bajor. In your official capacity. To treat the evacuees."

The doctor looked up again at him, sharply. "But this is where the action will be, where the casualties will be—all my nurses and interns are on the planet already. Did he say why I'm needed down there?"

"Why, yes, he did. There's been an outbreak of food poisoning. They're treating the symptoms, but they need you to help track down the cause and keep it from spreading."

"Oh, dear lord, what next?"

"I can't imagine," Garak threw in.

Outside in the corridor, someone—no, two or three, probably Security—ran by, boots throbbing on the deck in punctuation to the sense of urgency he tried to foster in Bashir.

Bashir pushed to his feet and crossed the infirmary, scooping up implements and treatments for an obsessed thirty seconds, but when he glanced up and their eyes connected, Garak realized too late that his timing had fallen prey to his solicitude. He had lingered too long.

The doctor passed by him a few steps before his natural clairvoyance kicked in. He stopped with his back to Garak, hesitated, and slowly turned. His brows were up, his head tilted, his lips pursed.

"Garak . . . are you trying to get me to abandon my post?"

They looked at each other across the cold floor.

Bashir strode cagily toward him. "Do you know something we don't know?"

Anxiety played through Garak's mind and he wasn't sure how much showed on his face, but he had underestimated Bashir's ability to pluck it out. Disquiet had plagued him since he last heard the High Gul's words, and he had come here as a result.

He knew he had been cleverly manipulated and had allowed it to happen. Until now the euphoria of his discovery had puffed him up, clouded his thinking. He had accepted the High Gul's mystique, and now as he looked at Bashir, the one person on the station who approached him without suspicious ginger, he accepted his doubts.

"Doctor," he began, forcing a cynical tone to disguise his apprehension, "you and I have spent many hours in pleasant conversation which has taken, shall we say, the edge off my uniqueness here. . . ."

"If that's a tacit manner of admitting friendship, I'm with you all the way. But it doesn't answer my question. Are you trying to get me off the station?"

Garak let the gauze fall away from his expression. He had failed in his gamble, in his ruse, even in his attempt to be glib. After that, there was nothing but vulgar anxiety to serve a gasping master.

"Let's just say I have an intuition," he admitted. "I'd rather you weren't on the station anymore."

CHAPTER
13

"MAJOR KIRA! Safety-grid crash!" an ensign shouted.

"Where?"

"Reactor failure ... danger imminent ... Evacuate to docking ring. Automatic shutdown in six minutes ... repeat ... six minutes to fail-safe ..."

"Say it again! I didn't hear you! Can you turn the volume down on the klaxons?"

"Yes—the crash is almost systemwide. It's a major reactor shutdown. Ordinarily the station's separate areas would self-seal, but with the malfunctions we've had all morning, the sealing panels are failing. There's a flush of radiation into occupied areas. Anybody who's not evacuated in five minutes thirty seconds is dead."

"Where's Captain Sisko?"

"Infirmary, I think."

"Have you got the comm links cleared yet?"

"Some, but not to the infirmary."

"Six minutes—damn! What areas are in danger?"
Kira Nerys peered over Dax's shoulder at the panels

whose readouts were frantically flashing schematics of the station, with certain sections blocked out in bright emergency orange.

Even though she knew Kira could see the monitors, Dax heavily said, "Look."

Before them lay a 2-D architectural diagnostic of the station, simple blue lines in the shape of a giant spindle on a black background. At the heart of the spindle, a jellylike marigold-orange plume boiled from one of the reactor areas, moving like a swarm of killer bees as Dax narrated its path.

"Radiation is flushing upward through the lower core. It'll contaminate sections four, five, nine, ten, eleven, and twelve of the inner lower core, several connecting tunnels, airlocks, cargo aisles, several labs. Shortly after that it'll overtake the infirmary, main engineering, and from there it'll encroach very quickly on the Promenade . . . and finally Ops. Just a matter of minutes."

"Dammit! Here? Where's the safest place?"

"Docking ring. We still have working seals there."

"All right, that's where we'll go."

Kira was embarrassed when her voice came out as almost a groan, frantic to hold all strings on all kites and not lose any. The whooping klaxons were driving her crazy, ticking down the seconds they had left. She swung around to the other people on post in the area.

"Anderson! Go down to sections four and five and evacuate everybody to the docking ring. Mason, you do the same in sections nine, ten, eleven and twelve. Get somebody to help you. Utang, you go. Never mind your station, just get those people out! Then go down to engineering and see if Chief O'Brien needs extra hands. You and the officers will be beamed out just before fail-safe. After that, it'll take a starship's phasers to get back in here."

Take a step, swing around, take another step, swing around again. On the screens, the creeping mange moved ever through the station, toward her. The station pulsed with the menace of changing allegiance, and she found the idea noxious. Handing over DS9—when had she become so possessive? Starfleet would come and eventually they'd get the station back, but to lapse even for an hour to the malefic power she had fought all her life was a bone-grating thing. The station was no shining prize, only a giant set jaw turning in space, a restive plaza acting as a side door to the wormhole, but it was all Bajor had to prove that somebody besides Bajorans would stand ground here or even cared to.

But DS9 had once been Cardassian, had been built by Cardassians, functioned under a constant veil of having once lived another persona, had survived a change of allegiance, and sometimes Kira felt that the station, like a captured ship under a foreign flag, was only biding time until it changed back.

She pressed her hands to the sides of her head and scrappily demanded clearer thinking. Didn't get it, exactly, but some things took time.

"This is all we need," she roiled. "To abandon Ops! Don't we have any option? Isn't this place double-sandbagged or something? Anything?"

"After a certain point, the computer gives us no choice but to leave," Dax calmly instructed. "The computer is going to do everything it can do to keep contamination from flooding the whole station. It'll force us to abandon these areas as it's programmed to do. As long as it reads 'radiation,' it won't allow traverseways to remain open. It seals them."

"With what? Forcefield?"

"No, energy can fail. The heavy portcullises roll into place. And that's it. We have to beam everyone off ASAP. After that, we won't be able to beam off through the radiation."

Kira stifled a groan. Her chest hurt. "How many people are left on the station?"

"We have a report that all but fifty-one people have evacuated to Bajor. Most of the remaining personnel are Starfleet Security personnel and our department heads, along with a few others who are still getting off."

"Get'em off! What's taking so long?"

"I don't know. Kira . . . did you authorize launch of one of the runabouts into the wormhole?"

"Me? No."

"Well, look at this. We've got one heading in there right now. There it is."

Pointing at a moving blip on the small screen, Dax fought with her controls for a few seconds; then one of the larger screens popped on, just in time to show a clear picture of the runabout approaching the mouth of the wormhole and the wormhole flashing into its visible mode, a swirling toy of lights and energy. The runabout plunged in without even pausing to adjust approach vector.

"Patch me through to that!" Kira demanded.

"Go ahead."

"Attention, runabout, this is Major Kira. What's your authorization to enter the wormhole?"

They waited. No response.

"Attention, runabout! Identify yourselves!"

"It's no use," Dax told her. "There's nothing coming back over the frequency."

"Is it damped out like the internal communications?"

"No, just no response. It's as if there's no one aboard at all."

"Could it be the saboteurs making an escape before the station is contaminated?"

"Of course it *could* be."

Rankled and flooded with suspicions, Kira knotted her fists. "Keep a monitor on the mouth of the wormhole. If they decide to come back, I want to know it. Explain to me what happened to the reactor."

Dax played her controls as if enticing information out of the mechanics, but shook her head. "I'm not receiving specific data. Some kind of rupture. I can only presume it was sabotage, not a breakdown, given circumstances."

"That doesn't make me feel any better. Six reactors on the station, only two of them operating, and one of those two ruptures. If it's not sabotage, we're going to go down in a record book somewhere. How did they tap into the technical connections necessary to rupture a reactor? And what disturbs me is that these people might be able to get to the other one and rupture it too. Then, on top of contamination, we're also out of power."

"By then it won't matter," Dax began.

She began to say something else, but stopped as Ben Sisko appeared, packed into the small opening of one of the access conduits, crawled out, unfolded his large frame, and hurried to them, shaking one foot that seemed to have fallen asleep as he crawled through the guts of the station.

Kira swung around. "Sir—"

"I heard it." He shook out his limp and surveyed Dax's readouts. "Whether we have power or not won't make any difference, Major, if we have to abandon DS9 because of reactor contamination. Status?"

"Three minutes thirty seconds to fail-safe . . ."

"Intrastation communications are still ragged," Dax said, "but there are alarms going off everywhere. The computer is about to shut down any traverseways on the station, thinking it can stop the radiation from spreading, but it can't. There are too many malfunctions in smaller grids. If we don't get out of the inner core and get our people out, we're all dead. And, Benjamin, four of our Security men were attacked in the lower core, probably by the infiltrators on their way to or from their sabotage of the reactor." She paused and looked up at him. "Our men are all dead."

His skin wine-dark in the shadows, eyes harsh, Sisko's face turned stony, cheekbones, lips, jaw cut on edges.

"Four more," he said through his teeth. "And infiltrators now have possession of their four phasers. Dax, issue Security Alert One to our personnel here and on the planet. We've got to stop supplying weapons to our enemies."

"I'll do my best to get the message through, Benjamin."

"Sir, somebody launched a runabout without authorization," Kira said, "and it went into the wormhole. It could be the saboteurs trying to escape into the Gamma Quadrant."

"Could be, but it isn't. I launched that runabout myself."

"You did?"

"Yes, I did."

"But why?"

"So it'll be there in case I need it. Or in case I need to use its impulse engines to blow up the wormhole by remote. I have to protect the wormhole as much as I have to protect the station. I have an obligation to the civilizations in the Gamma Quadrant not to let hostile powers go through there, and I have an obligation to us not to let the same come through from there. One can never be too prepared. I'm sure you agree."

"Well, I—"

"Three minutes to fail-safe . . . repeat, three minutes to fail-safe . . . all personnel evacuate specified areas . . ."

"Benjamin," Dax said, "we can beam out to the docking ring in the last four seconds, but after that even the transporter safety features will shut out these contaminated areas."

On the monitor, the marigold cloud spread toward main engineering. Closer, closer—it was almost there.

Kira watched Sisko, as curious as she was anticipatory of what he would do about this poison thundering down upon them. This wasn't a time for shilly-shallying or faintheartedness. She didn't think she was falling prey to either of those, but her hands were cold and her mind already spinning with ways to keep the fight going without having Ops as a command center.

Her hand was poised over the transporter's

automatic-evacuation panel. One tap, and the machine would grab any life-forms left in the endangered areas and deposit them in the docking ring.

But Sisko wasn't making any orders of that nature yet. He gazed at Dax's monitor as if he had the time.

They watched as the marigold cloud pressed toward main engineering and the labs down there.

Finally he glanced at Kira. "I've got two and a half more minutes. I'm going to use them. Just to be prepared, adjust the emergency evacuation transporter to put us in the docking ring instead of on the planet. Our Cardassian guests'll have to contaminate the whole station before I give it up, and they've got to breathe too."

"I've done that," Dax said.

"Sir, we don't know what kind of protective gear they've got," Kira pointed out.

"Maybe not, but I'm willing to—"

"Attention, aliens."

Sisko straightened and looked into the air as if to find explanation written on the ceiling. "Uh-oh . . . here it comes."

Dax leaned forward, her flawless expression crimped. "They've tapped into the general broadcast system."

"See if you can home in on it. Use the biosensors once you get close."

"This is the High Gul of the Order of the Crescent. I am speaking to Benjamin Sisko, commander of the intruders. You are in possession of Cardassian property. You will surrender it immediately. I have immobilized your command areas. Surrender or I will do likewise to the habitation areas."

Narrowing her eyes and feeling as if she were

waiting for a punch line, Kira waited a second to see if the voice would speak again.

When it didn't, she said, "Order of the Crescent . . . that's old-fashioned. It's from before either the Central Command or the Obsidian Order. Over seventy years! Maybe longer—I'm not sure. I heard some of the older Cardassians mentioning it."

Sisko nodded. "It could be an elaborate hoax."

Kira pressed her hand to her short hair as if to hold in her thoughts, then held the same hand out to him. "But the Order of the Crescent? How can that be? Who are these people? A history cult or something?"

Occult with contemplation, Sisko folded his arms as if he had all day and turned to face her. "I'll tell you who they are, Major. They're those corpses we found in the docking pylon, that's who they are."

"Corpses? You mean those *dead* Cardassians?"

"They weren't dead," he said, his low voice sequestered, bodeful. "They were in some kind of hibernation. Breaking into the chamber may have awakened them."

Smoldering, and suddenly angry that all her instincts had failed, Kira abandoned any composure and let her jaw fall. Her cheeks and hands turned cold. *"What?"*

He nodded slowly. "Those bodies are the people we're fighting. They didn't infiltrate the station at all, Major. They were already here."

"But that's—that's—"

"Spooky. Yes, it is. That's what we're dealing with, Major. A brigade of the dead." He crossed behind her suddenly to the other side of Ops and tapped the monitors and readouts.

"Fifty seconds to fail-safe . . . Evacuate immediately . . . repeat, evacuate immediately."

Watching them both, Dax held her poise as she said, "Transporter is activated and standing by. Benjamin—radiation is going into engineering. Shall I transport them out?"

Suddenly Sisko's expression changed. He crossed Ops again to another station and checked and rechecked the panels. All the readouts would say the same things—that they were about to die.

Dax turned and snapped. "Benjamin!"

"Stand by!"

The marigold plume began to flood main engineering on the monitors. Miles O'Brien's post. Had he gotten out? It was a pale, bitter assumption, a faint hope, that he had, and a gripping horror that they couldn't call and ask.

Kira felt her pulse hammer in her wrists and temples. What was wrong with Sisko? Was this some kind of breakdown? Had he snapped? Was this the time for the second-in-command to countermand?

As she watched him rush from console to console, searching for something he wouldn't explain, she thought of O'Brien . . . death by radiation poisoning. The tongue bleeds, the skin burns off in red flakes, blood vessels swell, pop open, eyeballs blister and swell.

Have I got my phaser? I'll shoot us all first.

"It's encroaching on the infirmary now," Dax said, her throat tight. "Benjamin, whatever you're doing—"

"I told you to stand by."

Holding silent, Kira felt her skin wither. While O'Brien could be anywhere on the station, working his engineering skills here or there, Julian Bashir wouldn't be anywhere but that little black area now turning orange with poison.

And Julian would stand his post until told otherwise. He would have faith in them, up here.

The transporter enact—it was right there. It was under her hand.

Dax's voice was very low, fierce. "Benjamin . . . the infirmary."

The infirmary was contaminated now. If Julian was in there, then he was dying a hideous death, slow and burning, and mercy would be to choke to unconsciousness before his skin was burned off his body. What was Sisko waiting for? A desperate shriek from a dying physician to get everyone else off?

"Sir," Kira attempted, "we *have* to get out of Ops and evacuate the whole central core! Our officers are standing by at their posts. They'll be killed by that cloud if we don't beam out! They're *being* killed now!"

"I said for both of you to stand by."

Sisko's tone was that of almost cheerful defiance. He hovered over a set of readouts that had held his attention since the cloud flooded engineering.

Kira watching him, drenched in shock, and finally spun to Dax and flagged her arms desperately. *What's he doing?*

Pushing back from her console, Dax stood up and with fluid motion abandoned her control center. "We don't have any choice. We certainly can't swallow that much radiation, and we can't defend the station if we're dead."

"Thirty seconds to fail-safe . . . Implement emergency evacuation immediately . . ."

Feeling her legs tingle with sudden resolution, Kira stared at him, held her breath, and tried again. "Sir, it'll be all right. I've been pushed back before."

The carpeted deck was uncomforting beneath her as she came to stand beside Dax, so the automatic transporter sensors wouldn't have any trouble finding her. Didn't make any sense, but she didn't care. Machines could break and she didn't want to be in the middle of one when it did.

"Fifteen seconds to fail-safe . . ."

Dax again placed her hand over the transporter trigger. "Ready, Benjamin."

Energize. Energize. Energize. Well? Energize!

Kira stepped away from Dax, toward Sisko. "Sir?"

He had pressed forward over the command center, his large hands spread like the feet of a giant hawk, his neck knotted and his eyes canted to one side.

"Ten seconds . . ."

Kira clenched her teeth.

Behind her, Dax abridged, "Benjamin?"

They both moved toward him.

"Five seconds to fail-safe . . ."

Kira drew a long breath. "Sir!"

Pushing to his full height, Sisko set his jaw and waited. There was nothing left to do. The decision had been made and there was barely time to unmake it. They were either cannily calling a bluff or they were trapped here, to await contamination and a slow and gory death by radiation poisoning.

Four, three, two . . .

And he had made his decision for all the Starfleet

personnel still left on the station—they were trapped with him if he was wrong.

Holding her breath for the last tick, Kira was swatted with the full impact of command authority, of Sisko's having made that decision and of his having the absolute right to make it for all of them. She had made decisions like that all her life, but only for herself.

"One . . . Fail-safe."

Ops fell silent, but for the soft whirrs of the computer systems working, and the occasional croak of a compromised system trying to get itself back on-line.

On the screen, the orange mange flooded the inner core of the station all the way to the top—to Ops. The picture looked like a spindle, but now with bright tangerine wool around it.

Quietly Dax said, "It's here."

Using only her eyes, Kira looked around. She listened.

She waited for her skin to start tingling. Like a sunburn—that's how it would begin. Then her tongue would swell.

"Fail-safe plus five . . . six . . . seven . . ."

No swelling. No sunburn.

"Fail-safe plus ten seconds."

No tingle. How long would it take?

She put her hand on the phaser at her hip. She closed her eyes. If she could save her eyes for a few seconds longer as her skin began to peel and her blood to boil, she would be able to aim, to shoot.

"Fail-safe plus twenty seconds."

"Captain?" a voice popped through the same hole Sisko had come in through. "Captain Sisko? Are you still here? Hello?"

Kira opened her eyes and looked.

Bashir's benign gaze preceded him as he crawled in and strode toward them, looking from one to the other, brows up like a child's.

"What's going on?" he asked. "Why wasn't I beamed out? My infirmary alarms went off. The computer said the whole place was awash with radiation, but the transporter never came on. I asked Chief O'Brien on my way here, but he didn't understand either. So what is it? Am I needed on the planet or not?"

"Julian!" Kira uttered, her throat raw with relief. Her pulse hammered in her throat, echoing in her ears. He wasn't lying on the infirmary deck with his skin flaking off!

He looked at her, then grinned in a completely confused and self-conscious way. "Have I done something?"

"Captain! Captain Sisko! Captain Sisko!" Another voice. This one not nearly so lyrical.

A gremlin appeared in the hatch, popped out, and screeched to them, eyes ringed with white as he clutched two large twine-tied bundles, one under each arm. "Where's the radiation? What's going on? What happened? The alarms started ringing and there was this terrible voice drumming about fail-safes and contaminations and I kept waiting to get beamed off! I thought you had things in hand up here! I wrapped up as much latinum as I could carry and I've been waiting to get off. And while I'm on the subject, do you know that two-thirds of my patrons evacuated without even paying their bills? They ran right out the door! I mean, they didn't even *pay!* Do you know what kind of sight that is? It's like watching money grow legs and walk right out! I have their names and I want them run down!"

"Calm down, Quark," Sisko said. "Dax?"

Tilting her reedy body just enough to peek at the panel as if watching an errant child, Dax allowed the computer systems time to read themselves out and put the diagnostic conclusions up.

"Atmospheric sensors read stable," she said. "The computer is blocking off the main accessways, but there's no actual contamination happening." She turned to look at Sisko without taking her hands from her panel. "Nothing at all."

"Fail-safe . . . code red, code red . . . all personnel in contaminated areas are now overwhelmed . . . fail-safe . . . do not enter contaminated areas without protective gear . . . fail-safe."

"See?" Quark pointed at the speakers. "That's what I mean!"

Bashir blinked at the booming computer voice. "I think it's trying to tell us we're all dead."

Quark rounded on him. "I *feel* dead!"

The doctor didn't respond to the Ferengi's remark, but pulled his medical tricorder out of his shoulder pack and fiddled with it. "This doesn't make sense . . . according to the tie-in with the station computer system, we actually read out as dead. This is amazing!" He turned the tricorder and picked at the controls. "Something must be interfering with its sensing mechanism. Is that possible?"

Low in his throat, Sisko chuckled, "Smart bastard."

Rattled, Kira swung to him and burst out, "A fake! They almost got us to abandon Ops! They could've walked right in here and taken over if not for you!"

Lips pursed, Sisko sighed in obvious relief. "He made the computer believe the station was being contaminated and hoped we'd act as we were trained to act. But I sensed a red herring. After all, if he wants to destroy the station, there are easier ways to do it. He wants possession of it, intact. And if it's flooded with radiation, he wouldn't be able to use it for a month."

"That's incredible!" Kira rapsed. "How did you know?"

"I didn't, Major, believe me. I could've easily been killing us all. I guess you could say I made a bet that he wants the station more than he wants us all dead. There's just something about him——"

Suddenly the alert klaxons very unceremoniously fell silent. The blunt quiet was both soothing and unnerving.

Shaking her head with relief, Dax slid back into her seat as if she had never come out of it. "All ventilation systems read functional and clear now. The computer is giving up its effort. It thinks we're all out of the inner core. That or dead . . ." Then she paused, tapped, and her ivory face crimped again. "Benjamin, the outer short-range sensor grid alert just popped on."

"Why?" He leaned forward.

Kira snapped around to Dax and looked at the readouts that showed them what the sensors were finding in deep space around the station. "Another fake?"

"No fake," Dax said. "I'm reading a Cardassian Galor-class warship . . . fully armed and coming in at high warp, full shields."

The short-lived touch of victory in Sisko's eyes fell away.

"It's begun."

CHAPTER
14

"THERE IT IS . . . a mass exodus. They have left from their hiding places and hurried into the docking ring. Soon the inner core will be ours. Hard radiation is a great fear for soft-tissued beings."

The High Gul of the Crescent Order peered between the massive shoulders of Elto and Ren at the tiny auxiliary screens in their covert headquarters. Shuttle after shuttle, craft upon craft, even down to the small single-pilot traders, had abandoned the station.

"Elto, tie me in to the general broadcast system. I wish to flush out any stragglers and squeeze the bravery out of those huddling in the docking circle."

"Yes, High Gul."

Elto picked at the bare circuitry inside the wall, made a mistake, hunted for the correct connections, then tediously made them.

"Go ahead, Excellency," he said ultimately, seeming relieved that he hadn't taken any longer.

The leader drew a sustaining breath, clinging to the

significance of even small accomplishments for a man so long dead to his culture. Now his men would hear what they had long deserved to hear.

"This is the High Gul of the Crescent. I have control of your command center; of your engineering section, from which I have access to all your reactors; and of your entire central core. I have retaken this sector of space in the name of the Crescent Order. Once again, as it was in the deepest beginning, this is Cardassian space. Any who remain on this station and wish to surrender will be mercifully sent out of Cardassian jurisdiction. Any who resist will suffer the scorch of radiation poisoning, as did those bold lingerers in the contaminated sections. In a symbolic gesture of my complete control, I am now putting the station's communications systems back on-line—" He paused to gesture for Elto to comply. "—so that you will be able to notify us of your surrender and your location. I will wait ten seconds. If I do not hear from those of you who are hiding, I will begin to wash the docking circle with radiation, and there will be nowhere left to hide."

Elto glanced up at him, hope lurking in his sunken eyes.

Since the haze of reawakening had fallen from the Gul's mind, his young men had all seemed more sunken, more skeletal than they had been in all those years past. He knew now that they weren't changing, but only that he had seen them through his affection for them and the sheen of their loyalty, as if seeing long-lost children and wanting desperately for them to be healthy, radiant, and well.

These young Elite were devoted to him and that was charming, but now, as the glaze faded, he saw the clear etching of skull plates, the depressions of nasal passages, the thinness of skin around bony arterial shells, and the shadowed cavities of their eyes.

Again, he wondered how he looked to them and hoped their devotion would haze their vision.

"Ten seconds, High Gul," Elto said. "No response from anywhere in the outpost."

"Perhaps there are none left," Clus offered from behind them. "Perhaps they're all out!"

"Then the station is ours," the High Gul told them simply. "This massive marvel is Cardassian once ag—"

"Attention, intruders."

They stopped, listened. In an instant the universe changed again.

"This is Captain Sisko of Starfleet, commander of Deep Space Nine *and regional supervisor of this sector. We have not abandoned the operations center of the station. Repeat—we have* not *abandoned Ops. We have control of this command center, of weapons, of main engineering, the infirmary, the Promenade, the docking ring, and we have secured all reactor chambers against further tampering. We know your radiation leak was faked. You have invaded Federation property, you've killed my people, you've assaulted my Security chief, and you've laid siege to my station. I'll give you time to surrender, but not much. Turn yourselves over immediately. Sisko out."*

A hush cloyed them as the deep voice fell away. Suddenly all they could hear was the faint murmur of ventilators that normally no one ever really listened to.

"High Gul . . ." Ren's astonishment littered his voice. "But—but—"

Elto pushed and jabbed at the naked controls as if deeming them liars. "Why is he still there?"

"He didn't abandon his command center," Clus gulped, abashed. "He dared the radiation!"

"No," the High Gul corrected. His arms tightened at his sides. "He dared *me*. He gambled not only his life, but all his people's lives. It could easily, *easily* have been no bluff!"

He paced away from them, his mind boiling. Anger pushed at his lungs as they heaved in his chest, still sore from reawakening.

"This man thinks like a demon . . . he risked all their lives that I wanted to occupy the command center more than I wanted their flesh. And he knows I'm Cardassian and require air and warmth as much as he does, for we looked into each other's eyes once and we understood each other. They're subtle sacrificers, these Starfleet people. They would've died writhing at their posts if he inclined that they should."

"We would do that for you, High Gul!" Fen blurted, a spray of saliva anointing his promise.

"Yes, High Gul!" two or three others echoed.

"But you are the Elite Guard! These people are no such thing!"

As the words shuddered out of him and he felt the rage build, he clamped his lips tight, paced himself, and demanded control of himself. Fooled! Imagine being fooled! He had been defeated before in battles, but only by the finest soldiers and strategists ever known. Not by outpost administrators, and he had never been made a fool.

Abruptly the narrow corridor fell to darkness, taking away the reassuring faces of his Guard. As blackness enclosed, the power within the walls dropped silent. Even their meager utility lights winked to darkness. Within the walls the faint noise of ventilators, generally so ignorable, sputtered and moaned to a halt.

Out of the darkness Elto's voice scratched, "Environmental support is off!"

"Off?" the High Gul swung toward the sound of Elto's voice. "What does this do to us?"

"We only have a few minutes of air, Excellency. With his hands upon the life-support controls, this man can drive us like animals through the outpost in any direction he pleases."

In the blackness the High Gul heard his men's breathing, every breath precious, but every breath filled the bellows of his fury.

No life support. No life. The station leader had turned the tables on them. Fooled!

For decades they had been held in hibernation, without heat, without air, and they had survived. Now, for want of a few more minutes of life support, he might be forced to falter away his advantage.

"Very well. Very *well!*" The High Gul balled his fists and struck at the walls on either side of him. *Thud. Thud.* "I should have killed him myself when I had the chance! I should've put my hand in his brain! Why did I hesitate? I place too much value on my own words. I gave them their chance as I promised Garak I would and they spurned it. We are now fully at war. Then very well! If he wants to drive us, then we will let him. We will take advantage of information Garak provided. We will let Sisko drive us, section by section, but he will drive us where *we* want to go—to the one place he thinks we don't know about. Ren! Fen! You wanted the honor—you have it. We'll entice

Sisko to track us, then you will bear away, head him off, and kill him."

"Yes, High Gul!"

"Painfully, High Gul!"

"How do you know it will be Sisko himself tracking us?" Elto asked.

"He's not the type to send others to do his work. And I know how to make him come to us. I know the one thing he will protect even more than this station itself. And we'll need someone familiar to help us with unfamiliar machinery . . . Telosh, Coln, you go with them and capture one of the command staff from this station. Any one at all—an engineer or something. A pilot or mechanic. It's time to abandon this outpost and launch our offensive into space, my young men. We will kill Sisko, then we will hail his supplicants from the bridge of their sequestered prize . . . their battleship *Defiant!*"

"How much does the crew know about where we are going and why?"

"I kept the number of crew to a minimum, sir, barely enough to run the vessel, and then I did tell them the nature of our mission—about the High Gul and the hibernation. It was the only way they would abandon their assigned posts without proper orders. However, I also told them that the High Gul and his Elites had been kidnapped by Starfleet and are being held on Terok Nor. That way, they'll willingly fire on the station."

"A nicely spun tale, Renzo. I commend you for that line of thinking."

"Thank you, but I don't know how much they believed me. I saw doubt and suspicion in many eyes.

Some of them know you were the High Gul's student, later his rival. They're sifting their memories for rumors and lessons long forgotten."

Glin Renzo kept his voice low, very low. There were only two others on the bridge, a navigator-helm and a science officer running the Galor-class ship's bridge, and he thought he could trust the two he had posted here, but certainty was a slippery fish in these circumstances. Not until he started choosing crew for this mission, started explaining to them the shaded facts, did he see just how twisted memories had become, how whitewashed the situation of eighty years ago was in their minds.

Their images of the High Gul were opaque and polished, had become history in all its grandeur or its coldness, and their opinions depended upon the loyalties, dreams, or sacrifices of their parents. He couldn't judge from their posture or the stiffening of their expressions whether their knowledge of this would turn sour. Yet, how many times had they both asked, "Is it true?"

And he had been forced to assure them that it was.

"Shall we run the ship silent, sir?" Renzo asked, suddenly eager to drive the fears from his mind.

"Silent?" Fransu leaned sideways in his chair and gazed into the open space on the screen. "No . . . they know we're coming. They couldn't miss the sector-wide communications block. Certainly they anticipate some action and will be ready. There is no such thing as silent approach to a facility with ears."

"They'll be powered up. They'll fight us with that station's weapons. Starfleet-installed weapons."

"I've fought before."

"Not with Starfleet."

"No, not with them."

"You're not worried?"

"Terribly."

"And the High Gul himself? He's formidable."

"Formidable and probably won't be sweetened when he finds out what I did to him."

"We don't know how much he knows."

"He'll know. He'll conjure it out of the past, Renzo, like a sorcerer conjuring a pot of smoke. That's the way he is. And the smoke will have my face on it. Say, how do you think I would look as a ball of smoke?"

"Not well, but you could make Gul Ebek cough."

"There! A bright spot in everything."

"Sir, have we considered—"

"Renzo!"

Fransu caught a movement in his periphery and was delivered a signal from his deep training, from the days long past of action in the field. No matter how frosted over by time, the flicker of assault was recognizable, if only resting in his memory like a fossil shape in dust.

He vaulted from his seat with a younger man's leap, shouldered Renzo out of the path of a descending blade, and took the blade himself. Pain erupted through the tip of his shoulder, numbing his entire left arm, but his right was his stronger arm and with that he drove their navigator staggering back against the helm console. His fist pressed upward against the navigator's jaw until the man grimaced, frustrated that his attack had been discovered an instant too early.

The navigator managed to squeeze his knee up between them. Fransu saw the knee push upward, but there was nothing he could do in time. With his enemy's leg pressed against his chest, soon his grip was broken and he was flying backward.

His head struck a hard object—he wasn't sure what—and the wince clamped his eyes shut for a moment. He knew that was a mistake. That moment was crucial. His skin crawled with anticipation.

He forced his eyes open and his right fist upward to be ready for the attack he was sure was coming, but all he saw was Renzo's flexing back.

The incessant spew of a sidearm whined across the cramped bridge. Echoing on the blunt walls, the sound was maddening because he couldn't tell what was happening.

"Renzo!" he shouted—pointless. Dangerous, too, to distract Renzo from what was going on.

So foolish. In his youth he would never have shouted so. His instincts were better.

Whose weapon was it? Fransu couldn't remember whether or not Renzo carried one today.

Seconds plodded past. Every movement of Renzo's form before him was gaudy, nightmarish, and when the speed finally returned Renzo stood gasping over the smoldering puff that had moments ago been a supposed loyal crewman.

The air around them bloomed with the stink of dissolved flesh and a pulse of heat from dispelled weapon energy.

Renzo's hands were shaking when he turned to Fransu, his lips parted in surprise, his eyes wide, and the weapon in his hand shuddering. It had been a long time for him, too.

He pointed at Fransu's shoulder and croaked, "Bleeding."

Fransu nodded. He climbed to his feet.

At the science console, their science officer stared in numb shock. Shock—but not lack of understanding. He knew what had just happened.

For that knowledge, Fransu sighed, took the weapon out of Renzo's hand, turned it on the science officer, and fired.

The astonished science officer raised his hands to cover his face and chest, wailed his protest, then sizzled into a puff of energy as his wail died away.

Renzo stared at the empty sacks of smoke that instants ago had been their two bridge attendants, and for a moment fear crashed across his face that Fransu might turn the weapon on him, too.

"Now we know," Fransu said, his throat raw. "Now we know, Renzo. There it is. Someone from my own handpicked crew. Now we can be sure of what will happen if news of this gets out, if it's discovered that the High Gul of the Crescent wasn't dead after all . . . that I didn't preside over his funeral, but in fact betrayed him and retook the planet he was about to take at a lesser cost . . . took it at great cost in my own favor, then claimed he died in the glorious battle and took the credit he deserved . . . that I slaughtered the two thousand of the Elite Guard . . . aren't these delightful memories, Renzo? Wouldn't you be proud if you were me? No wonder I've spent all my nights banishing the past. Ah, the things we do, Renzo."

The ship bucked over some gust of space wind, possibly from a nearby sun as they passed it, or possibly a belt of asteroid dust. There was no helmsman anymore, and therefore no one to report on the cause of the buck.

Handing the weapon back, Fransu began, "Perhaps we should man that position."

"The helm? Perhaps." Hesitation showed in Renzo's eyes as he settled the weapon in its holster again. His hands were still trembling.

"Call another helmsman and engineering assistant up from the lower decks." Fransu picked at the wound in his shoulder. "Someone you think you can trust."

"I . . . don't trust any of them now."

"Do your best. Just give the ventilators time to clear that stench from the air."

Renzo nodded, tapped the communications console on the science station, and passed the responsibility to the next in command to choose a helmsman from the engineering deck. When he was finished, he came once again to stand near Fransu, but not so near as before.

"Two more will be here in a few minutes, sir," he said.

"Thank you," Fransu responded, seeming distracted. "Do you remember those old uniforms, Renzo?" He plucked at the stiff shoulder pad of his jacket where the blade had sliced it. "How bright they were, the patches of color? Loose and comfortable, more elastic to the body . . . not stiff and metallic like these. Do you remember wearing those? You were so young."

Tactfully Renzo said only, "I remember, sir."

Fransu sighed. "Now you and I and this crew, we must all live with my actions from those days. I must destroy the High Gul and everyone who has seen him, which means the entire Terok Nor station. If he gets away and speaks to the Central Command, or if someone else speaks for him or about him, we'll be quite lucky if all they do is execute us."

Stepping near, Renzo pressed an elbow to the back

of Gul Fransu's command seat. "How will we explain the destruction of a Federation outpost without orders? Or a war? Or provocation? Or communication?"

Fransu gazed at the enormous screen showing open space before them. How black it was.

"I don't know," he said. "Everything is an unknown. I have no plan other than to kill him as I should have before. Kill, kill, it's all I do well."

"Nonsense," Renzo said flatly, then grinned. "You're a wild master at rotation minutie."

Fransu pressed back against the chair and bellowed in laughter. "What would I do without you?"

"Flounder."

"Ah, I wish I had a hundred like you. I wish I had ten. Even two."

"I could move around faster."

"You move fast enough." Fransu chuckled again, but there was remorse in his manner. "I hope we have luck today. This episode with the navigator—it shows the crack in this attempt. I had no chance to construct a plan, to build a web of confidences or a scaffolding of support. I have no one who will help me explain this or tell lies for me in the depths of the Central Command. Who besides you, Renzo, could I ever dare to trust?"

"There's something else we must consider," Renzo said evenly, without even attempting comfort for that other question.

Fransu looked at him. "Which is?"

"That perhaps the High Gul isn't on this station where we hid him at all."

"How do you think that?"

"Only because this tiny signal we received is indeed

only a *tiny* signal, not really confirmation of reawakening. There could be a malfunction, there could be a mistake. The High Gul's body may have long ago decayed or been moved, and something may have still triggered the signal device in the warming palette."

"But we saw his body eighteen years ago when the station was built, when we hid him there. All was functioning then."

"Yes, then. But even eighteen years is long, and the chamber where we put him was unheated. I don't know if the suspension palettes would continue to operate in space-zero temperatures. He may not be alive, may not be on that station at all. We may be attacking Starfleet without a reason."

"There's a chilling thought."

"Yes."

"But we have no choice. We can't go in and ask, 'Pardon, are you keeping our living Gul, or is our Gul dust?'"

"No, we can't do that."

"So we have to find some other way to justify the shattering of a Federation outpost, don't we?"

Fransu looked at him. "Yes."

In silence Renzo thought and nodded to himself, thought longer, then nodded again and went to sit at the helm, the seat still warm from the dissolution of the navigator's body. He spread his hands across the unfamiliar control panel and picked out the keys he needed.

"So . . . we discovered a distress call from a Cardassian vessel in this area. Here—I'm logging it now. When we arrived, it turned out to be a trap. We don't know if it was Starfleet or who, but they took over the station, lured us in, and attacked us. What could we do but defend ourselves? A lucky shot hit a reactor and completely demolished the station. We regret this tragedy. There."

He looked around, to see his longtime commander smiling at him.

"Most clever, my friend," Fransu said sincerely, chuckling as blood trickled down his arm on the inside of his jacket sleeve. "Lovely and simple. But don't worry—I know he is there. He's alive, he's there, and we shall dust the station. It's always easier to ask for forgiveness than permission. I'll apologize later."

"Only one ship? What kind of invasion strategy is *one* ship? Dax, confirm that."

"Scanning . . . confirmed. I'm only picking up the one Galor-class vessel, and that's all. There's no fleet behind it, not even any minor support vessels. It's coming in hot, not acting as if it's waiting for anyone else to join it."

"One ship . . . what can that possibly mean? Whatever it is, it's not a full-scale invasion. That changes everything."

As Captain Sisko prowled Ops, Kira watched him and tried to avoid asking questions every time he said something, but she decided she'd rather be embarrassed by ignorance now than foul up because of it later.

"Sir," she began, "what does it change? What was our strategy?"

"I deliberately didn't launch the *Defiant* until I knew what this was all about. I wanted to keep it inside the station's deflector envelope as long as possible, assuming an invasion force was on its way. If six or ten ships were coming in, what good would it do to get the *Defiant* cut apart? I was waiting for Starfleet to show up, then launch and join up with them. You have to understand, Major—if there's a war coming, a heavily armed ship like the *Defiant* could be more valuable to the Federation than this whole station." He held an open questioning hand toward Dax's board. "Now I've got one ship coming in. What's that supposed to mean?"

"Benjamin, they're moving," Jadzia Dax interrupted, fixing on another monitor than the one displaying the incoming vessel.

Sisko turned to her. "Who's moving? Mr. Crescent and his men?"

"Yes."

"Are you sure it's them you're picking up?"

"I've got partial internal sensors back on-line. O'Brien must be working pretty hard down there. I've got a faint biological reading on a cluster of what could be Cardassians moving inside the access conduits."

"It's cat and mouse," Kira said as the three of them huddled over the one screen, and she looked at Sisko. "Except now you're the cat."

"The computer thinks the station is flooded with radiation," Sisko murmured thoughtfully, "and that's reduced the number of places he can hide. Now all we have to do is further limit the funnel he can run through."

Dax played the keys of her panel. "They tapped deeply into the computer systems at the database level. That's how they faked the reactor rupture. I've just learned to trust the computer and believed what I heard and saw."

"It's not your fault, Jadzia," Julian Bashir uttered quietly from behind Kira.

It was the third time in five minutes that Dax had tried to explain what had happened. Since they'd so nearly been fooled, she'd become forbearant. She seemed even embarrassed that she'd accepted what she had seen in front of her and had nearly been driven from her post.

"He could've flushed the atmosphere out of these areas any time," Sisko said, tilting the subject in another direction. "But he didn't. Why didn't he?"

Kira paused to think. "Because they want us alive for some reason. We're valuable. Maybe hostages?"

"Maybe," Sisko said.

They all looked to their collective right as sounds scratched in the open tube leading to the rest of the station. Odo's masklike face appeared, his skin like melting candlewax, blue eyes dull and exhausted as he peered through.

How strange . . . Kira drew a sharp breath and found her stare drawn to him and she couldn't look away. He wasn't humanoid, this form was artificial, yet his fatigue was showing itself on the canvas of his mask as clearly as it would on her own face if she hadn't slept in a week. His features were less defined than usual, blurred at the edges, making him like a watercolor painting that had run in the heat. How many more hours could he go like this?

He lowered his head briefly, both hands on the rim of the tube, then summoned the strength to pull himself out.

"Odo," Bashir began. "I don't approve of your leaving the infirmary. You don't look good."

"Thank you," Odo sputtered, not attempting to hide his bitterness. "There's nothing the infirmary, or you, or anyone can do for me."

Silence fell and the words rang and rang. He was saying he would be dead soon, and had accepted that there was no help for him. In her periphery Kira saw Sisko glance for silent confirmation to Bashir, but thankfully no one said anything about getting him off the station. Their restraint was diplomatic, but no one, including Odo, was fooled.

Kira found herself shamefully glad that she wouldn't be the one to give that order. Like the old days in Bajoran history and Earth history—sending a loved one to a leper colony to die without the comfort of family. Through Sisko's calm exterior she saw the bitter rage that comes from the death of a friend.

Being crusty had helped her in her life, steeling herself and refusing to fall apart as others had, but she had changed. Being an adult was a lot different from being a teenager. Teenagers were indestructible, self-shielding, and took one day at a time. Over the years, her shielding had thinned, and she constantly gazed at the future.

How much could she take?

This was like being a fugitive in the Bajor's caves again. She didn't want to live that life again.

Sisko moved out of her periphery and came around behind her. "Constable, how are you holding up?"

The Security officer's weakness was palpable. He had to support himself on walls and consoles and chairs every step of the way to them. "Poorly," he admitted, his voice scratchy. "If I can concentrate on my job, I may be able to hold this form longer."

"You have to hold it," Bashir said.

"Either that," Sisko added, "or I have to put you off the station for the protection of everyone else."

"I understand."

"You were with the Cardassians for a while, so tell me—do you know anything about 'the High Gul' or something called the Crescent?"

"Crescent?" Odo tilted his head in puzzlement. "There's no such thing."

"But what about in the past? Seventy or eighty years."

Shivering with strain, Odo pressed both hands to the back of an empty chair and stared into the floor. His fingers blurred into solid mittens, then separated again as he concentrated.

"Crescent . . ." He sharply looked up. "The Crescent Order? You can't be talking about *that!*"

"Yes, I am. What is it?"

"It was the strongest order ever created in the Cardassian hierarchy! It was almost unanimous in its endorsement—the leaders were nearly deified in their own times. But it was almost a century ago! What's that got to do with us?"

"That's who we're dealing with."

Odo stared at him. "You're mistaken."

"Not a bit. That's who those corpses were. Some special force or ultimate unit, led by this individual who calls himself the High Gul."

"High Gul," Odo whispered, suddenly breathless. "High Gul! *The* High Gul? There's only one person with that title in Cardassian history!"

"And he's like George Washington or Christopher Columbus for Terrans," Sisko ratified. "Hard to see through the haze of legend and reputation that's grown around him over the years. But he's eighty years behind the technological times. That's got to work in our favor."

"I don't know," Kira interrupted. "He's learning pretty fast, to be able to take control of our computers that way."

"But he didn't get complete control over them," Odo picked up, "or he would've had atmosphere control and would simply have killed us all."

"Yes!" Kira blurted. "That makes sense! That's why he tried to trick us into leaving!" She looked at Sisko. "He didn't have all the control we thought he did!"

"And now we're getting control back on the inside," Sisko said, "while on the outside we've got one ship coming in, but only one. I still don't understand what that means."

Kira struggled for answers. "It could be they've launched a full-scale attack over a wide area and can only spare one ship for this station."

"That's not how the Cardassians work, Major," Odo wheezed. His face was glazed with effort, and he held on to the console as he spoke. "They have their logistical quirks, but spreading their troops or their vessels too thin isn't one of them. They'll launch their entire fleet at a square inch of space rather than fight a battle on a wide front. It's why they concentrated so hard on Bajor for so long."

"Benjamin," Dax quietly interrupted, "I'm getting a hail from the incoming vessel now."

Sisko stepped past Bashir to her. "Put it through. Let's hear what they have to say."

Dax nodded, tapped her panel, and said, "This is United Federation of Planets Station *Deep Space Nine*. Identify yourselves and state your intent."

"This is the Cardassian Imperial Warship Rugg'l. Who speaks for the station?"

Sisko blinked at Kira for a moment. He murmured, "What kind of name for a ship is 'Rugg'l'?"

Behind them, Bashir shrugged. "A Cardassian one."

"Sounds like a barn dance." He cleared his throat and spoke up. "This is Captain Benjamin Sisko. Just who the hell do you think you are?"

"I am Gul Fransu of the Cardassian Central Command and I'm ordering you to surrender peacefully or be boarded by force."

"You're in Federation space without authorization, announcement, or Starfleet escort. Please explain yourself. You have five seconds."

"We have come to rescue our greatest battle lord, the High Gul of the Crescent Order, whom you have kidnapped and are holding hostage in your facility. We demand that you hand him and the soldiers of his Elite Guard over immediately or your station will be laid wreck."

"I've had about enough of these people," Sisko said. "Major, fire up the *Defiant*'s engines. Get her ready for launch. Odo, if you're well enough, track those Cardassian intruders. We know the station better than they do—that's got to work in our favor. See if you can trap them somewhere."

The exhausted Security chief pressed his thin lips in determination, grumbled, "I'd be delighted," and struggled to the internal systems console.

"Open frequency," Sisko said.

Dax moved only one finger. "Frequency open."

"This is Captain Sisko. I refuse to drop my shields for any beaming purposes. This is Starfleet jurisdiction and I'm not handing anyone over to you. Any crimes committed on this station will be dealt with by Federation statutes. Any persons occupying this station are entitled to Federation sanctuary."

"Even if they are there to conquer the very sanctuary you offer?"

"Yes, even then."

"Perhaps I could lend you some soldiers who would be able to deal with the invaders on a Cardassian level."

Sisko smiled, but not nicely. "Thanks, but no thanks."

"Sir—" Kira interrupted.

"Stand by," Sisko said and signaled for Dax to cut off the channel. Then he looked at Kira. "What?"

She held out a beckoning hand. "Let's do it! Let's just hand the Crescent and his people over to them? That would solve all our problems! Let the Cardassians deal with these parasites!"

Sisko's black eyes hung on her as he contemplated the ups and downs of what she was saying. Could he see the eagerness in her face—how badly she wanted to get rid of the Cardassian scourge on their station? Sure he could. She wasn't hiding it.

"No," he said after a time. "Whatever their game is, I refuse to play it. They've made me part of the equation and I am not cooperating with either side until I sort out what's really happening here. Or until Starfleet arrives, whichever comes first. Dax, put me through again." He waited until the channels were open, then said. "There will be no compromises to my authority here. Stand down your weapons, turn your ship around, and consider yourselves evicted from this sector."

A long pause. The open channels buzzed faintly with effort, trying to override the damping effect.

Ultimately the voice came again.

"No."

Sisko vocally shrugged. "I thought you might say that. All right, we do it the hard way. Close frequencies. Phasers three quarters. Open fire. Let them know I mean business."

Kira bruised her hip as she slid hard into the chair beside Dax, once occupied by one of the officers she'd sent below to effect evacuation. The controls felt right under her hands as she adjusted the firing mechanisms, homed in on her target, took a fix, and struck the enable pad. It felt good, really good.

On the screen, red streaks of phaser fire broke from the station's weapons ports and chipped sparks out of the deflectors of the Galor-class vessel. Electrical results crackled bitterly around the vessel, then glanced off into space and dissipated into a salmon-colored fog.

"Direct hit on their forward screens." Kira gazed at Sisko appreciatively.

"That was pretty sudden, sir," the doctor commented, but didn't clarify what he meant.

Sisko didn't look at him, but continued scoping the ship on the main screen. "I gave them a chance. They were lucky to get the one."

"I'm all for that," Kira ratified.

"I thought you would be, Major."

"Damage is nominal," Dax said. "They've got their full screens up. They knew we'd fight. They're turning away now . . . coming to a new attack position."

"They're firing!" Kira pressed her feet flat to the

carpet and the heels of her hands against the edge of the console, but when the station shook with impact she still felt as if the world were falling apart around her. Planets, fine, ships, fine, but this station, hovering somewhere between land and vessel—she still wasn't used to fighting a battle from the free-floating halls of DS9.

"They fired!" Kira blurted. "They actually fired with their own people on the station!"

Sisko nodded. "That tells us they don't care as much as they're letting on about their Gul and his Crescent."

Dax reported, "Hit on our starboard deflector shield generators."

"Doctor," he said, "would you take the attitude control thruster position, please."

"Oh—of course, sir."

"Quark!"

The Ferengi cast him a fishy stare. "What! I didn't do anything! I've just been standing here!"

"Sit down over here and take these controls."

"But I don't know how to spin this top!"

"We'll tell you what to do."

"I protest strongly!"

"Go right ahead. Major, put the phasers on full power and fire at will."

Fingers tingling, Kira bit her lip and fired away freely. The Cardassian ship on the viewer took the body punches well enough and returned every shot, but didn't dare turn its strong forward deflectors away from the station while being bombarded from the strong weapons sails. From her vantage point before the monitors, Kira saw the heavy-bodied *Rugg'l* taking strike after strike, hovering just out of full-impact range, and returning fire between the station's shots. A straightforward siege, hit and be hit, head-on.

"Captain Sisko!"

His face melting for an instant until he got control, Odo swung around in his chair and almost fell before catching himself.

"The *Defiant!* That's where he's headed! He's figured out that we have a fully-armed warship docked here!"

Sisko glowered at him, then thumped the console with a knotted fist, not very hard, but hard enough to give away how he felt. "Dammit."

"How?" Kira pierced. "It doesn't show up on any schematics! It's not even logged in the station computer!"

"Officially, it's not here at all," Dax muttered.

"Yes, it is," Sisko said, "but it's a need-to-know property. It's pretty hard to hide a whole starship from incoming and outgoing traffic."

Sitting as if waiting to have her fingernails done, Dax let her eyes twinkle at him. "Not if you arrange the approach and departure vectors just so. You'd be surprised how many ships have come and gone without ever seeing the *Defiant.*"

Returning the cagey look, Sisko rumbled, "Old man, you *are* a devil in disguise."

"I know."

"So how could someone lurking around the bowels of the station, using sketchy plans and logged schematics to find his way around, discover that we've got a starship docked here?"

A few seconds went by before, then at the same time all five of them chimed, "Garak!"

Leaning away from her console in fury, Kira thrust all her fingers into her hair and grabbed on hard. "That snake! I should've locked him up at the first sign of trouble! That double-crossing, ungrateful *snake!*"

"Come now, Major, Garak's not all bad," Bashir protested. "He's been treated well here, he's got friends here, he's lived a decent life here——"

"And he's in exile here!" Kira seized. "He'd do anything to change the balance of power in the Cardassian government!"

"Kira," Sisko said sharply, "you come with me. Odo, you too. Let's get down to the *Defiant* before he does."

As her blood began to race, Kira pushed out of her chair. "Aye, sir!"

CHAPTER
15

THE SOUND OF choking is as old as time and as heartless. Pain, surprise, a graze of humiliation, of shock that the posturing has finally cracked open into violence—all are pieces of the body of battle.

Smoke boiled across the *Rugg'l*'s bridge. Gul Fransu waved pointlessly at the gushing black stuff as if to slap it away, but there was more coming in. "Get the ventilators working! And where is our bridge help!"

"Both killed in a corridor during the second hit." Renzo's throat was raw with smoke. "I've ordered two more, plus a weapons specialist. Ballistics are inhibited, warp power down one-fifth, sublight compromised one-quarter."

"Adjust forward and beam thrusters to push us back. Gain some ground. Put our strongest shields to the station, then all stop. All we have to do is keep hitting them. Can you see?"

"I can manage my way."

Hearing Renzo move off to his left, Fransu shuffled

across the bridge, still blinded by smoke, and burned his fingers twice on fused panels before he found the engineering console and tapped instructions to the lower decks, assuming they were still alive to take his orders.

Renzo stumbled to the middle of the bridge, cradling a wounded arm as he gazed at the calcimine claw of Terok Nor hanging in space before them on the crackling screen. "It's bigger than I thought it would be."

"It's a change-faced lodging," Fransu added, joining him at the command chair. "It looks Cardassian, but looks lie. If the High Gul has found out how long he lay there in dark cold, then he's a shocked man."

"Shock can twist a person," Renzo considered, by way of agreement.

Fransu only nodded. "Concentrate all our power to deflectors and weapons. We're a fighting ship, they are a station. We can take more than they can. Their shields will collapse before ours, and a station cannot run away. It will be just exposed metal to be cut to pieces by whatever we have left. And connect with the nearest communications drone and make it stop blocking this area. I want to hear the High Gul's voice one more time before I destroy him."

Renzo looked at him, paused, then thoughtfully said, "I shouldn't let you."

Fransu glanced at him knowingly, shifted his shoulders, and gazed again at the huge station slowly rotating, its dull rim spackled by white lights.

"But you will."

He gazed with satisfaction on the giant station that in a short time would be a relic. The only thing darkening his mood was the inevitable killing of his own crew when this was all over, and the abandoning of his ship. He and Renzo would survive in a life pod and make up a story to cover their acts of these hours. Anything could be said to have happened except what actually was happening.

It wasn't the end he had imagined for himself and the High Gul and the Elite Guard all those years ago when he had hatched the plan to depose the High Gul's power and turn the course of events as they were being laid out, but things had changed. And he was older now. He would have a chance to—

"Renzo!" Fransu jolted out of his chair. "What . . . what is that? What is *that!*"

"Where?"

"On the lower docking pylon!"

Below the station, just coming into view as the great structure slowly rotated, hanging like a spider on the glittering web, lay a blunt-cut vessel, dark against the fabric of space. Built low, round, and flat, it had blunt side-mounted propulsion units and a scoop-shaped snout protruding out the front—weapons or sensors? The clubhead ship would present very little target hull to the enemy on approach or vector. Painted in matte ink blues and grays, it bore no usual pride and smiles of Federation ships, but only the muscular essence of dirty purpose.

"That's the *Defiant.*" Fransu browsed the forward screen. "I heard reports about it. It was made to fight the Borg."

"If that ship is meant to fight the Borg, and *we* have to fight it—"

Moving hand over hand around the helm, Fransu stalked the screen, his eyes scanning again and again the blunt vessel that had changed everything.

"Why hasn't it launched? What's it doing, just sitting there at dock?"

"Maybe it's here for maintenance." Renzo was clearly working to hide his agitation at the sight before them. "Maybe they have no crew for it. Maybe the warp core is out of it—maybe—"

"It doesn't matter," Fransu rasped. "Everything is different now! If that ship is spaceworthy, we must act before they have the chance to cast off! I don't want to have to deal with that blockbuster—quickly, Renzo, more quickly than you have ever done anything, double our fighting power and sacrifice wherever we must. Close in on the station and gear up for heavier bombardment. We can no longer afford a simple siege. We have to storm the walls! We have to finish the station before that thing launches!"

"Talk to me, Dax, is this comm badge working?"

"—ing, but br—up, Kira. I'll boost—ain. . . . Is this any better?"

"It's better. Sir, the comm badges are back. Mostly."

From ahead of her in the dim, dusty causeway they'd been forced to go through to avoid areas the computer still had sealed off, Kira could just barely hear Sisko mutter, "Right."

The conduits were scarcely more than tubes in the internal skeleton of the station, meant for maintenance, not easy movement for anything larger than the eternal and unavoidable cockroach. Claustrophobic and encroaching, the conduits were especially crushing now as shudders and booming sounds shook the bones of the station from the constant throttling by Gul Fransu's ship. He fired and fired at them, probably hoping to chip away at the station's deflectors and eventually break through. It might work. If they let him have enough time.

On her hands and knees, Kira shuffled along behind Sisko, pausing every few shuffles to check behind, to see how Odo was doing. Each glance gave the same answer—poorly. Each progressive moment stole more strength. He'd been holding humanoid shape for a long time now and it had become a race. If he slipped, dared to rest, or was somehow driven unconscious and lapsed to his liquid state, then *boom*. In his guarded, background-man way, eternally outside even among outsiders, Odo knew his job and didn't mind doing it, even under the worst of conditions. Solitary as an eagle, soaring above and out of the crowd, but always on the lookout, Odo competed with Sisko for tacit authority over arrests.

Ordinarily nimble and lean, today he was shivering. Yet he still resisted Kira's concerned glances, in which lay offers to let him off the hook, that they would take care of this particular danger. He forbearantly refused, even if only with the weather eye of each return glance. In his sedately alien manner he insisted he would prevail, that the effort of tracking and capturing these infiltrators helped distract him from his fatigue. Maybe that was true, and maybe it was just something he was telling himself.

She wondered. She continued crawling forward.

"Major," Sisko said from in front of her as he crawled out of the conduit into an open narrow passage in the docking pylon, "I've been thinking about these two people we're struggling with. What do you think about them?"

She accepted his hand and let him lever her out of

the hole. "I think they're belligerent, pushy. . . . I think they're . . . well, they're Cardassian. But this High Gul—he's a wild card. We can't expect him to behave like Cardassians we're used to."

Still inside the conduit's opening, Odo looked battered and bruised, even though technically a shapeshifter couldn't be bruised. Danger of his condition fluttered before them—even he didn't know how much he could take, or not take.

"Unfortunately we don't have time to take a history course on the Cardassian past. Come on, Constable." Sisko's face gleamed with perspiration in the tawdry work lights as he hoisted their exhausted Security chief out of the conduit opening. "We've got this individual prowling our innards, and suddenly a sector-wide whiteout that has all the earmarks of a prelude to invasion, but culminates in the appearance of one, and only one, ship."

The station rocked hard suddenly, and made a sickening pitch. Sisko and Kira stumbled but managed to stay on their feet, but Odo skidded onto one knee.

Sisko plunged to catch him. "What the hell was that?" He tapped his comm badge. "Dax! What's going on?"

"Gul Fransu has moved in, Benjamin. He's not going to bother hovering out of range and potshotting us, apparently. He's hitting us with full power."

"Hit him back the best you can. We'll hurry."

"Understood."

"Sisko out." He stepped past Kira and snapped, "Let's get going. That kind of hit'll shake the station apart in minutes."

Forcing herself to let Odo follow them on his own,

Kira hurried to his side as he moved into the more open corridor. It was chilly here. Dax was right—she had apparently kept this docking pylon almost exclusive to use of the *Defiant*, so there wasn't usually anyone down here. There hadn't even been time to heat up the place beyond standby temperature.

"Sir, are you suggesting that we're caught between these two people in some private fight? A personal grudge?"

"You tell me." Sisko's voice was gravelly with frustration. "Gul Fransu flies in and demands that we hand over the 'hostage' we're holding, his supreme whatever-he-said, his High Gul, and when we don't comply and take action to drive him back, he fires on us with full-power destructive force. Would you do that if your High Gul were being held in a place?"

"No. You're right, I wouldn't."

"Unless you were the one who wanted to kill him." She turned for another custodial glance at Odo.

With those long legs Sisko got a stride ahead of her, so Kira hustled to his side once again and this time hurried to keep up. "Do you really think that? That changes the whole strategy of what's happening."

"Hell, yes, I do. Don't you feel those salvos? This guy means business. I don't know what the backstory is on these two, but I'd bet there's a big one. I'd also bet the Cardassian Central Command doesn't know Gul Fransu is here at all."

"You think he's acting on his own? Attacking a Federation—" Kira's words were partly lost in the thunder of another hit. They grabbed for each other and for the corridor handrail until the reverberations rolled away. "Attacking a Federation station on his own authority?"

"I hope so," Sisko said. "Otherwise it's war." He stopped at a loading junction and tapped his comm badge. "Sisko to O'Brien."

His comm badge blipped, crackled, then fell silent. In that instant of silence Kira's awareness fixed on Sisko as she realized what she had just heard.

War, and he was ready for it. In spite of all that had happened to him in his life, and in the past few hours, he was still being a Starfleet officer, more concerned about the station and defending Bajor than himself or even his son. For that moment regret sliced through her, a sliver of embarrassment that most Bajorans still acted as though they expected the Federation to abandon them at a feather's flight.

"Sisko to O'Brien. Come in, Chief."

Another *thrumm* cast them to a bulkhead, but there was no answer from O'Brien.

"Sisko to Dax. Are you still picking me up?"

"Dax here, I hear you, Benjamin. You're not clear, but I might be able—"

"I can't pick up O'Brien yet. Can you?"

"There must be some residual inhibitors in the system. The High Gul's a good wrecking ball, but he's not much of a repair man. I've managed to get contact with Chief O'Brien, but he's breaking up."

"Tell him to reserve power to shore up the deflector grid. Fend Fransu off with full phasers, the harder the better. Protect *Defiant* at all costs until we can get her launched and out into maneuvering space. Sacrifice other areas of the station if you have to. Just buy me time. Do you understand?"

"I understand."

"Keep these channels open. They might clear themselves if they're active. Sisko out." He took Kira's elbow and hustled her forward with particular urgency. "Major, when we get to the *Defiant,* I want you to handle the docking clamps by hand, in case Gul Fransu is scanning the—"

The corridor erupted into bright orange light and white sparks. A streak of destructive energy came so close to Sisko's head that his hair was seared as he ducked backward, shoving Odo back also. He drew his phaser and fired blindly down the corridor to a junction where the shots had come from.

Almost instantly another streak came in answer, and drew black artwork on the far wall.

Caught in the crossfire, Kira dodged wildly to one side and struck a bulkhead, dropped, and rolled for her life toward Sisko. He pulled her around the corner.

"How could they possibly miss!" she choked as the stench of seared metal thickened the air. "We were sitting ducks in that passageway!"

"I don't know," Sisko uttered. "Maybe their eyes didn't wake up all the way."

"Or, sir, maybe they have trouble using our phasers."

"Explain why you think that."

Kira pressed her shoulder to the cool wall. "Sometimes specially trained elite soldiers get special weapons and that's all they know how to use. When I was on Bajor in the caves, we were guerrilla fighters and the first rule is that the enemy supplies all your weapons. We could use anybody's weapon and make weapons out of anything. The Cardassians only knew how to use their own."

"Like flying the same runabout all the time. How many are there? Did you see?"

"I'm sorry—I didn't see a thing," she admitted.

Sisko pressed his lips flat and his face turned hard as he scanned the flashing corridor for a target and evidently didn't see one. "We don't have time for this. . . ."

"Let me draw them out, sir," Odo offered. "I can take a phaser hit."

"Not on your life, Constable. Or mine. Or hers. You don't have any idea what a high-energy burst would do to the fissionable material in your body. Besides, I just don't like the idea."

"Sir," Kira said, "that corridor comes around like a horseshoe and meets this one, down there, behind us. If they split up, they can trap us here without cover."

Sisko looked in the direction she was pointing, to a shadowed curve in the pylon's corridor where a darker shadow gave away another passage. "Go down there and stand ground. I'll try to draw them out. Odo, stay behind me."

"Reluctantly," Odo muttered. He clutched his own phaser, but his arm sagged. He pressed his shoulder blades to the wall and closed his eyes for a moment. His face had a sheen of melting plastic, scraped with patches of orange that fluxed and changed as he struggled to hold his form.

Resisting an urge to give him a reassuring pat on the shoulder, mostly because she was afraid her fingers might leave depressions that might give him even more trouble, Kira stayed low and climbed past him, then made her way to the other passageway opening. As she arrived, the thought occurred to her to keep going, to hunch her way down this bend, around behind the assailants. A blanketing shot could stun them all. Kill them all.

How many were there? Would she be facing two or ten? Had she and Sisko stumbled on the entire band of renegade Cardassians? Or was this a hit squad, come to get them before they reached the *Defiant?*

She tried to listen to the sounds behind her, to count the phaser shots scorching the other corridor. Sisko was shooting. That meant he saw targets. She almost called to him to tell her how many he saw, but that would telegraph their ignorance. Old bells went off from other battles, and stopped her from doing that. Ignorance was better than broadcasting favors to the enemy.

Frrrruuuummmmmm—the station was hit again from outside, a bone-shattering blow that echoed and creaked deep within the base structure.

Enemies outside, and enemies inside the station. It was still a blister. Abruptly defensive of the big old place, she gripped her phaser tight and scanned the dimness for movement. Unless they were fools, they would come here. She was ready.

Unless they anticipated her being here, guarding this passage—unless they had chosen this place on purpose. . . .

Had they done that? Was she falling into their plans, letting them separate her from Sisko? Weaken the force?

"Sir!" she began, and turned to look, but all she saw was Sisko's shoulders hunched and working, and Odo huddled behind him, struggling to brace himself on the shuddering wall. They didn't hear her over the whine of phasers down the pylon curve, and the drone of hits from outside, relentlessly rocking the station every few seconds. Like some ghastly bagpipe, the drones and the whine coupled to rattle her mind. She found herself wishing for five seconds of silence.

She saw phaser shots lance the air over Sisko's head, hopelessly missing their target.

"Sir!" she shouted. There was no time for anything else.

As the ceiling buckled over Sisko and Odo, Kira realized what she had failed to understand until now. These Cardassians weren't imbeciles who didn't know how to handle phasers. Instead they knew the architecture of the station, and that was their target—the ceiling struts.

A hellish noise in the foreground drowned out the drone of hits on the station from Gul Fransu's ship. Kira threw herself to the deck as the corridor collapsed around her, her eyes and mouth caked with metallic shavings and insulation dust. The whine of phasers broke off, then there were two more whines, then nothing. The air turned thick, musty.

All at once she wanted that sound back.

Plastered with debris and dust, she dragged herself forward, abandoning the passageway the Cardassians had fooled her into guarding. Masonry and ceiling stuff clogged her path.

"Sir!" she called again. That was stupid—if he didn't answer, then the Cardassians would know they'd forced him down and would advance to finish him off.

Sparks and fizzling noises erupted at the place where Sisko and Odo had huddled. Part of the wall was sheared off, exposing live electrical fittings that were gutted and arguing with the open air.

And there they were—two Cardassians in funny

clothes. Big ones, haunting the wreckage behind clouds of dust and electrical smoke.

Frruuuummmmmmmm Frruuummmm-fuuummm

The deck beneath her vibrated like an earthquake.

Lying low, Kira slowly brought her phaser around to the front, peering over her arms as she took aim.

Her hands wouldn't close on the firing mechanism. She looked at them—blood sheeted her knuckles. Spasms racked her numb fingers and her elbows both tingled. In a minute that numbness would go away, but did she have a minute?

She let the phaser fall sideways into her left hand and made her right hand into a fist, then opened it, then clenched it again. She had to get the feeling back! She had to aim . . . fire . . .

Out of the rubble like a swamp monster in a story, a huge dark form rose in a single heave. Chunks of masonry and metal shavings cascaded from Ben Sisko's shoulders and the top of his head. His face was gray with dust, powdered and skeletal, and for an instant he looked like a dead Cardassian. The whine of his phaser blistered the narrow corridor again, in two sharp chords—*bzzzt . . . bzzzt.*

One of the Cardassians shrieked and raised his hands, but the other never had a chance to make a sound or move. The air turned hot and stinky again, and the two forms melted violently away like burning flash paper.

Under Kira the deck rumbled. *Vuuuuummmmmm*

Another hit from outside. The station could only take so much. They had to get *Defiant* launched. They had to defend from a distance. . . .

She managed to get the phaser into her right hand.

Pain swept up her arms as the numbness began to fade. If she could just feel the trigger—

"Major?"

Smoke blurred her vision. Her shoulders hurt now. Was that a good sign?

"You're bleeding. Let me get you up."

The deck floated away under her and she hovered in midair, breathing heavily, her head light and spinning. As her head slowly cleared, Kira became aware of hands dabbing at her knuckles and wrists, squeezing her arms, probing for cuts and breaks. Over the pain in her shoulders, sensation was coming back into her upper body. She could feel her fingers again. Could she ever.

"Bet that stings," Sisko said. He still looked clay-gray and wasted, caked with insulation and dust, as he moved away from her to paw through the pile of collapsed ceiling. "Nothing permanent. Some abrasions, maybe a shock or two. I think you got the worst of it. Odo and I were insulated from the electrical jolts by the ceiling material."

Kira cleared her throat and forced her voice up. "That's the first time I've ever heard anybody being glad that a ceiling fell on him."

"Right. Well . . . those two were easy." Sisko glanced down the corridor expectantly, then hauled Odo to his feet. "Can you stand?"

"Yes," Odo croaked, and pressed a hand to what was left of the wall, determined to have spoken the truth.

"You call that easy?" Kira coughed as the dust crowded her lungs again.

"Easy to fool, I mean," Sisko said. "Once the

ceiling fell, they took for granted that I was done for, and came over here. That gave me my chance."

She brushed the hard bits of scrap from her tingling arms. "So did I."

"Anyway, it's two down. Adjust your phaser to leave a body. I want to be able to prove to Mr. Crescent that we've done what we've done. Major, how many of those individuals were asleep in that chamber? Do you remember?"

"Weren't there twelve? Eleven?"

"That means, counting the one who got killed before, that they're down to seven or eight." He glared down the pylon's forbidding corridor and gritted his teeth. Hot provocation shined in his eyes. "I can handle nine."

The High Gul chilled with satisfaction. Sisko had come to keep the *Defiant* out of enemy hands, and the enemy was already here.

"Thrust!"

It was his favorite battle cry. Much better than "action" or "rush" or "arms forward" as others had invented in his time. He enjoyed more than he could ever have anticipated shouting it once again. Oh! The surge of it! The *surge!*

His Elite Guard thundered through the tiny pass toward the three stunned faces of Sisko, his shapeshifter, and a Bajoran woman. Ah, the joy of pure shock! What invigoration to put such shock on the faces of the enemy!

The High Gul spread his arms and raised his chin, basking in the sensation as his young guards charged the enemy. Even knowing that Ren and Fen had failed, were probably dead, he suddenly captured a low-ranker's delight in the chance to destroy Benjamin Sisko himself.

Why hadn't he thought of that before?

Ren had wanted so badly to go. Fen had coveted a chance to act like a pure brute and had never had one until now.

The High Gul knew he had nurtured their desires to his own purpose. But that was what they were here for.

Before him his young heavyweights formed a barricade of shoulders and thick backs as they boldly charged the three stunned outposters. A few shots of energy creased the air, but no one fell.

There were shouts—not his men. The others.

Wild shots of energy weapons sliced into the bulkheads and ceiling, blasting the construction apart and raining rubble and dust. Blades flashed. Cutthroat hacks drew blood—the High Gul saw the smears of it on the wall, but couldn't see Sisko or the others anymore. Was that Sisko's voice? The huff of deep physical effort?

The High Gul looked for the solid dark shape, so familiar in his mind now. Sisko was a big man, but these young ones were big also, and there were four on him. Umdol, Elto, Telosh, Koto.

At the far end of this junction the High Gul saw the shapeshifter, barely able to stand, huddled against a wall, raising his energy weapon and struggling for aim that would skewer one of the Elites and not his own commander or their nurse. The High Gul was gratified by the shapeshifter's depleted condition. From moment to moment parts of his body were blurring, changing color, dissolving and reassimilating. All his energy was going into holding his form.

Yes, it was gratifying, but there was also terror in it. What if he was *too* tired?

Three others, Clus, Coln, and Malicu, were after the woman, but she was slight and difficult to grab. Twice as the High Gul watched she was caught and still managed to slip out of the Elites' grips. The second time she spun away from them, lost herself in their massive legs, danced underneath and out of the way, then turned a weapon on them.

Orange bands of light, scorching light, crackled through the air. Coln shrieked with agony and shock as his arm was severed from his body at the point of his neck artery, and half his chest went with it. He grasped the empty air where his arm had been, stumbled, stared at the disaffected limb lying in its own twitches in the dust, then gasped over and over with shock and confusion. He fell against the bulkhead and stared, suddenly oblivious of the battle around him.

Now his eyes sank and turned icy. He sank toward the deck, his mouth moving in soundless words. By the time his haunches touched the vibrating deck, he was no longer close to life.

Coln, who had been the High Gul's wife's favorite. A son she wished were theirs. She had felt that way about Elto, too. And about Ranan, who died with Malicu's spear through his body when the shapeshifter changed before him.

Perhaps the Bajoran wasn't a nurse after all.

She fired again, but this time her shot went wild as Malicu caught her around one shoulder and dragged her off balance, and Clus knocked the weapon from her grip. It went flying. This enraged her and she bellowed against the beachhead that she'd struck.

As the bitter stink of seared flesh and bone puffed at the High Gul out of the dimness and through his grief, he realized the meaning of energy streaks randomly grazing the immediate area and what might happen.

"Don't shoot the shapeshifter!" he shouted over the scream of the energy weapons. When the sounds continued, he shouted louder, "Cease firing! Blades only!"

He stepped through the clutter of fighting forms, rushed to the shapeshifter, and kicked the energy weapon from the shuddering hand. The shapeshifter sank against the wall, helpless to chase the weapon, helpless to put up a fight or use his natural abilities to confound the enemies who had cornered him. This was a defeated being.

The High Gul gazed down at him in intimate silent warning. Then he turned to the grunting mass in the middle of the junction.

And he drew his own blade. It was time to move this drama forward to the next poignance.

He moved slowly. Each step was calculated, not a charge or plunge, but a stride. He knew his target. Somewhere among the bright tunics and flags of his own men was the form of Sisko.

He saw flashes of the right colors from time to time—Sisko's black head, his burgundy clothing, blunted by dust. . . . The High Gul moved closer, pressed in deeply on top of the struggling mass, but was shoved off as Telosh howled in shocked pain and suddenly collapsed, clawing at his throat.

Under Koto, Elto, and Gobnol, Benjamin Sisko was fighting viciously, holding Gobnol by the face with one hand, Elto by the head in his bent elbow, Koto up on a pointed knee, and with the other hand clawing at the deck for the energy weapon that had apparently been torn from his own grip, but he was nowhere near it.

Roaring, Malicu suddenly charged in, pushed Elto aside, and plunged onto Sisko. Beneath them, Sisko was a demon given life. A beautiful sight, such possessive rage, and the High Gul gave himself a moment to enjoy what he was seeing. Worthy foes were neither cheap nor common, and he had hardly expected to find one doing paperwork on a cargo station.

His thoughts snapped when Malicu yelped like an animal and staggered back.

Sisko had apparently gotten his grip on a chunk of marble—who could tell what piece of discarded construction material this was?—and had used it on Malicu.

Time to stop enjoying and start eliminating.

The High Gul placed one hand on Koto's shoulder, and very gingerly felt his way through the tangle of large arms and torsos with his knife until he thought he had the right feeling on the end of his blade.

Taking his time and sensing his way through to the best flesh, he leaned forward, pressed the heel of his hand to the hilt, pushed hard. He knew that sensation as it rushed up the hilt, and he inhaled deeply to savor it.

Below, Sisko threw his head back and those white teeth flashed in a terrible grimace. He shouted something unintelligible—a roar of anger, perhaps, a good sound.

The pile of strong bodies collapsed suddenly. The High Gul stumbled back, drawing his blade back with him. Red blood ran down the blade to the hilt, and drained over his arm. Just right.

"No!" the Bajoran woman cried fiercely from behind him, kicking and slapping Clus and Elto, who were just now managing to catch and hold all her many limbs.

A surge of energy—he recognized the last panic of a dying man—blazed where a moment ago there was only the mass of Elite Guards and one human. Two brown hands came up, caught Gobnol by the head. Gobnol suddenly lost his balance, threw his arms backward, and there was a ghastly *crack.* He fell forward onto Sisko's sagging body.

All at once, the pile of effort quite simply heaved once and collapsed like a great dying animal. Abrupt stillness washed over the corridor. There was no more movement, other than the haunting twitches that came after a battle.

Gobnol and Telosh lay plainly dead. Close by, Malicu flinched and sucked his few last breaths. His head was cracked completely open from his eye socket to the top of his skull ridge. His sad eyes rolled toward his leader. Still alive.

Lying across the gore of Coln, Koto struggled to get up, slipping in his own blood and Coln's.

"Help Koto," the High Gul snapped to Elto. "Leave Malicu."

He paused briefly over the destroyed forms of his men, ignoring Malicu's gurgling pleas for help and the last pathetic wandering of his eyes.

"Malicu," he uttered. "My last student."

The syllables dissolved in his throat.

He turned away. He could look at the dead, but not the nearly dead.

Three of his Elites left. Three out of two thousand. A heavy price.

Stepping over the sheared pieces of flotsam left on the deck by the battle, the High Gul came ultimately to the site of his win, and looked down with appreciation on the dark lump in the rubble.

"Benjamin Sisko, leader of the outpost, king of the sector," he murmured. "A waste."

Dragging the Bajoran woman along with him, Clus drove his toe into Sisko's muscular side. When there was no reaction, he declared, "Dead."

"How do you know for sure?" the High Gul asked, almost quizzical. "You've never seen a human before."

"Looks dead," Clus offered.

"So did we." Enjoying his amusement at his soldier's expense, the High Gul moved a few steps to glower down at Odo.

Helpless, weak, the constable lay at the joint between a bulkhead and a support strut, unable to change shape, not strong enough to put up a physical fight, and stared up at his bane. The High Gul saw the struggle to remain in this form when it would have been natural for him to shapeshift into a whip or something and lash these invaders to a wall.

What a strange creature . . . his face was moving, melting in patches even as they watched.

Hoisting Koto at his side, Elto glared down at the creature too. "Kill him? I can do it."

"No," the High Gul said. "I wouldn't even know how to kill such as him."

"Bring him with us, Excellency," Clus suggested. "He can help drive the ship."

Tolerant of mood in the shade of his win, the High Gul turned. "Remember what we did to him, Clus? See how tired we've made him? He is a walking explosion. I don't want to have him anywhere near us."

"Then Garak," Elto said. "I'm sure he knows how to drive that ship."

"Garak?" The Bajoran woman came to life suddenly. Anger boiled in her eyes. "I knew that ball of spit's been helping you!"

The High Gul looked at her. "To his own purposes, you may be assured." Then he turned again to Elto. "I don't trust Garak entirely. I feel much more secure about this young woman. I do not trust her at all . . . so at least I know what I'm dealing with."

He held a graceful hand out toward the narrow end of the pylon, toward the main docking arm.

"Come now, my strong and young believers, and let us board our victory."

CHAPTER
16

"YOU ARE BAJORAN. What is that like?"

"Let go of me!"

"Please don't kick. It's unbecoming and will get you nothing. I've never been to Bajor, but I know the story of the place—Clus, don't clasp the lady so tightly. There's no reason for crudeness on any part. She's the first of these people I've been able to speak to in person and I'm very curious to have a conversation."

"Don't get your hopes up, mister."

"What is your name?"

"What's yours?"

"I am the High Gul of the Crescent."

"I'm the Mermaid of Flickernock."

In the dim shell of the lower pylon near where the *Defiant* lay off the docking ring, Kira Nerys cursed herself for getting caught before she could freeze the docking-clamp locks. She cursed herself for getting caught at all.

And it wasn't too hard to curse these guys in the clown suits either. Brigade of the dead.

Her left cheekbone hurt where they'd hit her. Was her lip bleeding or only swollen? Felt like both. She was still dizzy from the ambush, but fought to keep them from seeing that. In her periphery she saw a bruise rising under her left eye. Her hands were still numb, which was why she hadn't been able to fight them off.

Anyway, that was the story she was sticking to.

Before her, an elegant Cardassian man of indeterminate age scouted her placidly, as if he had a week. His face was sallow, but his eyes sparkled. There might be a lack of life in his skin, but there was plenty in his attitude.

He wasn't pacing, wasn't fidgeting, but simply standing, looking at her, almost eye-to-eye with her, a head shorter than any of his guards, princely in an alien way with his shoulders draped by a dusty dark purple cloak. Only when the ship, the whole station, was rocked by another hit did he put out one unconcerned hand to grip the corridor handrail for stability. He didn't seem particularly interested in the fact that the station was being pummeled every few seconds.

"My other two Elites—my men—are dead? Is that correct? I sent them to kill your leader, but I had to kill him myself. So I assume their deaths from that."

At first Kira thought to remain silent, but the answer blistered its way out. "You assume right."

That felt good.

He frowned openly, then motioned to his men. He led the way through the long docking pylon and without ceremony entered the husky fighting ship *Defiant*. Until now it had lain silent at its post.

Kira inhaled the cool air inside as they moved through the passage onto the bridge. *I'm gonna peel Garak when I see him.*

The bridge was quiet, cool, even pleasant in a tomblike way, as if waiting for rebirth at the conjuring hands of those who had brought it here to deep space.

The High Gul assigned his three remaining men around the bridge, then pointed at Kira.

"Put her at the helm."

One of the huskies stuffed Kira into the navigator's seat, and he wasn't gentlemanly about it. The physical roughness was designed to show her that she had no choice but to stay here and do as they bade.

The High Gul ran his hand along the back of the command chair. "You know, I'm confused. If Captain Sisko has had this ship at his disposal all along, why has he not launched it himself and done battle with my colleague out there?"

"He was waiting for the planet to turn blue," Kira dashed off, simmering.

"Docking clamps can be released from here," a Cardassian at her far left said, from the engineering subsystems station, "but I'm not sure how to do it, High Gul. It would take a day to learn."

"Don't worry, Elto," the High Gul said.

Something pressed against Kira's bruised cheek. She flinched and looked. A Starfleet hand phaser.

"Release the docking clamps," the brawny animal beside her said. "Launch the vessel."

Kira pressed her hands flat on her thighs and tipped her head sideways, into the pressure of the phaser. "Get stuffed," she said.

She felt foolish, sitting here, knowing Odo was back in that crumbled corridor, left weakened and unable to help, having to deal with the death-littered deck, to stare into the face of Sisko and think of the loss. It had been one of her biggest unspoken fears—to be wounded, weakened, helpless on the field, unable to move the future, waiting for capture or death, not knowing which would be worse, knowing that to be rescued meant a burden for her companions.

Those were thoughts she had banished daily, but thinking of Odo brought them all forward.

"If you do not help," the High Gul said, buffeting the rage of his young soldier, "I will go to warp anyway. Rip the station apart."

She pulled away from the phaser and turned to peer at him. "You aren't the type to do your enemy's work."

The High Gul smiled. "I like that," he commented. "I hadn't thought that particular item about myself, but it's something to live up to."

"Congratulations," she said, "but I didn't actually mean it as a compliment."

"No, of course you didn't. Clus, take Koto and go to the engineering deck. Learn what you can and get ready for battle mode."

"Yes, High Gul."

The big ugly one—now, there was a definitive choice—took the injured one and disappeared into the turbolift. That left only the High Gul and Elto on the bridge.

"Tell me about Sisko," the leader parried while Elto struggled at the engineering subsystems controls. "I've been collecting perceptions about him. To exercise my mind."

"You killed him," Kira condensed. "Isn't that enough for you? It's over, isn't it?"

"But I am a soldier. I gather enemies. The quality of them is how I measure myself. We are all reflections of our enemies."

"You're a reflection of a nightmare. Have you looked in a mirror lately?"

He smiled. "No."

"You might as well, because I'm not going to sit here and carry on a conversation with you."

"Then I will talk. You tell me if I'm right. Captain Sisko was a man with nothing to lose. Enduring, sometimes unremarkable, always shy of the collisions he has felt in his life, and this pocked nightwalk upon which we turn has been his sanctuary. That's why he defended it so fiercely. Am I close about him?"

"I wouldn't know," Kira rebuffed. "I didn't know him very well."

"Oh? Why not?"

"We didn't like each other."

"Are you an officer in the unit Starfleet? A field commission? To appease the Bajorans into letting Starfleet operate this outpost, I would surmise. What is your position in the rank structure here? At first I thought you were a nurse, but then I saw you fight, and you are no nurse. Why do you live upon a Starfleet outpost and wear the livery of its sentinels?"

She swung the seat a little toward him. "Look, Mr. Crescent, your goons jumped us and that's fair, but you're not going to get any information out of me. If you're going to have your gargoyles kill me, then make your point and get on with it."

"Yes," the High Gul said patiently.

Was the patience real or was he a good actor? Kira tried to read his face.

"Let me guess about you," he said, looking at her as

if regarding a painting in a gallery. "I fancy myself talented at this, so tell me if I'm wrong. You are a dauntless line-walker, yes? You have inborn vitality, sanded to perfection by the harsh fugitive life you once led on Bajor during the decades of struggle against my people's occupation of your planet. I have to confess to you I respect you and your people for throwing us off. Then, you grew up defensive. Fiercely self-willed. Ready to run on vague instincts when necessary. You're inquisitive. Let me see your eyes . . . they're cold, but in a hot way. You're diligent, demonstrative, and you possess a will of iron. Am I close at all?"

She stared at him and battled for control over her expression. She'd stopped saying yes, but he was still getting it out of her face somehow.

Though the invaders' leader was a smaller man than the other bruisers, physically he showed signs of once having been strong, and he had a confident kind of demeanor that didn't come from bashing heads. Every time he asked a question, he looked her square in the eyes and waited for an answer, gave her time, even though she might not say anything. He never made a threat, but simply went on to the next question. He had a nice voice, too, and that was somehow unsettling. Bad guys were supposed to rumble and rasp and cackle a lot. Even over the faint buzz of the translators that allowed them to speak to each other, his voice thrummed with easy drama. This guy could read poetry.

"I think your life on Bajor was a trial," the High Gul estimated. "The scars show beneath your youth."

How did he know?

Chilling thoughts of Sisko rang and rang in her

head, echoed grimly by the *frrruuuummm* of Gul Fransu's hits on the station above them, vibrating down through the ship every thirty seconds or so. They were like heartbeats now, part of the life and death of *Deep Space Nine.*

She sifted her fogged memory of those last moments in the pylon for signs of life in that heap of arms and legs and gushing bodies. She was in charge now. In charge of the station's last few minutes.

"Yes, it was a trial," she said, after weighing this answer's value too. "It was a brutal misery and a constant crippling resistance against barbarians like you."

"Me? Not like me," he said. "I am from much before all that. My legacy is from another time, another Cardassia."

"Are you?" she impugned. "Not from what I've seen so far. You can posture and delude yourself all you want, but let me tell you a little about what you spawned. Burned children . . . severed limbs . . . prisoners scalded with boiling tar as an example to others, survivors shown recordings of their writhing families, a civilization already beaten being beaten further down for no reason other than their captors' insecurity. Healthy Bajorans broken and shredded by generations of slavery . . . the planet stripped until it was useless even to Cardassia. Proud of your children, Mr. Crescent? They boldly carried on the legacy you've pretty plainly shown us today. That's what you slept through. Another time, my backside."

She knew she shouldn't talk, but desire to communicate her fury rumbled to the top. A feeling of dissection took her by the throat, just as this extra-large Cardassian hit man had her by the arms. Any of these monsters could snap her like a twig.

"You're a freak," she told him. "A fossil. I and my people lived out your legacy for you. And you proved it was yours when you walked over so casually and put your knife into my commanding officer while he was still fighting three of your men. That's grandeur, I'll tell you. You can kill me, but that won't kill the fact that I saw what you really are."

The High Gul's face had been impassive, he'd worked at that, she could see, but suddenly a single crease appeared across his brow, just a small change but still a suggestion that her words had plucked a string he hadn't wanted to hear vibrating.

He realized he'd given something away. Quickly he pressed his bloody palm to his head for a moment, and paced across the bridge away from her until he regained control.

"Madam, I need you to help me drive this battleship. Will you help if I promise to use it in defense of the station against the Cardassian force outside?"

She pursed her lips. "You're good with words. But you can't charm me into helping you."

His friendly manner vanished like a light snapping off.

"Seconds matter!" he raged, so sharply that even Elto flinched at the upper bridge console and turned to look.

Lowering her chin instead of raising it, Kira simmered, "Peddle it somewhere else."

Before her, the High Gul's hollow yet elegant face was crimped now, twitching.

She was doing it. She was getting to him. At least

she would have that. He might win, but if she had anything to do with it he wouldn't win happy. She could take torture. They weren't getting the *Defiant*. Judging from the rocks and shocks blundering through the very bulkheads, shaking the ship under them, the station wouldn't take much more of this relentless battering before its shields fell.

She stared at the High Gul and blindly hated him. She was in command, for the last minutes of *Deep Space Nine*'s existence. It was almost over. They'd lost. Now the only victory left was to not aid the enemy.

"Launch the vessel, sentinel," the High Gul repeated, "or, believe me, I *will* rip it off the pylon and take half of your station with it!"

Kira pasted him with a poignant glare and folded her arms across her chest. "Then rip it."

"You are maddening!" the High Gul spat. He swung away, then swung back without taking even one step. "You baffle me! You're obviously a survivor, a smart woman—can't you see what's happening here? Surely you've figured out that whoever is there is not a friend of mine! I am not the reason your station is dying!"

She pushed herself to her feet. "You're deluding yourself!" she blazed. Instantly she swung around to Elto—he was poised to jump her. "Don't bother! I'm not going to fight you." When he settled down, confused, she turned her back on him and faced the High Gul. "Who else but you is the reason? You can't charm this away and you can't hide from the moral blame. It's all yours. You and your poisoned culture."

A bone-rattling hit drummed through to them— possibly a hit right on the docking pylon, shaking the ship so hard that Kira grabbed for the helm to keep her balance. As if a figure in a dream, the High Gul barely moved, didn't even shift his feet through the shock wave, but stood still as statuary amid the blur of vibration. He seemed untouchable by the shaking, roaring, bawling of the station and the ship as their deflectors were shorn section by section.

"You're wrong about me, sentinel." He stabbed a conductor's finger at open space, as if directing the music of heavy hits. "This Cardassia is not me. I never tortured anyone nor made a single slave. I am not the Cardassia you know. Yes, of course we were conquerors, but in my time we were never squanderers. It was this new Cardassia who buried me in the vault, so my power would be diminished while they used my reputation, my banners, my pedestal of accomplishments to their own ends. Why do you think I was locked away?"

He came around the front of the helm and spread his hands upon the navigation board before her, leaned forward, and pleaded with his whole being.

"I would kill a million for a reason, but I wouldn't kill even one for *no* reason."

As she gazed back at him, Kira felt a change deep inside her chest. Pity?

She couldn't tell, but it was there and beating like a new heart. She'd been lied to by a hundred Cardassians in her life, she'd been deceived, bribed, courted by their every wile and had always turned a practiced deaf ear and responded with stony silence.

This time something moved in her at the beckoning of this ghost. It might be that she had weakened in these later few years, during which she had miraculously come to know a precious few honorable

211

Cardassians, knelt in tears at the deaths of some of these, an unthinkable turn of life for her.

Was she that weak?

"Tell me, sentinel," this man asked slowly, "what would entice you to throw off the yoke of Starfleet on behalf of Bajor?"

Everything about him had changed. He no longer threatened with either words or manner. Had he seen the change in her?

They stared at each other.

"How about a chance to see the Cardassia you know torn apart by civil war? . . . Would this win you over?"

CHAPTER
17

"THEY'RE GONE."

A faint electrical snapping and the sizzle of falling debris were the only sounds left after the portcullis closed between the pylon corridor and the *Defiant*. Now that avenue was closed.

"They're gone."

Something buzzed inside a wall panel. After a moment, it stopped.

A piece of the ceiling, dangling by a thread of insulation, strained its last molecule and fell with a short crunch.

"Tell me you're faking."

Before him he saw his hands melt and form again into hands. His mind was as blurred.

"Sisko . . . you're pretending."

Odo struggled against the blinding fatigue and dissolution of his physical form. He had never thought of dying, not this way, with the chance of taking the whole station with him.

He had been ready to rest when all this began. Now

the hours had drained him beyond his limits, and the pollutant in his body was making him feel ill. Each took more and then still more effort to resist.

Now there was this pile of knotted limbs and still torsos, and there was no noise coming from there. No movement. He had waited long seconds for it, but there was nothing. Sisko wasn't pretending.

He raised his numb hand to touch his comm badge. "Ops . . . Ops, do you read? Medical emergency . . . come quickly . . . Ops, can you hear me?"

The badge crackled weakly, as if it were also too tired to focus.

No one responded. Had they heard? It was barely possible that the channels were fouled, that they heard him but that he wasn't picking up their answer.

He clung to that.

With collected effort he drew his knees toward his body, slid them under and rolled onto them. The pollutant in his system was clogging his thoughts, fogging his vision, but he made his way to the pile of bodies and shouldered his way between them.

Two of the dead Cardassians slid off and thumped to the littered deck. Beneath them, still pinned under the third corpse, lay Ben Sisko. Blood puddled the deck beneath him, soaked his shoulder and neck and the left front of his uniform. His face was the color of clay.

Odo didn't bother speaking to him. There was nothing to say, no sense to any words. There was only the blood, bubbling from the wound in Sisko's chest.

Odo lifted his heavy hand and pressed it to Sisko's punctured chest. Slowly, ever slowly, careful to maintain the size of his form, he let his hand melt into the wound, sink through tissue and liquid, and take the form of the wound deep inside Sisko's body, and there he felt the struggling thump of Sisko's heart—not dead yet.

Gradually, concentrating, he let his limb take the shape of the edges of torn arteries and punctured muscle, until the pumping of blood was blocked off and the thudding of the heart became less panicked.

Now he would have to hold himself here, pressing into each vein as he found new bleeders, and he would tick off the minutes one by one.

A Cardassian civil war. Cardassians at each other's throats for a change, ignited by a hero of the past.

Kira's imagination bloomed like a ball of light. She knew instantly what the concept meant. Distracted by their own inner conflict, Cardassia would be finished as a threat to Bajor, or to anybody else. If this living corpse really was the one, the original High Gul of the Crescent Order, then Cardassia would rip itself apart over him.

He had changed completely in his approach to her. Had he been that much affected by hearing what Cardassia had become? She saw the tightening of his throat, the twitch of an eye, a faint flicker of revulsion that he didn't seem to want her to see. Nobody was that good an actor.

"I speak truthfully to you," he said, his voice much less dramatic than before, "about Bajor's best interest. I give you no word that I'll leave you alone if I am victorious. If I am victorious and I'm still alive, and Cardassia isn't smashed, you'll probably have to fight me someday. But Cardassia may be smashed. Certainly the current order will mutate . . . and I see in your eyes you don't think it can be worse." He paused, moved a step, looked at the deck, then looked up again. "What is your name?"

Fighting to continue hating him, she felt her animosity shiver. If he were lying, there would be prettier lies.

"Kira," she said.

He nodded. "Kira," he continued, "I offer you a holy war in my name that can only do well for Bajor and all its allies. We have a mutual enemy out there. Your station is falling apart. In minutes we'll all be dead. What are *you* going to do about it?"

She felt cold. All at once the weight of command was bigger than the station, bigger than the sector, and it made her back hurt.

Who could tell how a civil war would turn out? Whatever happened, those who were in power now would certainly be deposed by those younger and stronger. Current powers would be broken. Something entirely new might rise.

And the Federation would probably have a hand in the outcome—that could only be good.

If anything, a civil war would make Cardassia a nonfactor in the galaxy for fifty years or more. Take them right out of commission.

Imagine . . .

Could she make that decision? She didn't even know if Sisko and the others were still alive after that attack. The station didn't look good. She was on her own.

Was that a good enough excuse?

It might be.

She looked at the old man. Their motives were different, but sometimes that could work. Maybe after they drove Fransu off or killed him, the High Gul would abandon DS9. There was nothing for him here, after all. His front was at his home planet.

Sisko had been right—the High Gul could've killed them all any time he wanted to and possessed the station. Instead all he had tried to do was gain control over his environment and clear an avenue of escape. As soon as he lost control of DS9, he had abandoned it. It didn't prove he was gentle, but it did prove he was smart, too thrifty to waste havoc for no gain.

Kira moved again into the seat at the helm, tugged herself forward until his ribs touched the leather buffer, and tapped the flickering communications panel.

"Dax . . . this is Kira."

She looked at the High Gul, searched his face for satisfaction or gloat. There wasn't any.

"If you can hear me," she said, "release the docking clamps. Prepare to launch the *Defiant.*"

CHAPTER
18

ON DEFIANT'S COOL BRIDGE, a slim woman pressed her elbows to the panel in front of her, tightened her lips in frustration, and punched the comm. "Jadzia, this is Kira, do you read?"

The system crackled, then, *"Dax here, Kira. Are you on board?"*

"Yes, and I've got the High Gul on board. He'll be off the station. We're ready to launch. Release the docking clamps, please."

"Kira . . . you know I need command authorization to do that. Where's Sisko?"

"I left him in the docking pylon with Odo," she said dispiritedly, with meaning. "It's my call now, Jadzia."

There was a pause.

"Understood. Releasing docking clamps."

With a heavy, sonorous *chachunk,* the docking clamps receded and the ship's hull was free of its umbilical hookup to *Deep Space Nine.* Kira felt as if she had just listened to the sounds of her own legs breaking.

"Station umbilicals are in. You're clear for launch," Dax said. *"I'll keep the station's shields around you as long as possible. Good luck."*

"Thanks, but protect the station. We'll take care of ourselves. *Defiant* out."

The ship moaned, the engines warmed, the ventilators breathed fresh warm air, and the wide forward viewscreen blended to life, showing a disjointed view of the other two lower pylons, giant claws descending beneath the station in graceful curves.

"Alert status," the High Gul said from behind her. He was in the command chair.

Pressing her lips flat, she touched the red-alert control. The bridge fell to eye-forgiving red lights, which made everything on the control board show up more clearly.

"We've got to keep away from Fransu for a few minutes," Kira said, "until I can energize the shields."

"Do as you must. Departure angle."

Still nauseated by the twisted logic of what the High Gul had said to her, Kira complied. Before them the main screen wobbled and changed.

She pressed her hands to the helm. Beneath her scraped and tingling palms, the hard strong vessel angled down and away from the pylon, until they could see the vast underside of the station turning over them.

"There it is," he murmured. "The bespangled spool of Terok Nor. *Deep Space Nine.* Have you ever looked sincerely upon the thing you defend? Look how the grizzled prism turns in space. Ah, it's a tribute to science that it floats here, so similar to the spacedocks of my time. But in my time we had trouble living on them for very long. Look at the shadows upon her, like spilled wine. . . ."

"I always hated the place," Kira said, willingly crass.

"Then why do you defend it?"

"Because it's mine now."

"And as it is yours, so is the guardianship it provides to your fragile planet. I understand. How is the ship feeling beneath you?"

"Undermanned," Kira said. "We can fight, but as systems go down, there won't be any way to bring them back up."

The High Gul straightened and faced the main screen, the picture of the station's gunmetal rim with its pearl-string of lights, at the broken windows and shattered hull, parts only creased, some sliced right out like forkfuls of pie.

"I will order them to cease," he said. "I am the High Gul. Now I have this strong ship. I'll fight him and I'll win. In respect for Captain Sisko, I will leave your station intact. In respect for you, sentinel, I shall leave Bajor alone for now. Then I shall do as I promised—put all the factions of the galaxy up against each other until they mutually shred. They will play like puppets for me, and I will rename this sector Little Chaos."

"Hold very still . . . one more moment . . . now slowly begin to withdraw—slowly, Odo, slowly! I'll get each bleeder one by one as you release them . . . good . . . oh—look out! . . . all right, I'm sorry about that . . . almost done . . ."

They were both sprayed with blood, sweating and

working in intolerable conditions. The pylon was cold, and now dust-clogged and stuffy.

"He's not dead, is he?" Odo asked, exhausted. Plugging off Sisko's bleeding from the inside had been grueling.

Julian Bashir appreciated the ability, however, and had already commented several times on its effectiveness. "You did a remarkable thing here, Odo. Just another moment or two . . ."

Below them, a low voice croaked, "No, I'm not dead yet."

"Captain," Bashir chuckled, "I'm sorry. I didn't realize you were conscious. Are you in pain?"

"Hell, yes, I'm in pain, Doctor."

"You'll be stable in just one moment. Odo managed to retard the bleeding until I could get here."

"Situation . . ."

As his mind fogged in and out, Odo forced himself to find the energy to speak. "Kira was taken hostage aboard the *Defiant*. I heard them launch about five minutes ago. The High Gul is down to four men, counting himself. The station is under heavy bombardment. I don't know the details."

"Have they moved out of the shield sphere yet?"

"I don't know that either."

"What about me?"

"You sustained a six-inch puncture wound to the upper left quadrant," Bashir said. "It went down at an angle and missed your heart, but punctured a lung. Odo kept you from bleeding to death and also from . . . well, exhaling yourself to death, for want of more technical terminology. All right, Odo, slowly withdraw and I'll close the wound."

"Patch me together."

"That's what I'm doing, sir."

"I mean right now."

"Now? Captain, your heart nearly stopped. You need a good twelve hours of recuperation time."

"Pump me full of whatever it takes."

"You already are full of anesthetics, antibiotics, and cordrazine. That's why you're talking to us and not screaming in agony."

Odo looked at Bashir. The doctor was overstepping. His young bronze face was tight with concern at this field-treatment business. He didn't like it. He wanted a nice clean infirmary around him, with support staff and sterile fields.

Understandable. The situation was intolerable to Odo, the lack of control, of order, the unpredictability. He grimaced with anticipation of disaster as he brought his physical matter back to his side and reintegrated it into a humanoid hand, but no bright light came to signal the end.

Before him, Sisko struggled to roll onto his elbow. The effort drained him as if he'd been climbing a cliff. "There are bullies on my playground, Doctor. Neither deserves to win. The High Gul is like the soldier left on an island who doesn't realize his war is long over with. If I don't stop him, he's going to keep fighting until it breaks all our backs. You shore me up and get me out there."

Irritated, sopped in blood to the elbows and speckled with it up to his neck, Bashir didn't argue. Staidly he prepared the right hypo.

As he waited, Sisko looked at Odo with concern that embarrassed the shapeshifter, then fingered his comm badge. Sweat poured down the sides of his dust-plastered face as he forced his legs under him. His complexion was ashy as a Cardassian's. "Sisko to Ops. Come in, Dax."

"Benjamin? You're alive? Kira said—"

"Mostly. Status?"

"Fransu knows what he's doing. He's concentrating his firepower on our shield grid and he's broken it in several places. Overall shield power is down to one-third, structural integrity is ruptured in sixteen outer areas, and the lower core is uninhabitable. There are fires in at least ten sections. Weapons power is still up, but I don't know for how long. O'Brien's giving them priority. The docking ring is—"

"How are the transporters? Is *Defiant* still in range?"

"Impulse engines are just warming up. It's taking a while because of the complete maintenance shutdown. They're coming up around the station to meet Gul Fransu's ship."

"Have they moved out of the station's shield perimeter yet? And are their shields up?"

"No to both. In thirty seconds they'll be out of our shields and they'll have no choice but to put up their own."

"I want you to beam me over there, quick."

"Specifically—?"

"The bridge is transport-shielded. Send me to the engineering deck." He looked at Odo again. "You coming?"

"I want to," Odo offered automatically, and even the offer caused a reserve of strength to surge through him. He sat up straighter. "But I can't. If I could only relax completely for just ten minutes, I could hold this form again long enough to help you. But that's not possible. I'm coming to the end of it. I have to get off the station."

Sisko gritted his teeth and grimaced with pure effort as Bashir hoisted him to his feet. Then the doctor gave him the last hypo, the one that would mask his pain, clot his blood, sustain his strength, keep his heart hammering, and hold him upright for a few critical minutes longer.

"Don't use the transporter," the captain said, struggling for every thought. "We don't know what that would to you. The dissolution of particles might—"

He stopped. He didn't say it.

"Ignite me," Odo droned. "I understand. I'll find O'Brien. He'll get me into a runabout."

"Benjamin, you have ten seconds."

"Odo, I'm sorry," Sisko grated with clear sympathy. "I'm ready, Dax."

"Are you armed?"

"A phaser, two fists, and a lot of teeth." Sisko stepped out of the clutter of bodies, and as Odo gazed up at him and wondered what he was thinking, he said, "Energize."

"Fransu! Fransu . . . Fransu . . . so it's you."

On the main screen, the picture of Gul Fransu was incongruously clear, considering the sector whiteout and the bombardment that had rattled down through the station to the *Defiant* until a few minutes ago.

The High Gul stared and stared at the man he obviously knew.

Kira Nerys paused and watched them. What did they look like to each other? To Fransu, the High Gul must look not so different from the last time they'd seen each other, eighty-some years ago. But Fransu was an old soldier now, hammered and wizened, only an echo of what his youth must have looked like.

The High Gul glanced at her in an accusing way, then dropped the fact that she hadn't told him the identity of their attackers. As she returned his glare with her own, he seemed to accept that it hadn't been her job to tell him. The opposite, rather.

He looked again at the Cardassian man on the screen.

"Fransu . . ." he murmured again. "I had hoped it would not be you."

On the screen, Fransu glanced to his side at one of his crewmen, then rubbed a sweaty hand across the front of his silver-gray uniform.

"Excellency," he began. *"Central Command is thrilled that you are alive."*

"Oh, yes," the High Gul drawled. "Yes . . . I certainly would be, to see an anchor of the past resurrected."

Kira held her breath. What was the relationship here? Had Sisko been wrong about these two?

"Fransu," the High Gul began, dwelling for some unspoken reason on the name, "patch me into the Central Command. I wish to speak to them."

"Excellency . . . I cannot do that. The sector is blanked out."

"Unblanket it."

"I can't do that without collecting the string of drones manually."

"I see. Fransu . . . I want you to cease firing on the outpost of Terok Nor."

"Very well."

Kira squinted. Too easy. Way, way too damned easy.

"Where are my Elites, Fransu?" the High Gul asked. His voice had a terrible one-dimensionality about it. "Where are my loyal two thousand?"

"During the conquest of Tal Demica, in the later years when it was almost won, I sent the revive signal. They arose, but you did not. You were gone. Someone had moved you. The two thousand went on to fight as ordered, to conquer Tal Demica as planned. Your name is revered through the Empire."

Before Kira, the High Gul smiled a deep sentimental smile, but also one of warm amusement. He strode to the other side of the deck, pulling his hand along the helm as if drawing a line, gazing first at the deck, then back up at Fransu.

"I would like, when this is over, to go back to Tal Demica and see what really transpired and what has developed there as a result."

Fransu paused, struggled for control over his expression, glanced to his side again. *"If you will beam aboard,"* he said evenhandedly, *"I will take you there."*

"Thank you, Fransu. Thank you most deeply. Now I know without a doubt what to do. I'm glad we had this moment of deception between us. I've enjoyed this," he said to the face on the large screen. "Unfortunately, all things end."

"Deception?" Fransu returned, but he knew.

The High Gul nodded. "Didn't you learn anything from me in those early days? I don't think you allowed my two thousand to survive their hibernation. You've not only become a coward, but a butcher as well."

"Why do you say these things, sir?"

"Because you're preparing to release the outpost only in order to engage this ship in battle."

Fransu sighed, glanced to his right again, then asked, *"How do you deduce this?"*

"Because you've brought only one ship. Central Command has no idea you've come here, have they? Otherwise there would be either celebrations and a welcoming fleet, or a fleet of blatant attack, depending upon how things have really played out. But there is only you. You were ambitious enough to betray me, but too cowardly to kill me. You try to act in secret, to protect yourself from your past actions, but you've learned nothing in these years. The truth always leaks out, Fransu. There is no perfect silence. Whatever you do here will find its way back home. Cardassia has nothing to gain from the destruction of these people."

"No," Fransu finally admitted. *"But I do. I should have killed you when I had the chance, but in those days I could not raise my hand so high. Fortunately, my awe for you has faded with my youth."*

"How do you intend to explain the slaughter of this outpost?"

"There will be nothing but a smoldering wreck. I learned long ago not to explain wreckage."

"I'm glad you learned something," the High Gul said. "Now, my bold student, let me ask you this and watch the shade of the decades fall from your eyes . . . do you remember what you're up against?"

CHAPTER
19

WITH THE HELM under her hands and the ship murmuring softly against her thighs, Kira Nerys faced forward but still felt the High Gul's eyes upon her, scoping the back of her head, her shoulders, and she felt his tempered smile.

"We're coming out of the station's shield sphere," she reported. Her throat was raw. "I'm putting up our own shields. They're almost fully charged. Do you have a heading for me? Something tells me you're not the frontal attack type."

"What are the strengths of this ship?"

When he asked that, ignoring her comment, instinctively Kira stopped underestimating him. He might be out of date, but smart then was smart now and he was smart enough to know that she knew how to fight with this ship.

"Heavy weaponry," she said, "heavy shielding, tight maneuverability. It's a one-of-a-kind ship, so Fransu won't know its abilities."

"Weaknesses?"

"Our weaknesses are simply lack of crew. If something goes down, there's no way for the five of us to get it back on-line. Second, our photon torpedoes are out of the equation. We don't keep them active and loaded—they're too dangerous. It takes crew to load them. We'll have to do without ours, but Fransu won't have to do without his."

"And as I recall, photon torpedoes are quite formidable at close range."

"Right."

"Things have not changed so much. Weapons are weapons, ships are ships, Fransu is Fransu. While we pass him, I want you to open fire. Let him have a taste of this vessel in his teeth."

Kira hunched her shoulders and pressed her cold fingers to the helm. "Coming about."

Squat and tankish, tilting as efficiently as a dish spun across a galley floor, the *Defiant* turned up on one fistlike nacelle, swung on an invisible lead line around *Rugg'l*, and jumped into a sudden burst of speed.

Like a prowling hound the Cardassian ship hung against the ageless black shroud above *Deep Space Nine*. A beautiful sight in its way, and a strange drugged feeling, this reawakened challenge. It raced in Kira's veins. Again she was fighting the Cardassians, this time at a Cardassian's side. There was always a cost to peace, and if she paid Bajor's today she would be gratified. Deals were made every day, but few for the sleepful nights of a whole civilization, possibly a whole sector. Bajor's peace had been allowed lately, but unfinished. If the High Gul wasn't lying, and she didn't think he was, then she might have purchased a few generations' nights of peace, whose mornings were unafraid.

Seconds were suddenly swallowed and she shook herself out of her thoughts and put her hands on the firing controls, but Fransu beat her to it. The Cardassian ship opened up on them at close range, pounding blue bolts across the open sky between the two ships, incising *Defiant*'s shields across the critical midpoint.

The bridge became sharply hot—a sure sign of power loss somewhere on board. The ship was in survival mode and sacrificing comfort for compensation.

"Equipment failure in something called PDT crossfeeds," Elto reported from the upper bridge.

"That's the primary slush deuterium tank—impulse fuel temperature. We can't go without that."

The High Gul calmly searched for the comm unit. "Bridge to Clus and Koto. If you can hear me, please go to the auxiliary control area and compensate for temperature control in the impulse fuel tanks."

"They're turning," Kira said as she watched the other ship on the forward screen and the small displays around her that measured what was happening out there.

As *Rugg'l* began its swing to meet them, Kira opened fire. Heavy energy bolts racked the bridge, so powerful that their noise came up through the ship as an earsplitting whine—*pew-pew-pew-pew*.

The bolts rapid-fired into space and caught *Rugg'l* under the chin, knocking the big ship upward against its own artificial gravity.

The High Gul inched forward in the command seat and cracked, "Wonderful!"

"Not bad, not bad, not bad," Kira murmured, gritted her teeth and came about again. When the beam of *Rugg'l* presented itself, she fired again.

The Cardassian ship heeled downward on one side now as its shields absorbed the pummeling with almost visible effort.

"This is a wonderful ship we have!" the High Gul uttered genuinely.

Kira nodded, but her mind was on something else. "We can hang out here forever and pound on each other until one of us breaks down, and it'll be us because he has a crew and we don't."

"And he knows by now that we have no photon torpedoes, or we would have used them at this range."

She peered over a shoulder. "How do you figure he knows that much about Federation technology?"

"I must assume he does, or we could all die of my shortsightedness. After all, *he* has not been asleep for eighty years."

Kira made a ragged grumble in her throat and faced the bow again. One battle at a time.

"Shoot again," the High Gul said. "We can cut and cut him until he faints."

Without confirming—she couldn't bring herself to aye-aye this guy—Kira leaned into the controls, brought *Defiant* up on an edge, rolled around *Rugg'l*'s stern, and opened fire again. *Pew-pew-pew—*

But this time Gul Fransu was ready. He had readjusted his shields to deflect the heavy bolts away from their critical sections, and that bought them precious seconds. They returned fire, anticipating Kira's piloting and sledgehammering *Defiant* continually until Kira managed to pull the ship completely around and veer off.

"They've got our number," she choked. "Guidance is shuddering, fusion reactor pellet injectors are backflushing . . . I'm losing plane-to-thrust balance—I've got overthrust! What are your men down there doing anyway!"

Defiance.

Its own kind of red alert. A brew of possessiveness and insult, and the effect of having damned near died. A rush of invincibility, enough to sustain the critical minutes.

Might have been the drug. Didn't matter. Any rage was good rage.

The sizzling of a transporter beam was the last sound that should've gaggled through the engineering deck of this taut-muscled ship of the right name, but here it was, ringing in the ears of Benjamin Sisko. He watched the battleship's innards coalesce around him as if the room were doing the beaming and he was just standing here while the universe changed around him.

It was an illusionary by-product of beaming. In his rational mind he knew exactly what was going on, but down inside he'd never quite gotten used to it. Lights flashing where there was no fixture, energy crackling where there was no source.

He pressed his shoulder tight against the corner of the chief engineer's office doorway. Dax had put him into a sheltered area. Outside on the main deck, two Cardassian soldiers hustled about trying to run a ship meant to be run by a crew of couple dozen. They were probably rushing to put as many systems on automatic as they could, but there was a limit to that. Some things just couldn't be replaced by computer programs and autopilots. Some things just required the leaps of logic that only living beings with common sense and flashpaper innovation could make.

He struggled through blurring vision to see the readouts. What was the ship's condition? Had they taken any hits yet?

Yes, there was one . . . another . . .

The two ships were engaging, perhaps just testing each other, but there were shots being exchanged. Were *Defiant*'s shields up yet? Yes—he could see the bright lime-green lights confirming shield integrity. They'd gotten the deflector grid on-line. They had a few minutes, time to maneuver.

How much was Kira cooperating on the bridge?

Threats wouldn't hold much ballast for Kira. Something more compelling had moved her.

He seethed to get these people off his ship. Was that sensible? Who would run the ship if all the Cardassians were gone? The *Defiant* would be a doomed creature tied to a stake.

Back and forth the arguments wrangled in his aching head. He found no answers and battled to make a plan without them. Yes, he would take engineering. He never again wanted to be helpless on a possessed ship. His pulse drummed in his ears—he had no idea how long Bashir's concoction would keep him on his feet. Stimulant this strong would kick back on him before very long. All the clocks were ticking.

Before he was ready one of the Cardassians heard the scrape of Sisko's boot on the doorframe and turned to face it, saw him, reacted with shock, clawed at his side for his hand weapon and brought it around. For an instant Sisko was shocked too, almost too long an instant. His depleted body and mind jolted at the sight of the Cardassian's hollow face and that weapon swinging around and up, but his own weapon was already in his hand. He gave over to instinct and opened fire. One hard squeeze.

His phaser was set for wide field and found its target without relying on him for good aim. Narrow ray, and he would've missed.

The Cardassian raised his arms to protect his face, made a choked yell, broke into torn pieces of flesh and squiggled to bits of floating ash, leaving only the stench of burned living matter to puff back toward Sisko.

What the hell? Sisko thought. He checked his phaser, which was set on heavy stun. Apparently the long dehydration had made the Cardassian's body unstable.

Where was the other Cardassian? He'd slipped out of Sisko's view—when? He couldn't see. . . .

Of course—the engineering deck was only half lit. It wasn't just his eyes after all. The lights were down fifty percent. Dock standard. He'd forgotten about that. No one had bothered to turn them up. Or more likely the Gul's men didn't know about dock standard. That was why everything seemed blurry, diminished, colorless.

A movement at his side—a hard force struck his phaser arm, numbing him to the shoulder, driving the weapon from his hand. He heard it skid away, scraping pitifully across the open deck. Pain blinded him for a crucial instant. He raised his elbow sharply, taking the one chance he had, and amazingly made contact.

Driving backward into the point of contact, he threw all his weight into that elbow and felt his attacker's balance skid out from under them both.

The Cardassian's own phaser dashed out to one side, though he managed to keep a grip on it. Together they struck the side of the pulse drive monitor unit with a deafening crack, and the Cardassian's phaser went off.

The surge of raw phaser power whined so close to Sisko's ear that it raised the hairs on the backs of his hands and neck. With both hands clutching the Cardassian's arm around his neck, he looked in time to see the phaser beams slice a glaring orange burn crack across the control panels on the other side of the complex.

"Stop it!" Sisko ground out, his lower lip pressed into the Cardassian's rock-hard arm. "Stop it! The deflector grid! You're heading for it! Idiot, you're—"

The phaser kept screaming at his ear. The Cardassian's hand clenched hard on the weapon, firing the wobbly orange flame as if drawing his name on the engineering panels, going like a child's scrawl toward the deflector grid.

From behind the Cardassian bear-hugged him and kept firing, either didn't understand or didn't care, or was caught up in the fever of the wrestling match.

"Stop firing! Stop—firing!"

He dug his heels into the ground and dropped his weight out from under, trying desperately to pull the mighty Cardassian off balance only a few inches. But this was like wrestling with an iron statue. The Cardassian roared an unintelligible curse and wouldn't give. In front of Sisko's aching eyes, the phaser and the fist clutching it shuddered and buzzed, draining violently all over the engineering deck housings—those critical housings where the important stuff lay.

Sisko raised one foot, searching for a wall or

something to brace against—too late. The phaser beam went like scalpel through the deflector grid housing, and in a pathetic instant the shields were down. That was it. They were down.

A tough ship . . . without shields. Fransu's weapons would cut into bare unprotected hull plating.

"You blundering ass!" Furious, Sisko tucked his chin under the Cardassian's arm, found a hole in the Cardassian's armor, peeled back his swollen cheeks, and sank his teeth in where it counted.

The Cardassian gasped, dropped back, and tried to pull his arm up.

Sisko brought his knees up, dropped out of the stranglehold, and rolled away. His hands scratched the deck, the corners, the housings for a crowbar, a mallet, a piece of the ship, anything he could use as a bludgeon to make this end somehow in his favor. But there was nothing.

He had as he turned only swollen hands and numb legs, equilibrium shot to hell and judgment not far behind it. He cranked his head around to the Cardassian—something about seeing death coming, about facing it head-on and not being shot in the back.

Pressing both hands to the side of a repair console, he pushed all the way to his feet.

His back muscles withered with anticipation of the Cardassian's phaser slicing the same scrawl in his spine as it had in the deflector grid.

He rose to his full height at the same second the Cardassian stumbled up and was swinging around to him. The soldier's face was twisted, growling, and the weapon was coming around, too.

The deck lit up—more electrical buzzing, more hot

streaks. Sisko squinted, knowing it was coming. He didn't have anything to throw.

The Cardassian's expression changed, but only for the briefest instant before changing quite suddenly again—eyes grew wide within their bony goggles, mouth fell open as if to gulp a protest, when abruptly his body tucked forward to accept a blow and dissolved into a puff, then fizzled out of life.

Sisko stared at the empty space before him, wondering during that last instant if he had in fact died and come back as supernatural and now his very thoughts could destroy.

He spun around, caught himself, chest heaving and legs fighting for balance, and struggled to focus his vision on the figure there. With a gurgling wheeze he snarled, "Garak!"

Garak loosened his grip on his weapon—he didn't want to fire it accidentally at the man he had just saved.

"Captain Sisko," he said. "You look as if you've been through a shredding. I heard you were dead."

"Where'd you," Sisko heaved, "hear that?"

"Oh . . . tailor's privilege, Captain." There was an attempt at smugness, but it was shallow. Garak attempted a dispassionate grin and failed.

"What are you doing here?"

"Throwing in with you. My hopes have crumbled." There was a veil of sadness that Garak couldn't hide. "Only grim alternatives now."

"I hope there are alternatives left. Do you know anything about Federation technology?"

A flicker of the smugness came back. "Captain . . . don't you know by now? I'm a *very* good tailor."

"Then stay here and man engineering."

He stepped to Garak and glowered, feeling his stiff face groove with permeating disgust. Then he tipped one shoulder toward the deflector grid station and lingered only one more bitter instant.

"We'll talk later," he said.

"Our shields just collapsed! Can't you get through to your men in engineering? What are they floundering around with? They've got to bring our shields back up!

"Clus, Koto, this is the bridge—give priority to bringing the deflectors back on-line. We have no deflectors. Clus? Koto, do you read? Clus?"

Putting her shoulder down and digging her feet into the carpet as if pushing the ship herself, Kira drew a shuddering breath. "I don't know how long we can do this. We're dead without shields, there's no doubt about that."

The High Gul abandoned the comm unit and told her, "Break away from him and go to the sun."

She twisted around. "Say again?"

"The sun," he said with a casual motion outward into the solar system. "Go to the sun. Go close."

"You want to play tag right next to the sun?"

"No, around it."

"Why?"

"We need something in our favor. Fransu will have photons, we will have the sun."

"If we leave, he might take the opportunity to cut up the station."

"No, he knows I'm on board here. He will follow me."

"How do you know?"

"Because he is Fransu, sentinel."

Irresolute, Kira shook her head and faced front again, where all their troubles lay. "All right . . . he's Fransu."

She sheared off on her course, wheeled *Defiant* around on a rim, and belted all the speed she could get out of the struggling impulse drive. She could almost feel it sucking, tapping fuel as best it could. A little better now—maybe the Gul's men had figured it out and put the PDT back in balance.

But still no shields.

They could go to the sun, all right, and about all they could do was hide behind it. One shot of full phasers from a ship the size of Fransu's would buckle the hull somewhere or slice off an engine, and that would be it.

"They are following, High Gul," Elto reported. "Firing again—"

His voice was cut off by a blistering hit that sent sparks from the ceiling and smoke pouring out the port subsystems. But it was a grazing hit—Kira still had helm integrity under her hands. She squeezed speed out of the ship and the ship dug in.

The sun was in front of them, blinding bright in spite of the main screen's compensators that saved their eyes. Bajor's unforgiving apricot sun, now a strategic point in a space battle. Not the destiny of most suns, certainly.

Kira aimed for it. It stayed the same size for damning minutes, then began to appear steadily larger.

"He is pursuing," Elto reported. His voice squawked with tension. "Gaining!"

"Go around the sun, sentinel," the High Gul said, "as far as you can go, but stay on a horizontal plane."

"What'll that do for us?" Kira asked, to avoid another automatic aye-aye.

"I know how Fransu thinks. He was never very good at this. He's too cautious to be good at it. Rather than chase me and risk my turning on him, he'll wait on this side. We'll come up underneath him, hit him hard, then disappear around again. It will completely unnerve him."

"And you're enjoying it."

"Yes, I'm enjoying it."

"Playing sun tag isn't my idea of strategy," Kira said. "Without shields, we can't get too close or we'll fry. He's got shields and he can—"

"It doesn't matter what he has," the High Gul insisted. "We will prevail if we outthink him."

Kira bit her lip. "Doesn't always work . . ."

She adjusted her vector to avoid slamming into the sun—although the abandon of it was insanely enticing for a second or two—and brought the ship around just as the temperature warning klaxon came on.

"Proximity alert . . . veer off immediately . . . proximity alert . . . veer off immediately"

"Yes, shut up," she muttered, and switched it off.

She was sweating. Her clothing began to chafe around her wrists and neck. Her hair slowly began to matte. She could feel it becoming heavier, strand by strand, as the heat increased. Without shields, the ship couldn't fend off the sun's beating.

They looped around the sun at the axis horizontal to themselves, pretending that up was really up in space, and down was down.

Kira watched her displays cautiously. "We're opposite to DS9 . . . now."

"Loop under the sun and meet him. Come up firing."

Understanding the picture, Kira appreciated the High Gul's restraint in explaining every detail and ordering every move. She knew what to do and the order was to just do it. He was also taking the still-ripe risk that she was truly willing to work with him. This would be the time for her to turn on him. She felt his eyes on her, knew he was betting his life on her.

It was a kind of field-of-honor trust, and though it failed to unnerve her, it did keep her from thinking about anything but the task at hand, distracted her from imagining ways to betray him.

The bridge was getting hotter. Sweat drained down the sides of her face. Beneath her clothing she felt it puddle on her chest, under her knees, and on the bottoms of her feet. Every movement now had an annoying squish.

On the screen the sun grew closer, then scooped upward to the top of the screen, then all but its bright light vanished and they were underneath it.

She piloted as sharply as she could manage, but without shields she could only cut so close.

Fransu's ship was right where the High Gul said it would be, hesitating, wondering if it should come around. Something about that bothered Kira, but she ignored her inner voice and came up firing as instructed.

Phaser streams incised the deflector grid underneath Fransu's vessel, and without even looking at the sensor displays she could see the crackling of energy cutting through the grid. There had obviously been some previous damage done by DS9's phasers, and now she was cashing in on it.

Fransu's ship shuddered off to port, trying to gain range, but Kira kept *Defiant* at full speed, never mind the dangerous reality of being overtaken by the sun's powerful gravity.

"It worked!" Elto called, panting with excitement.

"Worked," Kira breathed to herself.

"Loop around the sun again," the High Gul said.

Without responding to him Kira piloted a tight path around the brilliant field of heat and light, keeping *Defiant*'s stronger topside hull to the sun. The engines moaned with effort so taxing that the sound thrummed up through the deck under them.

"All stop," the High Gul said when they were on the other side again. "Come about and hold position."

She maneuvered the ship as instructed, facing the sun, ready to leap or plunge in any direction.

"Holding position," she said. "The next move is Fransu's."

They began the most awful, nerve-wrecking thing in battle—they waited. Ten seconds . . . twenty . . . forty . . . a minute . . .

"Where is he?" Kira asked the main screen, the sun sizzling upon it, hurting her eyes in spite of the screen's compensators.

The High Gul coughed on a thread of smoke coming up from one of the port side panels. "I told you he wouldn't follow. Elto, can you pick up his location on the other side of the sun? We can go and hit him again."

"My readings are confused," Elto choked on the

electrical smoke. "I see several images of his ship . . . but none is complete."

"Those are sensor ghosts," Kira said, turning to look at him. "Switch to tactical sensors and look for propulsion residue instead of a ship."

"Thank you."

She shifted around again, nauseated by her decision to help them.

Bajor, Bajor, Bajor, the galaxy was bigger than Bajor. There were millions of innocent families in the Cardassian culture, too, whom she'd never considered before coming to her position on *Deep Space Nine* and widening her field of vision. And others who would be affected by a Cardassian civil war—she scoured her mind for the impact of what she was doing, and plaguing doubts ate at her.

"When we've made him tense," the High Gul said, "we'll again loop around beneath the sun and pound his unprotected underside. Fransu will never expect that. He'll be protecting his bow and beams, expecting a flank action. Sentinel, if you would prepare us for—"

"I see him!" Elto stumbled to the lower deck and took the navigation station and weapons, giving Kira the chance to concentrate on the helm. "He's coming out of the sun's corona! Here he comes!"

CHAPTER
20

"FIRE! FIRE!"

"Firing." Kira heard her own voice as if in a distant crowd. She lunged into the phaser mechanism and blasted freely, but Fransu's ship barreled down upon them from inside the bright disk of the sun.

"Our phasers are only skimming their shields," Elto reported, gripping the edge of the console in front of him. "At this angle, we need photon torpedoes."

As if in bitter mockery, Fransu's ship opened fire with its own photons, and the *Defiant* boomed like a cannon going off in a cave as she was hit by *Rugg'l*'s strafing run. Fire broke out in three places around the bridge, sparks fanned from deck to ceiling, and smoke boiled along the starboard side.

"Fire again!" the High Gul blazed.

Kira abandoned her controls and swung around to him and fought for stable tone.

"We've got to get out of here. You've got to accept the fact that we can't fight him without deflector shields. You can't outthink a photon torpedo! Let me veer off!"

With her fierce expression she dared him to respond, to cough up some poetry that would shield the ship.

Stiff in the command seat, the High Gul's voice was ragged. He looked from the screen to her, then to the screen again, at the far-distant silver scratch of Fransu's ship swinging about to come back at them.

"Very well, veer off. Any course."

As she swung back to the helm, Kira felt a sudden stinging pain run up her left arm—the port side lateral sensor array subsystems station had just blown up. The carpet beside her was burning!

She managed to stay in her seat and field the hot sparks that scorched her face and left hand, winced, and wiped the sparks off on her leg. She turned the ship up on its blunt nose like a clumsy dancer and struck off with full impulse speed straight Z-minus around the bottom of the sun—the course the High Gul had fancied would surprise Fransu. Now it was just an escape route.

The Cardassian legend gripped both arms of the command chair. "Why did we not see him coming? These modern sensors should've been able to pick up anything moving toward us!"

"I tried to tell you!" Kira shouted over the crackle of shredded electrical systems. "It's eighty years later. He can get a lot closer to the sun than you think! That's how he came around without being seen! The reason we don't play this game is that our shields have gotten better than our sensors!"

"I see no particular wisdom in what's happening here," the High Gul said. "A battle is a battle—time-tried methods should operate in any age. And Fransu is a known element. . . ."

She cranked around, still keeping both hands on the controls. "Well, maybe the raw technology's improved in eighty years! And maybe he's got eighty years more experience than the last time you saw him! And maybe, just *maybe,* he doesn't think of you as a hero-god anymore!"

Pure gut fury blew into the High Gul's face as he stared at her.

Uh-oh . . . trouble. She'd hit a sour chord with that one.

He rose from the command seat and glowered down at her, his arms arched out at his sides, hands slightly raised as if he were about to backhand her. But she didn't care. A crack across the face wouldn't change anything.

She stiffened her jaw, ready to take it.

But abruptly the turbolift door swept open and raw orange phaser fire creased the bridge. Not just outside on the bare naked hull, but right here, inside, ten feet way, where no one could possibly get away from it.

Phasers blared like stampeding macaques across the bridge of the fighting ship. There wasn't even time for Kira to plunge out of her seat once the turbolift opened and the lightning started. She could only duck forward over the helm and cover her head—a silly instinct that could do nothing against the attack of hot phasers. But it was one of those things that made a person feel better just before dying.

None of the phaser energy hit her, though—a mind-boggling surprise during moments in which she prepared to be vaporized. When the sounds fell off, she was still sitting at the helm, digging her fingernails into her hair, peeking up from the crook of one elbow.

"Sir?" Slowly she let go of her hair.

Before her was a ghost of Ben Sisko, drenched in blood, plastered head to foot with dust, hunch-shouldered, gruff, armed and dangerous.

Such a death mask . . . Sisko was furious. Ghastly and sunken with purple bruises, his eyes were ringed in white and boiled with anger. Sweat cut shining trails through a blood-flecked gray plaster of dust on his face and neck, and his soaked uniform was torn in front and across one shoulder, revealing a slate-blue bandage over half his chest and secured to the bare corded muscles of his shoulders and upper arm.

On the starboard helm deck, the High Gul was kneeling at a smoldering collapsed body.

"Elto . . ." he called softly. He lowered himself to his young guard's side.

A long purple burn cut across the front of Elto's smoldering uniform. His eyes were open, his mouth gaping in amazement, but he never took another breath.

"Oh, Elto," the High Gul moaned. Grief-stricken, his face flushed, he looked up and motioned to the body. "This was unnecessary . . . this wasn't in my plan!"

Sisko gazed down at the High Gul and spoke to him in person for the first time. "I didn't read your plan."

The High Gul looked at the body of his assistant again. "I would have protected him over my own life. I'd rather you had killed me instead. Whatever you think of me, he deserved to live."

"You made that choice for him," Sisko said. "I didn't."

The old soldier nodded, then shrugged and accepted what he had just heard.

"Thank you for leaving his body for me to touch in the end. I wouldn't want him disintegrated. He has a family."

Sisko kept his phaser up. "I wanted physical proof of all this. And of who did it."

"And you came back from the dead to get proof." The High Gul patted one hand on the lifeless chest of his assistant. "I understand. My others . . . in the engineering area . . . gone also?"

"Yes, gone."

Keeping one eye on the High Gul, Sisko sidestepped along the perimeter of the bridge until he was over Kira now and looked down.

"You all right?" he asked.

From behind the hand across her mouth, she actually felt a moist laugh blurt between her fingers. The laugh was pure nerves and naked relief. She looked up. "I'm *so* happy to see you."

"Same here. Stand by."

Abruptly light-headed as the weight of responsibility poured off her shoulders, unable to take one more shock, she could only manage a silly nod.

"She's a scrappy one," the High Gul said. "Your sentinel, here. I played to her fears, but she had none. She was as fearless as an Elite. I told her I would cut out her heart as I tried to cut out yours, and she gave me the knife. I was an inch from success, and a woman stood in my way. I'm very impressed."

"Fransu was lying to you, you know that," Sisko said. "You've been betrayed."

"Yes. So you tapped into our conversation?"

"Some of it. The part about the two thousand

soldiers. I'll bet he never awakened anybody. He probably slaughtered anybody associated with you."

"I know. He likely took over the conquest of Tal Demica and took credit for what I and my men had built. Today he comes to make sure the truth never shows itself. The battle between us has been for nothing. He's going to destroy the station."

"Attacking the station with a foreign-flagged ship is an act of war," Sisko said.

As she watched him, Kira thought he was testing the water, trying to see what the High Gul thought of the prospect.

"That doesn't frighten Fransu," the old warrior said. "Your Federation will have only a melted-down hulk in space and a mystery." He shrugged with his eyes and faced Sisko. "The strong taste of battle shows on your face. You're too good at this not to enjoy it, Captain. Instead of standing against me, stand with me and we will rule here."

"It's my duty to stop you," Sisko said.

The High Gul held out a beckoning hand. "Stand with me, and duty will be what *we* say."

Sisko didn't offer an answer, but only looked at Kira.

Aware of the High Gul, she responded to Sisko's silent question. "Sir, the other ship is bearing down on us and we don't have shields."

"I know we don't. Take the helm, Major. Come about one-half, then give me a two-second warp-speed burst, heading four-one-one-four."

"Aye-aye, sir! Coming about!"

CHAPTER
21

"WHAT ARE YOU that you cannot be killed?"

The High Gul of the Crescent stared up at the ragged, shredded form of Benjamin Sisko in all its bloody stature, and in the old soldier's eyes there was undeniable, perplexing relief.

"A man with a good crew," Sisko croaked, wavering like a marionette, twitching a dozen muscles at a time to keep on his feet. Only his phaser hand was absolutely stable.

Sisko could imagine what he must look like to the Gul, and to Kira, his half-swollen body demanding each two steps as they came, his hair and face plastered with bloody dust, his uniform in shreds, showing the bandage across his chest. On his bare left shoulder and arm he felt the heat of the burning port bridge and felt the icy spritz of the fire retardant that had automatically come on.

On the helm deck he saw Kira poised, only one hand on the piloting controls, as if ready to step between the High Gul and the command chair. She wasn't going to let the Cardassian go there again.

Sisko appreciated that. He knew it was all for him. He could see that in her face.

"Stand aside," he said to the High Gul. "It's over for you, do you understand that?"

"Yes," the High Gul said. "I've lost my battle. We must do whatever we can to save your ship and your station. Though I do not know what. The ship is shutting down around us, with no one to repair it. I don't know what to do."

Realizing the power of personality it took for a man like the High Gul to admit something like that, Sisko unlocked his knees and winced his way to the lower deck, where he scooped up Elto's phaser and made extra sure the younger Cardassian was dead. He was done trusting even his own eyes.

"Do you think you can get Fransu to follow us?" he asked.

"Technology may have changed," the High Gul said, making a conciliatory gesture toward Kira that Sisko couldn't translate, "but the nature of men has not. Fransu is like a puppy that grows up always timid of the older dog, even though he is bigger now." He gestured at the aft angle being shown on the main screen, of Fransu's ship following them but not over-taking. "Notice that he's pressing his advantage, but pressing it from a distance. He expects to be disciplined. It's why he couldn't kill me all those years ago, and I can tell in spite of all this that he's having trouble killing me now. Yes . . . I can make him follow."

"I'll stay out of the picture," Sisko said. "Let him think you're still in charge."

"Captain Sisko," the High Gul began, "I've lost. There is no reason for you and your people to die. Hail Fransu . . . raise your phaser and kill me in front of him. Then he might break off the attack."

"No!" Kira burst in. When they both looked at her, both surprised at this sudden accommodation, she added, "It won't work. We've all seen you. He's not going to let any witnesses survive. You know that."

The High Gul smiled at her. "She has a keen mind."

"She has," Sisko agreed. But he knew there was more. Somehow in these past reckoning minutes, Kira had come to respect the High Gul. So that was why she had cooperated.

Better than torture.

He decided not to pry. For those minutes Kira had been in command and had possessed the prerogatives of office. She didn't owe him an explanation, though he thought he might have just seen it.

"Coming out of warp, sir," Kira said. "Two minutes on the button."

"Full impulse and maintain course."

"Maintaining course. We'll come up with the station on our starboard and the wormhole on our port side."

Sisko pawed the comm panel on the command chair. "Garak, can you read this?"

Seconds ticked by.

Kira looked at him. "Garak? He's here?"

"He's here. Garak, this is the bridge. Come in—"

"I'm reading you, Captain, barely."

"We need thrust, not weapons. Do what you can."

"I was working on the shields. I think I can give you one-quarter deflector power."

"I'll take it, but I really want impulse thrust."

"Thrust it is."

"Sir"—Kira gulped as her displays flashed—"shields at one-quarter!"

"Put them all forward and keep them to Fransu."

"Forward, aye—here he comes, sir!"

Sisko dropped into the navigation/weapons seat beside her. "Skimming phaser power over to the shields . . . shields coming up to forty percent. . . ."

Kira squinted through the smoke at the console displays around her scorched hands. "He's looping deep . . . coming around in front of us . . . he's maintaining . . . well, quite a distance."

"You see?" the High Gul said.

"He's too far away," Sisko ordered. "If we turn around, he'll make the same loop again and he'll still be too far away. I need to lure him in closer."

"Cut thrust," the High Gul told him, "then slowly drop your shields again."

"We just got'm up!" Kira leaned forward past Sisko and stared at him. "One photon and we're dead!"

Sisko motioned her down. "I've been dead. Do what he says."

She rubbed her hands on her knees to scrape off the sweat, then picked at the controls until the shields dropped.

And here they sat.

In the visible distance, Fransu's ship hung in space, just out of phaser range.

"Dammit, he smells a trap," Sisko gritted. "He's not coming in."

"His only real fear, Captain," the High Gul said, "is that I might somehow escape. The one thing he cannot have is my escape."

Sisko looked at him appreciatively.

"Then let's give him your escape," he said. "Major, move us toward the wormhole. Bring us to proximity that'll make it open up." His right hand was almost completely numb as he punched in another code on the comm panel. "Sisko to *Deep Space Nine.* Dax, do you read?"

"I read you, Benjamin, are you all right?"

"Still in one piece. All of you stand by at station controls. This is it."

"Standing by."

"Here he comes," Kira rumbled.

On the main screen, Fransu's ship drew closer, slowing down cautiously. He didn't trust them—but the High Gul was right . . . he wasn't bearing down like a locomotive either.

Closer, closer—

Normally invisible, the fabulous natural phenomenon of the wormhole sensed the ship's proximity and burst open. Out of empty dark space came the sudden bloom of its white-blue spiral, a great maw beckoning them to come through and abruptly be somewhere else, far away. It was a door to another quadrant, a bridge over tens of thousands of light-years, as valuable to the Federation as it was guarantor of Bajor's critical position.

It whirled and whirled, waiting for one of these ships to take it up on its temptation. Even now, in the middle of battle, it was enchanting and hypnotic.

"Sir," Kira said, "Fransu's coming between us and the opening. He's cutting us off."

She sounded despondent.

"It doesn't matter. I'm not going in there." Sisko

eyed the screen. "Sisko to Quark—shut down the station's starboard weapons. Flush radiation out the portals. Make him think there's residual damage and we're making a last-ditch stand. Dr. Bashir, I want you to activate thrusters and rotate the station as if you're trying to bring the port weapons sails around to fire."

"Yes, sir . . . thrusters on."

For a moment, nothing happened. Then, on the wide vision of space before them, backdropped in one corner by the planet Bajor, ten million metric tons of station began to slowly pivot.

"What're you doing?" Kira asked.

"Giving him something to concentrate on. Making him think the station's about to fire on him. I want him to turn his forward screens toward the station."

"Why?"

He didn't answer. This wasn't a classroom.

When Fransu's ship responded on the screen, Kira came up in her chair and pointed. "He's doing it! He's swinging around! He's putting his bow to the station."

Calculating distance and speed ratios in his head, Sisko picked at the controls in front of him, eyeing Fransu's ship at the same time. "It's where his stern is that I'm interested in," he said cagily.

Kira looked at him, but didn't ask.

The wormhole's mouth was now directly behind Fransu's ship.

"Get ready to veer off, Major," Sisko uttered, eyes fixed on the wormhole and Fransu's ship.

He tapped his controls.

Out of the wormhole came a tiny dot, shooting out and up toward Fransu's ship, a pea attacking a shark.

"What's that?" Kira asked.

Sisko ignored the question and shouted. "Veer off, Major!"

She scrambled for her controls and the *Defiant* dropped out from under them like a broken turbolift.

Just as the pea got to the shark's tail, Sisko gritted his teeth and whispered, "Detonate!"

He punched his remotes.

The pea blew up into a ball of sparkling shards with such violence that there couldn't have been a piece of it left bigger than a human fingerprint.

Whining, howling, the *Defiant* rocked bodily and went up on a nacelle. At the helm Kira scrambled to keep control, to keep the ship from going into a spin. With effort she brought the ship to a balance and swung around. The whining faded away.

"Just right!" Sisko shouted, and lay a fist into the helm. "Nothing like a little physics to level the odds!"

At the station's outer firing perimeter, the Cardassian ship twirled like a top, canted badly off its gravitational center, cocked to one side with the power of the blow, and it wasn't righting itself. It hung in space, wounded and smoking, with part of its tail section blown clean off and green liquid dispensing into space in a spitting funnel of spray.

"Brilliant!" the High Gul offered. "Splendid, Captain!" He laughed. "We've each been beaten by dead men!"

Sisko glanced at him. Somehow they had come to be standing side by side. "For two dead men, we did all right."

"But it was just a runabout!" Kira gasped. "It doesn't have that kind of ballistics!"

Sisko glanced at her with narrowed eyes. "It does

when you pack its impulse core with antimatter, Major."

She gawked at him and slammed her palm to the navigation center. "A booby trap?"

"Right. Hail the booby, would you, please?"

"I would please!"

Shaking her head in amazement, Kira worked at her controls to call up the right frequencies and tap in the right codes for what was really a function of the communications station over her right shoulder. It could be done from the helm, but it took a couple seconds.

"Go ahead, sir," she said finally, burying a smile.

Sisko nodded. "Visual."

"On visual."

The screen crackled, forcing its damaged circuits to pull in a picture of Fransu on his bridge—a smoldering place littered with bodies. Fransu himself was scorched in the face, his severe gray-silver uniform smeared with blood and bluish lubricant. He was kneeling beside his command chair, with the gory body of a dead Cardassian officer cradled in his arm. The officer's skull was imploded. Blood and brain matter drained down Fransu's arm.

Crouched in unshielded misery, Fransu glanced at the screen, and it was obvious that he saw them.

Offering a few polite seconds to his aggrieved enemy, Sisko squared his shoulders with painful effort. "This is Benjamin Sisko. Surrender immediately and prepare to be boarded, or I and the station will fire on you. Without shields, you can't stand against us. Respond."

Fransu looked for a few moments at the body of the officer he cradled. He seemed almost to forget what was going on. Palpable grief traveled between the two ships, and there was a time of silence during which animosity between enemies broke down.

Gently Fransu let the body of his companion slip out of his arms to the deck. Slowly he pushed himself to his feet.

Then he looked up at Sisko.

"Is the High Gul alive?" he asked.

The High Gul moved closer to Sisko's side. "Yes, Fransu. I am still alive."

Fransu swallowed with difficulty, once, twice. He motioned to his right.

"Then, look."

He stepped out of the picture, and someone else moved into it—a thin, withered figure, of faded skin and frosted hair, whose eyes were nearly blind and teeth were worn to points, whose skin was parchment and whose arthritic hands were clenched like the claws of a dead bird, as if sprayed with the rime of extreme old age.

Paralyzed with shock, the High Gul stared at the fossil on the screen, and into the dusty past which to him was yesterday.

The ancient figure squinted its one functioning eye, stretched its thin cracked lips until its cheekbones showed like rocks under a spider's web.

And it spoke. Its voice was paper ripping.

"Husband?"

CHAPTER
22

"WOMAN . . ."

An old music played in the eyes of the High Gul and his million-year-old wife as they gazed at each other in bizarre harmony, and the many years fell away.

Ben Sisko stared at the crone on the screen and knew they were in trouble. Fransu was smart—he'd kept this as a last-ditch move, and it was working.

Now what?

Certainly Sisko knew they couldn't fire on that ship anymore, not with a hostage on board.

Nearby, the High Gul's face became strangely pacific. His voice was hardly more than a scratch.

"You are . . . beautiful. . . ."

She may once have been. Sisko tried to imagine her empty cheeks filled out, her eyes clear, her hair dark, color in her skin.

During this tense breathing spell he tried to imagine her as an enchantress, strong and alluring, but somehow that didn't fit with what he saw. Or perhaps it just didn't fit the High Gul.

He realized he was looking at the grande dame of a whole civilization, a duchess of bedlam for Cardassia, part of the hinge upon which the change had swung that even now affected him, the Federation, Bajor.

"This is a divine gift before I die," the dowager said, *"to look into your face once more and know the rumors were lies."*

"They were lies," the High Gul confirmed. "Have you been well treated?"

"As the wife of the High Gul, I had the best care."

"Have there been birds in your life? Ornamental grasses?"

"I lived in the mountains. The wild grasses rustled every night."

The answer seemed to accommodate the High Gul's dreams. He smiled wistfully. Then his eyes widened and he asked, "How long did the dog live?"

The old woman grinned so hard that her blind eye disappeared, leaving only the tiny sighted one and its thin flap of skin. "Six more years!"

Together they laughed as a hundred wounds healed.

All at once Fransu came up behind the woman, almost casually, without the slightest violence, wrapped his arms around her and put the blade of a short, sharp knife to her throat. He hugged her tighter and tighter, until her smile disappeared and the High Gul's smile did too.

Fransu's expression was almost passive, shallow, heavy with grief and weighted by what he apparently saw as a lack of choice. His back was to a stone wall, his foe armored before him, and he was playing his last card.

"Beam yourself over here, Excellency," he said,

"and I will turn your woman over to the Federation. She can live an even longer life wherever she pleases, and become even older."

The High Gul's expression bluntly changed. "Fransu, you are an insufficient person, do you know that? In all our years as husband and wife, in all the decades of a most spirited life together, I never made a single decision for her. The woman will choose for herself."

"That's acceptable. She's no fool." Fransu raised the blade until it forced the old wife to tilt her head. "Well? Tell your husband what makes sense."

The ancient woman wheezed against the blade, her nearly sightless eyes blinking rapidly as she tried to see the husband of her youth on the screen before her. She obviously wanted very much to see him, to believe the miracle that he hadn't changed at all in eighty long years, and that he still had a chance for the life that had been taken from them.

"Husband," she croaked to him across the void of space, as if the knife at her throat didn't even exist. "You are the High Gul. No one has ever come up to that title since you lived. This hour, I have serenity. You are the one and only High Gul . . . and I am old enough."

The High Gul's smile drifted away. He nodded. He shared another second of communion with his wife.

Then he stepped forward, and his hand came down on the helm's phaser firing controls. The *Defiant*'s weapons fired, blooming out toward *Rugg'l*.

"No!" Sisko shouted, but it was too late.

On the screen, the bridge of *Rugg'l* was disintegrating around Fransu and the old woman. Fransu defiantly raked his knife across the old woman's throat. The only color on her body appeared in the bleeding gash.

Unblinking, the High Gul watched the slaughter of his wife with nothing less than pride. There might have been a thousand other emotions at play, but he kept them to himself. If he was shocked, there was no sign of it.

Suddenly the main screen's picture blew to orange, then gray, then flickered off. *Defiant*'s sensors automatically shifted back to a wide picture of space before them—

Fransu's ship was smoking more and more, but it managed to return fire. The *Defiant* rocked again, sending Sisko and the High Gul stumbling. Clinging to the helm, Kira managed to keep her seat.

Before Sisko could claw his way to his feet and react, two spears of highly concentrated phaser power lanced across the screen from one side to the other, the kind only a very big ship could generate, and converged on Fransu's ship.

The *Rugg'l* folded in upon itself as if someone had doubled it over with a gut punch. Immediately another bolt of a slightly different shade of orange hit the ship and it was cleaved in two. Half the aft section and the remaining part of the tail went spinning off into space.

With a numb fist Sisko hammered the comm panel. "Dax! Cease fire!"

But he was too late. Fransu's ship hung sizzling, smoking and coughing blue and white sparks and noxious yellow-green gases. It would be hell in space over there.

"Dax, Bashir, come in!"

"We read you, Benjamin, but we didn't fire on Fransu's ship."

"Who did?"

"They did."

"Who's 'they'?"

"Change your screen to aft wide angle."

Kira glanced at Sisko, and when he nodded she found the right controls and shifted the screen.

Before them on final approach were three massive Galaxy-class starships and one almost-as-massive Klingon battle cruiser. They were coming up in attack formation, beautiful and frightening in their gleaming strength.

"You were right!" Kira said. "The whiteout! Starfleet didn't ignore a silent sector!"

Sisko could only glance at her and breathe in and out. Relief washed through him to know not only that he could count on the simple logic of invasion tactics, but also that he could count on Starfleet to back him up. Even the Klingons weren't willing to let a whole sector go dark without investigating.

"We're getting a hail," Kira said.

He cleared his throat. "Put them on."

"This is Captain Gamarra, Starship Exeter. Also the Starships Potemkin *and* Hood, *and the Klingon Imperial Warship* N'gat. *Do you require assistance, Captain Sisko?"*

Completely balked, Sisko gaped like a slapped kid at the fleet of bright ships. "I don't think I do anymore. . . . Is anybody left alive on that Cardassian ship?"

"Picking up a handful of life signs in the lower deck areas. And one on the bridge."

"Beam a Security team to the inner areas and take

charge, Captain Gamarra. The one on the bridge . . .
beam the life sign to me."

*"Confirm that—you want him over there, with
you?"*

"Yes, right here."

"Right away. Exeter *out."*

Without further complication, a funnel of transporter energy began to buzz almost immediately on
the starboard side of *Defiant*'s bridge. Sisko held his
breath.

The funnel sparkled, changed to bands, and formed
itself into a humanoid body. But hope sank—of
course, if wasn't the Gul's wife, despite fancy's flight.

It was Fransu.

He stood before them, saying nothing, but only
gazed at the High Gul with a strange allure on his
face. No contempt at all. Just the bewitchery of
watching fate play out, twisting like a pennant in the
wind, unpredictable.

Sisko turned to the High Gul. "I'm sorry," he said
with intimacy that surprised him. Not for his win. But
for the other things. Both their wives.

The High Gul didn't look like a soldier at all as he
gazed back at Fransu. "I felt this was *my* duty."

Sisko tipped his head in a gesture of the thinnest
forgiveness. "I'd be lying if I said I didn't understand."

The High Gul gazed at Fransu dispassionately, then
at Fransu's hands, which were stained and glistening
with the old wife's blood.

"What my wife said," he began quietly, "it's part of
being out here, in space. She always understood the
gravity of being the wife of a soldier, a leader . . . she
bore the danger of following. To the bitter end, she

never expected to be put before my duty." He looked at Sisko. "You must have had a similar woman."

Weighted by a graveside obligation to say something nice in response, Sisko felt his throat knot up and his lips go flat. He couldn't find words, or the strength to say them.

Suddenly a bright ball of light erupted on the other side of *Deep Space Nine,* throwing the station momentarily into silhouette. An instant later, shock waves rocked the ship.

Grabbing for the helm, he plunged for the sensor readouts. "What was that!"

Kira beat him to the display. The color dropped out of her face.

"Five thousand kilometers off the station," she rasped, "an Element One-ten fission explosion."

Sisko blinked at the screen, at the quickly dissipating ball of glitter. "Odo . . ."

He felt terrible, hollowed out, because he had forgotten all about the shapeshifter and that private torture going on over there.

He stared at the screen. "He must've gotten off the station just in time."

Tears welled in Kira's eyes. She did nothing to hold them back.

"The last casualty of this battle," the High Gul said. "I do not apologize, but I am sorry for that. It's unfortunate. We are soldiers and you understand."

Sisko kicked the navigation chair and sent it clattering. "I'm tired of being a soldier," he dashed off bitterly. "I'm tired of what it costs me."

His lungs heaved in and out, strength fled from his limbs as the six-inch puncture wound in his body charged its true cost. He slipped backward against the command chair without the will to catch himself and stay upright.

It was the High Gul who came in quickly to catch him and keep him from falling too hard to the deck. To his right, Sisko saw Kira whirled around as if afraid the High Gul might be grabbing for Sisko's phaser.

"No, Major—" he choked, holding up a staying hand as the High Gul lowered him to the steps between the command deck and the turbolift. "It's all right. I'll be all right. Take the prisoner below."

Kira pushed stiffly away, her legs shuddering, and she never took her eyes off the High Gul. But, sensing something in the old Cardassian's sunken gaze, she spoke to Sisko. "Sir . . ."

There weren't words, apparently, for her fears, or sense to them, but the High Gul seemed to understand.

"My honor to serve with you, sentinel," he offered quietly.

She stared and stared at him, her hands closed into fists; then abruptly she looked at Sisko.

"You have your orders, Major," he said evenly. "Take Gul Fransu below."

Again she looked at the High Gul as if clutched by foresight. She stepped away from the helm. Her voice was caught in her throat. "Yes, sir."

She didn't push Fransu, and Fransu didn't resist as she led him to the turbolift.

Sisko didn't look as the lift's doors gushed open, then shut, but he felt Kira's eyes scoping him and the High Gul.

The soft whine seemed loud as the turbolift whispered away, heading toward the lower decks.

Sisko settled his weak body against the step, aware of the High Gul's supportive grip.

The old soldier wasn't looking at him as he crouched there, though. He was looking out at the three starships and the Klingon battle cruiser, his eyes full of appreciation for the scalding martial beauty and power he saw out there.

After a moment he asked, "Are you ready for a holy war, Captain?"

Still fuming and thinking about Odo, Sisko simmered, "What's that supposed to mean?"

"Let me ask you first . . . what will you do with me now?"

"You've killed Federation people. It's not up to me. You're going to be remanded to Starfleet custody, and probably drown in a tangle of diplomatic yarn."

"Trial? Prison?"

"Probably."

"So your Federation will incarcerate one of the founders of the Cardassian Empire. A historical figure. Almost a god, in the minds of many Cardassians. The trial will gain great publicity. Cardassians will rise in numbers and come for me, there's no doubt."

"So?"

"Wouldn't it be better if you let me go?"

"Let you go?" Sisko grinned viciously over it.

"I'll retire . . . I'll go to an agricultural community until my dying day."

A few seconds plodded by, and then the High Gul laughed openly at Sisko's struggling expression.

"I didn't think you'd believe that one," the old soldier said. "You know me as well as I know myself."

"Well enough," Sisko accepted.

The High Gul paced across the bridge, touching the

helm, the battered consoles, ultimately picking up a piece of broken housing that had been blasted right off. He turned the burned shard over and over in his hands.

"Can you imagine what a powerful narcotic it is to have millions ready to go to their deaths at a single word from you? I have had this. No matter the tons of soil I tried to till, I would be drawn into politics as the years passed, I would be successful, I would eventually raise an army, and still we would be at war."

Softening through his anger and grief, Sisko shifted from one hip to the other.

"I don't understand the galaxy anymore," the High Gul went on. "I saw in your friend Garak's face the beginning of doubt. Like him, everyone will expect me to have a magic elixir that will turn Cardassia back to invincibility. But I have no such stuff. Better, I think, that no one man have it."

"Oh, I don't know," Sisko declared. "There are some men I'd follow . . . if I believed the same as they did."

The High Gul smiled at him. "Thank you." He sighed. "I am an antique. I wanted to restore the Empire as it was intended to be by those of us who framed it. I had so many victories, I began to believe what people were saying about me. But people tire of deities . . . unless each miracle is bigger than the last. But it is too late for Cardassia to dominate anymore. I understand now why it was destined to stop expanding. You have done me a favor, Captain Sisko. I may have been the destruction of my own people, had I gone to war with the likes of you."

He waved one hand at Sisko, the other at the main

screen and the fleet of starships martialed across open space before them.

"The galaxy has grown up in eighty years, but some things resurrect themselves. If I am incarcerated by the Federation, I am certainly out of commission . . . but word leaks out . . . Cardassia tears itself apart over me. They go to war with your Federation to get me back. Or to destroy me, depending upon which table you drink over." His eyes changed, narrowed, and he gazed at the screen as if into the future. "A holy war, on behalf of a not-god . . . In an effort to 'rescue' me, Cardassia will force the Federation, the Klingons, the Romulans, and all these to rise up and destroy it. I can't have that. . . ." He paused, thought of something, and asked, "What about Fransu?"

"Fransu may talk," Sisko added. "But he's going to do it while rotting in a Federation penal colony. He won't get much of an audience."

The High Gul nodded sadly.

"Captain, I don't want it to be my legacy that I was the death of my own people. That idiot Fransu should have killed me all those years ago. Or let me live, but this was the worst thing he could do. I am more than flesh . . . I am legend."

He turned to Sisko.

"Better I stay that way." He held out his hand. It held a small device, to be used only in extremes. "Better the High Gul never awakens."

"Recorders on visual," he said.

"Recording," the computer's voice said.

The High Gul took a step away from Sisko, then decided he was still too close and stepped even farther across the bridge. He tampered with the hand phaser for a few moments as if curious about the way the hardware worked, the funny markings in language different from any he had seen in his lifetime. Beam width . . . photon spill . . . emitter . . . beam intensity . . . trigger . . . Then he found the combination he wanted and adjusted the controls.

In a flashing spectrum of bare energy, as Sisko raised a hand to protect his face from the glare, the High Gul of the Crescent fried himself out of existence, and back into legend.

CHAPTER
23

"I DON'T BELIEVE IT!"

Ops was cool, dim, and there was even a fresh breeze coming through from the ventilators. On the main screen, the *Starship Exeter* and the Klingon warship hung in princely fashion, with the *Exeter* taking the wreck of *Rugg'l* in tow.

Standing together, Sisko and Kira stared baldly at the subdued, ever-haunted proctor of their station. Before them, the shapeshifter was obviously exhausted, but no longer physically strained. The poison was gone and Odo was still alive, standing right here, uneasy under their stares.

"How'd you get it out of him?" Kira asked as she glanced at Julian Bashir.

"I didn't," the doctor said casually. "The chief did."

He in turn gestured to Miles O'Brien.

Weak and battered, Sisko pressed a hand to the Ops console and levered around to the engineer. "How, Chief?"

"The same way we've used for centuries," O'Brien said with a quirky glint in his eyes. "A centrifuge. We put him in a big cargo drum, spun it with antigravs, and let the Element One-ten go to the outside, and filtered it out, then beamed it into space and let it blow its merry heart out."

Kira shook her head. "I don't get it!"

O'Brien tilted his grin at her. "You keep thinking of him as a solid. He's liquid. We just separated out the adulterant. Why didn't you just ask me to begin with?"

Self-conscious, Odo lowered his gaze, plainly hoping that would be a signal for all of them to stop gaping at him. He'd survived, and that was that.

Sisko glanced custodially at the people around him. Hovering nearby like the low notes on a French horn, Jadzia Dax stood nearby, gazing at them with an expression strangely similar to the High Gul's timeless wife's. Beside her, Julian Bashir eyed Sisko, certainly waiting for the right moment to order him to the infirmary for those twelve hours of recuperation.

At his side, still stained and frayed from these last hours' events, Kira was feisty as Peter Pan, but now somehow subdued, maybe ashamed—Sisko couldn't tell and offered her the respect of not asking. By leaving the issue alone, he gave her tacit approval of her actions on *Defiant*. He knew she walked a line, and he wasn't going to push her off.

That was how things were in this hard-bitten, untrusted, castaway garter of a station. Their electric Kira did a little command, a little security, weather-eyed Odo slopped over into defense or engineering, Sisko would do security or defense or anything else he wanted to, for an engineer O'Brien had broached more than his share of dangerous decisions, and nobody was really sure about Dax. They were an undefined collection, and that, in many ways, defined them.

Around them the grey walls and aniline black shadows of *Deep Space Nine* were as comforting as a summer glade.

Ultimately he looked again at Odo, unable to restrain his appreciation for the station's vigilant background man. "Well," he said, "that'll make quite a tall tale around the sector, I'll bet."

"Absolutely not, Captain!" Odo said, tight as a strung bow. "The indignity of having an engineer as my doctor, of being separated like the ingredients of some foul cocktail . . . if you don't mind, I'd rather not have it talked about. Chief, thank you very much, and that's the end of this."

"Come in! Come in! You can get autographs right here, only a modest fee—something to show your grandchildren! We have the entire episode recorded and we're re-creating it at zero nine hundred in the holosuites! Right this way . . . Odo! All these people want your autograph!"

"Quark!" Odo backed away as if approached by a snake.

Some people would describe Quark that way, but Sisko had come to think of their local Ferengi moonshiner as less a swindler than just a guileful shortchange artist who hated his own honest streak.

"Quark," Sisko demanded, grabbing the little charmer as he passed, "where'd these people come from? The station is supposed to be evacuated."

"Oh, it is, Captain," Quark said, "except for one transport ship that got stuck in its docking claw.

Security just got them out, and, well, there didn't seem to be any sense in sending them down to Bajor at this point, is there? I mean, they're here—why not take advantage? And I've been in contact with the refugee station on the planet about Odo's centrifuge show! We're already booked up through Wednesday afternoon! Ladies and gentlemen! If you'll follow me, I'll conduct a brief tour of the Operations Center of *Deep Space Nine*. It's a privilege to be here—as you know, Ops is generally off-limits to anyone, but—"

"Quark," Sisko snapped. "Not now and *not* here."

With false piety Quark crowed, "Of course! I understand completely! Ladies and gentlemen, this way! We're disturbing the heartbeat of the station, the very core of function, the command center—if you'll follow me, I'll lead you to the holosuites, and the first show will begin!"

Sisko grinned as Quark ushered his tour group around Ops, taking the long, long way back to one of the turbolifts. "Don't worry, Odo," he assured. "It can't last more than a month."

"I can't even do anything about it," the eternal misfit moaned. "I have to go back to my quarters and rest. If I don't come out for a month . . . don't come in after me. Good night."

Gazing at the deck, Odo made a controlled dash for the nearest lift while Quark was still pointing out the ships on the main viewer to his audience.

"Poor Odo," Sisko uttered. "All right, everyone, back to work. Doctor, deal with the wounded and collect any bodies on the station and conduct appropriate autopsies. Dax, let's begin bringing station residents and visitors back up from the planet in a calm and organized fashion. Priority goes to families with small children and merchants dealing in perishable goods. Chief, you're in charge of repair teams. Let's put this station back together."

As his crew broke up and headed back to their posts and Quark squeezed every last second of letting his tour group get a gander at Ops, Sisko indulged in a few winces and a telling groan, and for the first time let himself notice how hurt he was. His right leg was numb at the knee, his shoulders ached all the way up to his ears, and breathing was a struggle—that punctured lung. He could feel Bashir's masking medicine wearing off. His wounds were beginning to pound for attention. He'd have to get patched up before he could beam his son back up from Bajor. Couldn't let Jake see him this way.

As she came to Sisko's side, Kira eyed Quark's tour group, then glanced at the main screen. "The *Potemkin* went out to gather the communications drones that were blocking the sector. The *Hood* is securing the immediate area. The whiteout is over."

"Good. Thank you." Sisko leaned back on the Ops table.

"Now what?" Kira asked. "How do we report all this? It's going to make a big, ugly, bitter tangle between Cardassia and just about everybody else."

"First," Sisko said thoughtfully, "we'll dawdle around making repairs and offering shore leave to the crews of those starships. It'll drain the intensity out of the moment. That way we can stall making a report for a week or so, and let the matter fizzle out."

"Stall? Why?"

"Because if we make an immediate report, investigation will seem more urgent. The longer we take, the less critical any action will seem. We'll let the diplomats sort out the unwarranted attack on the station. We'll suggest that Gul Fransu was a rogue, not acting under authority of the Cardassian Command. We'll downplay the amount of damage and normalize relations quickly. I respect the High Gul enough for that. He ended his exceptional life rather than provide a reason for Cardassia to rise up in these times, because he knew it couldn't stand up to modern powers out there. I'd be betraying that gesture if I handed over the whole truth with all its colors. So . . . I think I'll just hang on to it, Major."

She gazed at him keenly, at first perplexed, then gradually more heartened by his logic. Her dilated passions found their way around what he was trying to say, and Sisko watched as, second by second, the tension went out of her shoulders and she became at ease with what he had decided to do.

The change in her made him believe he was doing the right thing.

He was going to do it anyway.

"What do we report about the High Gul himself?" she asked quietly. "I don't know what I feel about him anymore. At first I hated him, but later . . ."

"At first he was just a faceless enemy," Sisko abridged. "Then he got a face. It happens, Major."

She nodded, still mystified. "But he was here, the events did happen, and now he's *not* here. What are you going to tell Starfleet about how he died?"

Sisko drew a long breath and let out a sigh. "Let's just say he immolated himself on the bodies of both our wives."

He pushed off the Ops table, found his center of balance, and limped toward the turbolift.

"You have the conn, Major," he grumbled on his way out.

Kira watched him go. "Will you be in the infirmary, sir?"

"For a while." He cast a glance over his bare, bloody shoulder. "Then I'm gonna go watch the Odo Show. Quark! What's the ticket price?"

STAR TREK
THE NEXT GENERATION®

**Make It So: Leadership
from The Next Generation™**
by Wess Roberts, P.h.D., and Bill Ross
52097-0/$22.00
(available now)

Star Trek The Next Generation®: Blueprints
by Rich Sternbach
50093-7/$20.00
A beautifully packaged set of detailed actual blueprints
unavailable in any other form elsewhere — every fan's dream!
(COMING SOON)

Crossover
A novel by Michael Jan Friedman
89677-6/$23.00
With Spock imprisoned in the Romulan Empire,
the generations must work together to prevent interstellar war.
(Available mid-November 1995)

POCKET
BOOKS

Simon & Schuster Mail Order
200 Old Tappan Rd., Old Tappan, N.J. 07675
Please send me the books I have checked above. I am enclosing $_____(please add $0.75 to cover the postage
and handling for each order. Please add appropriate sales tax). Send check or money order--no cash or C.O.D.'s
please. Allow up to six weeks for delivery. For purchase over $10.00 you may use VISA: card number, expiration
date and customer signature must be included.

Name _____

Address _____

City _____ State/Zip _____

VISA Card # _____ Exp.Date _____

Signature _____ 1135-02